Brother
of the Bride

JACK CALDWELL

WHITE
SOUP
PRESS

For information, address Jack Caldwell, 15060 Germany Oaks Blvd, Prairieville, LA 70769.

https://cajuncheesehead.com
http://whitesouppress.com
http://austenvariations.com

ISBN: 978-0-9891080-9-6

Front Cover: *Two's Company, Three's None* by Marcus Stone (1892)
Back Cover: *Prospects* by Edmund Blair Leighton (1883)

Layout and design by Ellen Pickels

Dedication

To Barbara,
the light in my world

In Appreciation

To Debbie Styne and Ellen Pickels
for all their hard work.

To Abigail Reynolds and Maria Grace
for all their sound advice.

Author's Note

This work uses characters invented by Miss Jane Austen in her Regency novels. It is intended to honor Miss Austen and the immense pleasure her words continue to bestow upon the world.

This novel is Book Four in my *Jane Austen's Fighting Men Series*. It is a sequel to my earlier works: *The Three Colonels* (Book One), *The Last Adventure of the Scarlet Pimpernel* (Book Two), and *Persuaded to Sail* (Book Three). It is a prequel to *Rosings Park* (Book Five). It features characters from and references to events in those novels.

While *Brother of the Bride* stands on its own, the reader's enjoyment will be enhanced by reading the earlier books, especially *The Three Colonels*.

— Jack Caldwell
Prairieville, Louisiana

Dramatis Personae

Pemberley

Fitzwilliam Darcy: owner of Pemberley Estate, Derbyshire, head of the Darcy family, nephew of Lord Matlock and Lady Catherine de Bourgh

Elizabeth Darcy: wife of Mr. Darcy, daughter of Mr. and Mrs. Thomas Bennet

Bennet Edward George Darcy: son and heir of Mr. Darcy (b: 1814)

Georgiana Darcy: sister of Mr. Darcy

Mrs. Reynolds: housekeeper at Pemberley

Mrs. Nivens: nanny for Master Bennet

Mr. Thompson: steward of Pemberley Estate

Witherspoon: valet to Mr. Darcy

Sally: personal maid to Mrs. Darcy

The Rev. Franklin Southerland: rector of St. George Parish, Kympton

Kitty Southerland: sister of Mrs. Darcy

Others

Mr. and Mrs. Thomas Bennet: of Longbourn, Hertfordshire, parents of Mrs. Darcy

Charles and Jane Bingley: of Mayfield Manor, Nottinghamshire, sister and brother-in-law of Mrs. Darcy

Susan Frances Bingley: eldest daughter of Charles and Jane Bingley

Elizabeth Jane Bingley: daughter of Charles and Jane Bingley

Mary Tucker: sister of Mrs. Darcy

Thomas Tucker; husband of Mary Tucker, solicitor and partner in the firm of Phillips & Tucker of London and Meryton

Lydia Wickham: sister of Mrs. Darcy, widow of Major George Wickham (m: 1812–1815)

Chloe, Phoebe, and Rosanna Wickham: daughters of Lydia and George Wickham

Sir Percival and Lady Marguerite Blakeney: of Richmond, Surrey

Colonel Christopher and Marianne Brandon: of Delaford Manor, Dorsetshire

Ernest and Doretha Carlyle, The Honorable Baron and Baroness Higginbottom: of Bolehill Abbey, Derbyshire

Henry Crawford: of Everingham Manor, Norfolk

Mr. and Mrs. John Dashwood: of Norland Park, Sussex

Lady Catherine de Bourgh: of Kent, widow of Sir Lewis, mother of Lady Fitzwilliam, and sister of Lord Matlock

Dawson: personal maid of Lady Catherine

Colonel Archibald Denny: British Army

Mr. and Mrs. Robert Ferrars: London

Hugh Fitzwilliam, The Right Honorable 5th Earl of Matlock: Derbyshire, head of the Fitzwilliam family, brother of Lady Catherine de Bourgh

Alexandria Fitzwilliam, The Right Honorable Countess of Matlock: wife of Lord Matlock

Andrew Fitzwilliam, The Right Honorable Viscount Fitzwilliam: eldest son and heir of Lord Matlock

Eugenie Fitzwilliam, The Right Honorable Viscountess Fitzwilliam: wife of Lord Fitzwilliam

The Honorable Sir Richard Fitzwilliam, C.B.: Colonel, British Army (retired). Owner of Rosings Park, Kent and son of Lord Matlock

Anne, Lady Fitzwilliam: wife of Sir Richard, daughter of the late Sir Lewis de Bourgh

Mrs. Jenkinson: companion to Lady Fitzwilliam

Lord Frederick and Lady Henrietta Montgomery: Scotland. Lady Henrietta is daughter of Lord and Lady Matlock

Mrs. and Mrs. Edward Gardiner: of London, uncle and aunt of Mrs. Darcy

John and Isabella Knightley: of London

George and Emma Knightley: of Donwell Abbey, manager of Hartfield Estate, Highbury, Surrey

Stanley Preston: of London

James Rushworth: of Southerton Court

Mr. and Mrs. John Willoughby: of Combe Magna, Somersetshire

James Woodhouse, The Right Honorable 2nd Earl of Wakeford: of Wakeford Abbey, Surrey

Catherine Woodhouse, The Right Honorable Countess of Wakeford: wife of Lord Wakeford

Algernon Woodhouse, The Right Honorable 7th Viscount Llewellyn: son and heir of Lord Wakeford, of Ambervale Lodge, Derbyshire

Captain the Honorable Cornelius Woodhouse: British Army, son of Lord Wakeford

The Honorable Rev. Thaddeus Woodhouse: son of Lord Wakeford

Lady Penelope Woodhouse: daughter of Lord Wakeford

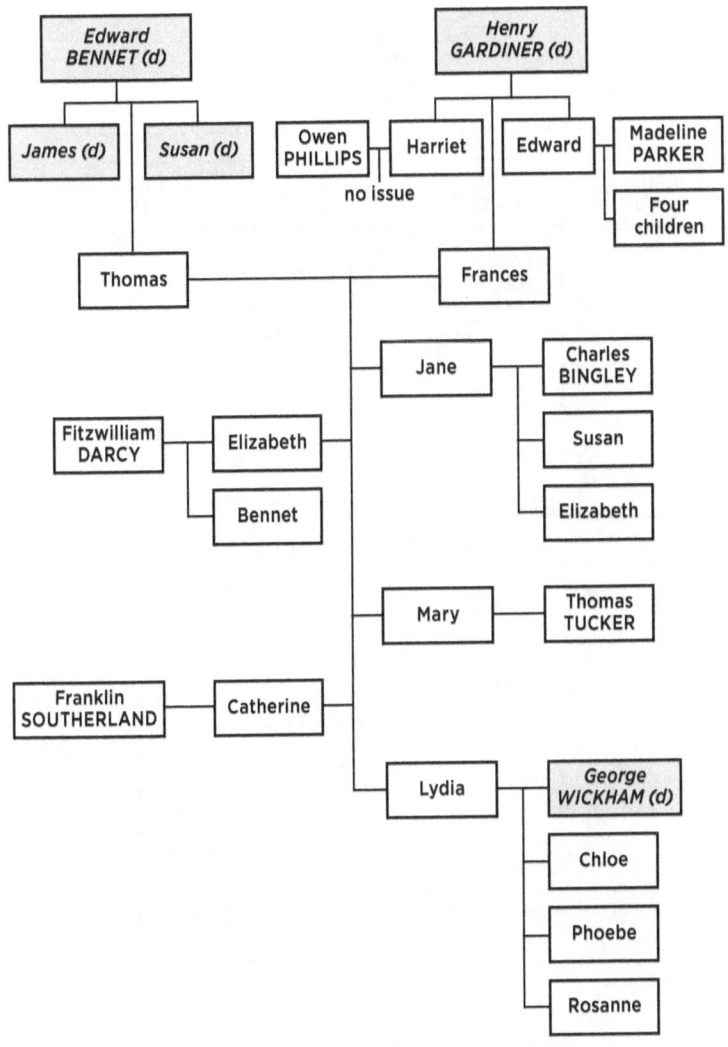

BENNET/GARDINER FAMILIES
as of January 1, 1816

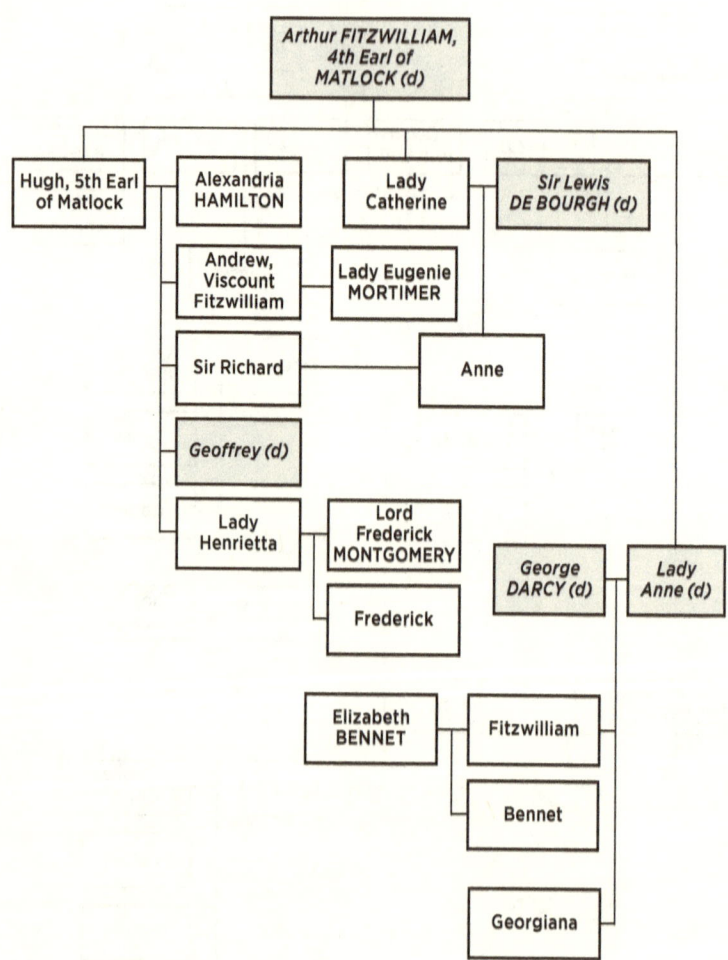

FITZWILLIAM/DARCY FAMILIES
as of January 1, 1816

Arthur FITZWILLIAM, 4th Earl of MATLOCK (d)

Hugh, 5th Earl of Matlock

Alexandria HAMILTON

Lady Catherine

Sir Lewis DE BOURGH (d)

Andrew, Viscount Fitzwilliam

Lady Eugenie MORTIMER

Sir Richard

Anne

Geoffrey (d)

Lady Henrietta

Lord Frederick MONTGOMERY

Frederick

George DARCY (d)

Lady Anne (d)

Elizabeth BENNET

Fitzwilliam

Bennet

Georgiana

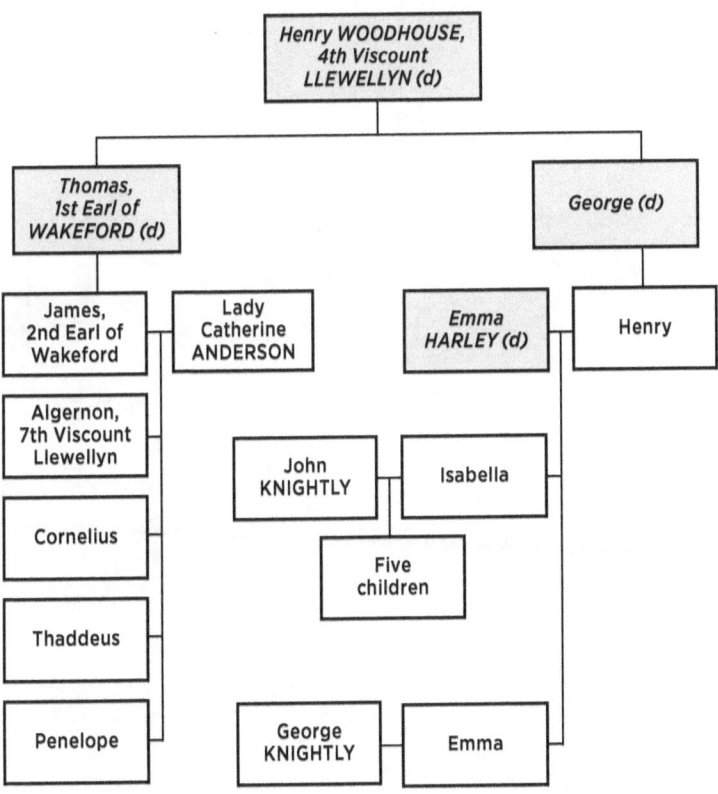

WOODHOUSE FAMILY
as of January 1, 1816

Henry WOODHOUSE, 4th Viscount LLEWELLYN (d)

Thomas, 1st Earl of WAKEFORD (d)

George (d)

James, 2nd Earl of Wakeford

Lady Catherine ANDERSON

Emma HARLEY (d)

Henry

Algernon, 7th Viscount Llewellyn

John KNIGHTLY

Isabella

Cornelius

Five children

Thaddeus

Penelope

George KNIGHTLY

Emma

Chapter 1

Fitzwilliam Darcy sighed with pleasure as he sat before the fire, sipping a glass of wine and observing the subjects of his happy, private kingdom gathered together in the library of Darcy House on Boxing Day.

That Darcy was king of his kingdom was indisputable. It was a rather select realm consisting of the vast estate of Pemberley in Derbyshire, a small estate in Ireland, and a house on a fashionable street in London, but it suited him.

His subjects suited him too. There, sitting on the floor, was his laughing, beloved wife, Elizabeth, and dear sister, Georgiana, playing with his giggling, cherished son and heir, Bennet. The uproar of the festive season was behind them. There would be no more parties, balls, or family dinners. Today was a day of peace and quiet.

Of course, calling Elizabeth Darcy his *subject* was somewhat absurd and potentially dangerous. She was his wife, friend, lover, and closest confident. He entrusted her with his deepest dreams, secrets, and desires. As such, she fell under his protection, as did all his subjects. Indeed, if Darcy were king of all he surveyed, she was the revered queen, and one did not anger the queen—especially Queen Elizabeth.

He gave in to the pleasure of gazing upon his adored consort. Elizabeth was one of those ladies who were more beautiful at four and twenty than at twenty. Always a handsome woman, she was now striking to his eye. True, her form was not so light as when first they met, but motherhood had accentuated her curves, and her daily walks kept her trim. Her cheeks and lips were as soft as ever, as was her deep auburn hair. Her eyes shone with laughter, good humor, and in their private moments, love and desire. She was the heart of the Darcy Kingdom.

Georgiana, too, had grown—something Darcy found a mixed blessing. There was no doubt now that his dear little sister was a woman full grown, and a lovely one at that. She was the image of their late mother. Her terrible shyness had moderated into a quiet reserve, not unlike his own. Her debut was considered a success thanks to Elizabeth's calming presence. Darcy knew that the day some young buck would steal her away from Pemberley was fast approaching.

Bennet was a combination of his father and mother. The boy tended to be quiet, speaking only when he had something to say, but he was good-natured, clever, and affectionate. Bennet was quickly growing from toddler to boy.

Darcy took another sip, happy to see the end of 1815. It had been a difficult and distressing year. The peace the country had expected twelve months before had been shattered by a renewal of war on the Continent. Thank God, Colonel Fitzwilliam and Colonel Brandon had escaped the horrors of Waterloo with nary a scratch, for there were many others who could not say the same. Poor Colonel Sir John Buford barely survived. There were personal tragedies too. Elizabeth's sister Mary Tucker had lost a baby.

Life had a way of balancing the bad with the good, Darcy reflected. His cousin Richard received the Order of the Bath and married Anne de Bourgh before leaving the army while his sister Kitty Bennet wed Franklin Southerland, the young rector of Kympton Parish. The Brandons welcomed a son into the world, and the Bufords a daughter.

The year had been too eventful for Darcy's liking. All he wished for this Christmas was a boring 1816.

A knock on the library door broke the domestic tranquility. "A Colonel Denny to see you, sir," said the butler. "Are you at home?"

An irritated Darcy set down his glass, tempted to send the man away. But, curiosity engaged, he said instead, "Show him to my study."

Apologizing to Elizabeth and Georgiana, he passed through the door connecting the library to the study. He was behind his desk when the butler showed in Colonel Denny. The colonel—a comrade-at-arms of Richard, Brandon, and Buford—had earned his rank at Waterloo. He was a changed man since his days as a mere lieutenant of militia in Hertfordshire in 1811. Once joining the regulars, Denny quickly rose through the ranks due to hard work, dash, vacancies, and luck. Wellington was a patron, and Brandon thought the world of the man. His red coat was slightly faded, a few light stains on the sleeve. *Not his dress uniform*, Darcy noted, *but that of a working soldier*. After a greeting and offering refreshments, Darcy took his seat, hoping the colonel's business would not take long.

"Mr. Darcy, I am very sorry to interrupt you. I shall get right to the point if you do not mind."

From a young age, Darcy had been taught to read a man. Colonel Denny sat rigidly, almost at attention. He was clearly nervous. "Pray, speak on, sir."

"You see, I had hoped to court your sister Mrs. Wickham once the first mourning for George—I mean Major Wickham was done."

"Yes." Brevet Major George Wickham had fallen at Waterloo, leaving a wife and three daughters. The entire family was aware that Colonel Denny fancied the Widow Wickham, although Darcy, for the life of him, could not fathom why.

"Well, sir, the six months will end on the eighteenth of January."

"I am aware of that, Colonel."

"I believe you know I had hoped for a posting in India. The War Office has seen fit to approve my request."

"My congratulations."

"Thank you. But that is the problem with courting Mrs. Wickham."

"Does Mrs. Wickham know of your desire to go to India?"

"Oh yes, sir. She is excited by the prospect."

Darcy frowned. "Am I to understand you have already spoken to Mrs. Wickham about your plans? Not only for your career but your intentions involving her?"

Denny colored. "Yes, I have. I had no choice! You see, the army wants me to sail for India by the end of January."

"What does Mrs. Wickham say to your intentions?"

Denny smiled. "She has honored me by accepting my suit. We will marry by common license in early January."

"My felicitations. It is unfortunate you could not follow the usual forms regarding mourning, but it is clear events forced the matter." Darcy spread his hands. "If you are here for my approval, you have it, as unnecessary as it is. You have spoken to Mr. Bennet, yes?"

Denny nodded.

Darcy rose. "Then our business is done."

"Pardon me, but it is not."

Darcy slowly lowered himself back into his chair. "I do not understand what else you want of me."

Denny cleared his throat. "You see, sir, there is a small complication."

After Darcy left the library to meet with Colonel Denny, Bennet became quite boisterous, so the party repaired to the blue parlor, Mrs. Nivens, the child's nursemaid, joining them. They were there only a short time before a footman entered.

"Are you at home for Lord Llewellyn, ma'am?"

Elizabeth was pleased to say, "Show the viscount in." She hid a smile when Georgiana quickly straightened her dress as they rose to greet their guest. Not that Lord Llewellyn was a stranger to Darcy House. Oh no, not at all!

The Darcys were acquainted for years with the Earl and Countess of Wakeford through Darcy's uncle, Lord Matlock. They had not met any of the Wakeford children, however, until Georgiana's debut last year. Their eldest son, Lord Algernon Woodhouse, Viscount Llewellyn, was by far the most pleasant of the young men calling on Georgiana. He was young, about five and twenty, but his gentle and quiet nature hid a solid brain. Darcy reported he was impressed with Llewellyn's estate after a day of riding it with the viscount. That it was only half a day's distance from Pemberley was agreeable. There were no whispers of scandal attached to any of the Woodhouses—another plus in the viscount's column. He was a sportsman enamored of riding, hunting, and fishing, London holding little interest. *Better and better*, Elizabeth considered.

A moment later the ginger-haired young gentleman was before them. "Mrs. Darcy, Miss Darcy, Master Bennet." His bow was crisply delivered; the ladies hardly had time to curtsy. Lord Llewellyn nervously worked his fingers as he held them by his side, his hazel eyes constantly flicking in Georgiana's direction.

As usual.

Elizabeth took pity on the young nobleman, offering a chair where he could easily converse with both ladies in the parlor. Because he was a regular guest, Elizabeth allowed Bennet to remain for a time. While Llewellyn was always kind to her son, she knew he was not there to visit with Bennet!

The young man relaxed after sitting down. "I hope your Christmas was very happy. Is your family well?"

"O-Oh yes, very well," Georgiana managed.

Elizabeth almost rolled her eyes. This was not the first time her sister acted rather timid in the viscount's company. Fortunately, she suspected it was for all the *right* reasons.

"And your family, milord? I hope the earl and countess are in good health."

Llewellyn assured them that they were when Bennet decided he wanted his share of the conversation. Escaping Elizabeth's hold, the Pemberley heir quickly waddled over to their visitor.

"Time for up!" He held his arms out expectantly.

The viscount's upraised hand stopped Elizabeth from reclaiming her son. With a smile, Llewellyn scooped Bennet from the floor and placed him on his lap. "And how was your Christmas, Master Bennet?"

"Horsey!" cried Bennet.

"A new rocking horse in the nursery has become his favorite toy," explained Elizabeth.

"I see." The viscount turned a stern expression upon the child. "A horse is a serious business, Master Bennet!"

Bennet blinked, obviously having no idea what the gentleman meant.

"Riding, sir," continued Llewellyn. "You must ride your horsey every day."

Bennet beamed. "Ride! Ride now!"

"Hmm. There seems to be no horsey about." The viscount looked around the room. "Perhaps this will serve." To the ladies' enjoyment and the happy squeals of the boy, he proceeded to bounce Bennet on one knee.

Elizabeth was charmed by the sight. Llewellyn was such a dear man. She turned to her sister and was transfixed by what she saw. Georgiana was more than pleased. She was *entranced—delighted—beguiled*.

"Mr. Preston, ma'am," announced the footman.

Instantly, the air left the room. Mr. Stanley Preston had also been a persistent caller on Georgiana while the Darcys were in town. Unfortunately.

The handsome and elegant Mr. Preston was everything Lord Llewellyn was not. Owning brown hair and average height, he was sarcastic, droll, supercilious, and ill informed. He spent the majority of his time in town rather than at his small estate. The grinning gentleman strode into the room as though he owned it. His foppish clothes were perfectly fitted, set off by an elaborately knotted cravat. He came to an abrupt stop upon perceiving he was not the only gentleman caller. Doing little to hide a scowl, he bowed to the ladies.

"Mrs. Darcy, Miss Darcy." Looking down his nose, he spoke to the gentleman. "Have you become a nanny, Llewellyn?"

"What a shame Oxford did not improve your manners, Preston," returned the viscount coolly. "You must pardon me. I am having a conversation with Master Darcy about horseflesh."

Mr. Preston snorted. "Each to his own level, I suppose. With such lovely diversions available, it would be a waste not to attend them." With a smirk he sat next to Elizabeth as there was no seat by Georgiana.

A small gesture by Elizabeth was signal enough for Mrs. Nivens to gather up her charge and retreat to the nursery. The remaining quartet proceeded to engage in the usual empty conversation found in the better saloons of the *ton*, the obnoxious Mr. Preston dominating the visit. Compared to the playful words shared between Lord Llewellyn and Bennet minutes before, the discussion was a painful bore.

About halfway into Mr. Preston's visit, the gentleman gave the viscount a particular look. Elizabeth knew Mr. Preston presumed that Llewellyn should be preparing to leave. Just then, Darcy entered the parlor.

"Ah, Llewellyn! Good to see you, milord! Mr. Preston." Darcy bowed from his shoulders and took a chair that allowed him to observe the entire room. "Llewellyn, I have the agricultural pamphlet you inquired about. Later, we shall retrieve it from my study."

Darcy's familiar manner with the viscount was a clear statement to Mr. Preston. Elizabeth busied herself preparing her husband's tea and observing the others out of the corner of her eye. Mr. Preston scowled, while both the viscount and Georgiana were relieved and smiling. In her estimation, her husband had proved again that he was the best of men!

After much more inane chattering, Mr. Preston's time was up and he took his leave, promising to return soon. This was information that pleased no one. Lord Llewellyn could no longer delay his own departure, but to Elizabeth's surprise, Darcy took the viscount to his study. Apparently, the farming pamphlet existed, and the viscount did desire to read it.

She should have known. It was simply impossible for her husband to lie.

It was unfortunate that Darcy would then farewell the viscount. Elizabeth knew Georgiana would have been delighted to walk Lord Llewellyn to the door. It would have delighted Elizabeth as well.

Goodness! Am I turning into my mother? Heavens!

Elizabeth was lost in such thoughts until Darcy reentered the parlor with news to share.

"*India?*" cried Elizabeth. "Lydia is sailing for India in a month's time with Colonel Denny?" To say that both Elizabeth and Georgiana were shocked would be an understatement.

"Yes, and they will marry in little more than a fortnight," reported Darcy.

"My goodness! I knew Lydia liked the colonel...but *India?*"

Darcy rolled his eyes. "It seems a settled business."

"Yes," added Georgiana. "Do you not recall the evening he visited after returning from France with Richard and Colonel Brandon? He said he desired a posting there." Elizabeth nodded and Georgiana turned to her brother. "This seems quite sudden, do you not think?"

"Perhaps," he replied. "Richard has often spoken of the Army's habit of having troops stand about at one place for weeks at a time before demanding they be at a new location as quickly as may be done."

"But what of the children?" injected Elizabeth. "Lydia is just recovered from Rosanna's birth! The baby cannot sail so soon!"

"Yes, about that..." Darcy would not meet his wife's eye. "Mrs. Wickham does not mean to take the children with her."

Silence descended upon the room. The ladies stared at Darcy with a mixture of emotions: surprise, disbelief, repugnance.

Finally, Elizabeth asked, "What is to become of them?" Her voice was level and composed, a sure sign of her deep anger.

"That has yet to be determined. I was told she thought they would live at Longbourn," Darcy said dryly.

"Longbourn! That is absurd! My parents are too old to raise three children under the age of four!"

"Very true, my dear. That was Colonel Denny's impression as well. Thus, the reason for his visit."

"Did he speak to my father?"

"He did."

"And we have received no letter? Oh!" cried Elizabeth bitterly. "My stupid sister! My indolent father! That I have brought you *such* relations! I am mortified!"

Darcy moved close and took his wife's hands. "You must not speak so. I would have you if you came with a score of Lydias. And your father I like very well, despite his eccentricities." He noted Georgiana had turned her head, giving them a modicum of privacy.

Elizabeth dashed away a tear from her cheek. "Oh, Fitzwilliam, what are we to do?"

That caught Georgiana's attention. "Do? Are Mrs. Wickham's children to live with us?"

Darcy grimaced at the thought. "I believe this is something we must discuss within the Bennet side of the family, but do not be concerned, Georgiana. Your wishes are to be considered."

"I only wish the children to be safe, wanted, and cared for!" Georgiana's chin jutted out in a Darcy-esque manner, something that brought a smile to her brother's face.

"Well said. *Where* remains the question. I must write to our brothers."

Elizabeth got to her feet. "And I to my sisters! We must move quickly. We have but a fortnight!"

Chapter 2

January 1816, Hertfordshire

Netherfield Park being available, Darcy leased the house for the month of January. The family arrived at the estate from London three days before Lydia's wedding, leaving Georgiana in the loving care of the Matlocks in town. Jane and Charles Bingley, traveling from their estate, Mayfield in Nottinghamshire, were expected the next day, as were Kitty and Franklin Southerland from Kympton in Derbyshire. Mary and Thomas Tucker had a house in Meryton and joined the Darcys for dinner.

"I take it you have not yet gone to Longbourn," said Mr. Tucker after the couple greeted their relations in the parlor. Thomas Tucker was a partner in Mr. Phillips's practice, and the serious, talented, and ambitious solicitor had secured both Darcy and Lord Matlock as clients. He met, courted, and married the former Mary Bennet in 1813, their common interest in religion and music assuring their felicity.

"No, Thomas," replied Elizabeth. "We were in no humor for the turmoil my mother has undoubtedly produced, and we wished to discuss this matter of Lydia with you and Mary in a more peaceful setting. How does Lydia fare?"

"I wish I could own myself surprised by our sister," replied Mary sadly, "but I cannot. Since her return from Newcastle after Major

Wickham's death at Waterloo, she has behaved much as she did before her marriage."

At the Darcys' alarmed expressions, she quickly continued. "Do not suppose she is flirting with any visitors! Of that she cannot be accused. I mean to say she has not raised a finger to help Mama; she believes herself to be ill-used and is only pleasant when Colonel Denny calls—which is as often as his duties allow."

"So, there is affection there. Does she spend any time with the children?"

Mary sniffed. "She was attentive enough before her lying-in, but since her confinement, she has time only for the babe, Rosanna."

"And yet she would leave her at this time?" Elizabeth's eyes flashed with indignation.

"Lydia employs a wet nurse. Rather, I should say our father does."

"That is not what I meant, Mary."

Mary colored. "I know. It is not for me to judge."

Darcy hid his growing disdain for Mrs. Wickham's behavior. Things were so different in his house. Every moment that Elizabeth and he could spare from their duties was spent with Bennet. How could they not? The boy was sweet and loving in his own quiet and gentle way.

Mrs. Reynolds claimed that Bennet was her master reborn, given his looks and behavior. This appeared to delight Elizabeth, who took it upon herself to have her son laugh as often as may be. She also teased her husband out of his worries that his heir might be *too* much like his father. She would often say, *"I fell in love with you. Surely, Bennet will capture the heart of his own impertinent lady, and both will strive to amaze the room with four-syllable words and witty banter!"*

Good God, he loved his wife!

Darcy was struggling for a comment that would not denigrate Mrs. Wickham when there was a knock on the door.

"Beg pardon, Mrs. Darcy," said a footman after allowed entrance, "Cook says the dinner is ready to be served."

It is just as well the discussion is at an end, Darcy mused as he rose and offered Elizabeth his arm. No decisions could be made before the Bingleys and Southerlands arrived.

AFTER DINNER, DARCY AND TUCKER TALKED POLITICS OVER THEIR port while the ladies visited with Bennet in the nursery. Given the shortness of the day, the Tuckers then left for their house while it was still light, and the Darcys retired to their rooms. It was Elizabeth's idea, for she was tired, and not just from the short trip from town.

"How does Mary fare?" Darcy asked Elizabeth after he joined her in bed.

She embraced her husband, seeking his strength and affection. "Mary hides it, but she remains distressed over losing her baby."

"Indeed? It has been months."

Men! Will they never understand? "I can assure you she does. Ladies do not forget such things. She will grieve her lost little one for the rest of her life."

Darcy began stroking Elizabeth's arm, and her tension and irritation faded. "I am very sorry for it. I should have recalled my mother's misery over her losses. But Mary is young yet. Surely, there will be other children."

"Mary fears there may not."

Darcy was quiet for a moment. "Perhaps we may remedy that," he said carefully.

Elizabeth raised her head. "Remedy? How could you do that?" Suddenly, a thought occurred to her. "Fitzwilliam, are you thinking of them taking one of Lydia's girls?"

"They will need a mother, particularly the babe. Can you think of a better choice than Mary?"

"Yes—Jane!" But she smiled. "I do like your idea, husband." What a good man she had married!

He returned her smile. "Pleasing you is my duty and my pleasure."

She encircled his neck and drew his face closer to hers. "Only a duty, Fitzwilliam?"

"I did say it was my pleasure."

She wet her lips in anticipation. "And *my* pleasure, sir?"

"Your pleasure is mine, sweet Lizzy," Fitzwilliam whispered before claiming her lips. She thought of nothing but him for some time.

THE NEXT DAY, DARCY STOOD WITH HIS BACK TO A WALL, WITNESS-ing Longbourn in full chaos. It was a sight he had not seen in... well, ever.

To begin with, the Gardiners had arrived with their four children. Being the eldest cousins, they had decided to teach Bennet Darcy, Susan Bingley, and two of the Wickham girls the fine art of screaming and laughing at the top of their lungs. Their mothers were in the far corner busy greeting each other while being fussed over by Mrs. Bennet and Mrs. Phillips. The nannies were upstairs with Hill, preparing the nursery. Furthermore, Mr. Bingley and Mr. Phillips amused themselves by encouraging the uproar.

Two years ago, Darcy would have fled the joyful commotion with a pounding headache. With the birth of Bennet, however, he acquired more than a son. He received the gift of fatherhood and developed a tolerance for such noise, instantly knowing the difference in a child's scream between delight, pain, or terror. While it was never to his preference, he could now endure such a hubbub as long as it was from the children.

Mrs. Bennet's exclamations were another matter altogether. Her squawks, as always, grated on his last nerve. But Darcy knew to persevere, for who would interrupt the heartwarming sight of the Bennet sisters' reunion, perhaps for the final time.

There was his Elizabeth in the midst of it, Jane Bingley on one side and Mary Tucker on the other. Kitty Southerland embraced her former favorite, Lydia Wickham, as though no time had passed since 1812. Tears and smiles adorned all their pretty faces. Mrs.

Gardiner and Mrs. Phillips were part of the circle, and Mrs. Bennet's cries of joy were heard over the clamor.

"Quite a noise, eh?" observed Mr. Bennet at Darcy's elbow. "I dare say one can hear it all over Hertfordshire."

Darcy did not reply. The years had not softened Mr. Bennet's sardonic manner. Instead, he glanced at the other gentlemen. Mr. Tucker looked as though he would stop the uproar if he had any idea how to do it. Mr. Gardiner, as a father of four, was far more sanguine. The Rev. Mr. Southerland was shocked and a little terrified. Colonel Denny simply ignored it.

Darcy found that interesting. Had Denny become immune to such a din due to his experience on the battlefield? He would have to ask Richard at his next opportunity.

Finally, the nannies made their appearance, rounding up the children and escorting them above stairs. The gentlemen reclaimed their ladies and took seats about the parlor. It was comfortable even though the windows faced due west. Once the expected inquiries as to the health of the various families were made and answered over tea, the real business of the day commenced.

"Colonel Denny, it is my understanding your ship sails for India in a little over a fortnight." Darcy began, as he was the acknowledged head of the family, being the most prominent of the sons and Mr. Bennet having no taste for the position.

"That is correct," the colonel replied. "I must present myself in Portsmouth a few days before she sails."

"So, a little over a se'nnight after the wedding."

Denny nodded and took Lydia's hand. "Our wedding trip will be abbreviated. We must call upon my family in Wiltshire."

"Lydia," cried her mother, "must you go?"

"Oh yes," Lydia insisted. "I cannot be separated from my dear Archie!" She gave her intended an overly intimate look.

Bingley sat up. "Archie?"

"Yes, sir," replied the colonel. "Archibald Denny. Mrs. Wickham likes to call me Archie." His slight grin earned a look from his intended best suited for the bedroom.

Darcy immediately dismissed any consideration of his sister's glances. "Let us speak of the children. Is it your wish that they remain in England?"

Lydia sniffed and Denny handed her a handkerchief. "Mrs. Wickham and I discussed this. While Calcutta boasts a considerable British presence, we feel it would be safer for the girls to remain with the family. The voyage is dangerous, particularly for small children."

"Oh, I shall dearly miss my three little girls," cried Lydia. "I cannot think of leaving them without weeping! But as Archie says, they will be safe in England, and they will have opportunities to make excellent matches thanks to my relations."

"Of course they will!" returned her mother. "Look what matches your sisters made thanks to your brother Darcy! When the time comes, he will certainly put them in the path of rich men!"

Darcy clearly saw that even after all these years, Elizabeth was mortified by her mother's thoughtless comments. If her face were any redder, she would burst into flame.

Tucker asked, "What of your family, Colonel?"

It was Denny's turn to be embarrassed. "I have few relations, Mr. Tucker. My good parents died years ago, and those I have left are elderly and poor."

"Lydia's girls go to strangers?" Mrs. Bennet gestured wildly. "Certainly not! They must stay here in the bosom of their family!"

Most of the gentlemen refrained from rolling their eyes, while Mary and Jane assured the colonel that Mrs. Bennet was motivated by her deep affection for the girls and meant no insult to his family. Colonel Denny claimed no offence.

Darcy felt all eyes on him. "If, as you say, Colonel, your family is unable to take in any of the children, it then falls to us assembled to determine where they will reside."

Lydia seemed confused. "I thought they would stay here at Longbourn!"

Mrs. Bennet began to wring her hands. "Oh, my dear Lydia, nothing would give me greater pleasure! Such beauties and such well-behaved little—"

Just then, the door crashed open and a blonde-haired blur dashed towards the couch. Mrs. Nivens entered right behind.

"Chloe! Chloe Wickham! Stop this instant!"

The child did not stop but, instead, dodged the nursemaid's outstretched hands, crying, "No! No bath! I want play!" She then leapt into Darcy's arms and attempted to bury herself in his coat.

Darcy resolutely gripped the arms of his chair. "Mrs. Nivens, I believe your charge is here." Chloe Wickham, Lydia's eldest, squirmed deeper into her hiding place.

"Forgive me, sir! The child is quite the handful." She pulled away the screaming, flailing, three-year-old. "Now, Miss Chloe, you must be a good girl and take your bath."

An ear-splitting cry of "NO BATH!" filled the parlor. Mrs. Nivens shook her head and marched out of the room, Chloe loudly complaining the entire time. A footman closed the door.

Unruffled, Darcy looked about as though this were an everyday occurrence. "I believe we were deliberating what to do with Mrs. Wickham's girls."

BY COMMON AGREEMENT, THE GROUP SOON BROKE UP BY COUPLE, the better to discuss the matter. Darcy and Elizabeth retreated to her old bedchamber. He doubted Mrs. Bennet changed much in the room, decorated as it was for a young lady.

"I never thought myself ever in *this* room," he remarked.

"Indeed?" Elizabeth graced him with a saucy smile. "You said you thought well of me when first in Hertfordshire."

"I did." Darcy ran the back of one hand down his wife's cheek. "I will admit to improper thoughts, but they involved a very different room." He came close. "My chambers at Netherfield."

"Fitzwilliam, we do not have time for this."

"Pity." The pair reluctantly sat upon the bed. "What are your thoughts?"

Elizabeth bit her lip. "The children cannot stay at Longbourn, for my parents are too old. My uncle and aunt Phillips have never raised children, and Uncle and Aunt Gardiner have four of their own." She glanced at her husband. "The girls' care must fall to Lydia's sisters."

Darcy saw she was troubled and took her hand. "We are of one mind about that."

"If all agree that Rosanna goes to the Tuckers, that leaves Phoebe and Chloe."

"Yes." Darcy frowned. "Phoebe…and Chloe."

Elizabeth huffed. "Our godchild is Lydia reborn."

Darcy pinched the bridge of his nose. "Pray remind me how that was brought about."

"I recalled it was Wickham's idea for us to stand as Chloe's godparents." Elizabeth squeezed his hand. "It was very good of you to accept the honor."

"It was solely for the girl's protection. I never thought Lydia's affections would last long enough for her to have more children."

"Wickham was very persuasive."

"I thank God you never fell under his spell."

"Fitzwilliam! I was never in danger from him." She smiled with that teasing sparkle in her eyes. "You were the only one I found irritating enough to love."

"Whatever the reason, I am thankful." Darcy raised their joined hands to kiss her knuckles. "So, back to our dilemma. What is to be done with the two eldest girls? Should Mary and Tucker accept Rosanna, what of the Southerlands for one of them?"

Elizabeth grew pensive. "Kitty and Franklin have not been married a year. I do not know whether she is ready for a family."

"Or perhaps she is. What of the Bingleys?"

"Jane would certainly welcome one of the girls. She might take both." She turned to him. "Do you think that wise?"

Darcy knew she was speaking of the Bingleys' near disaster in 1814. Charles made a foolish investment and was in danger of losing half his fortune. Most of the rest of his funds was tied up in their new estate, Mayfield, and their steward was a thief. It took Darcy and Tucker months to untangle the pickle his great friend had gotten into and recover as much of his money as possible. When all was said and done, an abashed Bingley was five thousand pounds poorer and a hundred times wiser. He pledged to do nothing unless Darcy, Tucker, and Mr. Gardiner approved it. Of course, that meant Darcy was more involved in Mayfield's issues than he wished.

"Bingley can afford it…now," he answered.

"So can we."

"*Both* the girls?" cried her husband.

"Then which should we choose?"

"I would hear your opinion, my dear."

"No," she returned with a grin. "*You* are the one with the particular tastes."

"As you well know, for I chose you over the finest jewels of the *ton*."

"I thank you for your pretty words, sir, but you have not answered me."

Darcy pulled a face. "I know Chloe is our godchild, but Phoebe is of an age with Bennet, while Chloe was born the same year as the Bingleys' Susan. Now, what is your opinion?"

"I would be content with either, but you make a good point with the ages of the children. And Phoebe is quieter."

"A troop of dragoons is quieter than Chloe Wickham."

Elizabeth laughed. "Very true! Phoebe it will be."

THOSE STAYING AT NETHERFIELD BROUGHT CLOTHES FOR DINNER, so the family assembled for the meal, the upcoming decision over

Lydia's daughters ruining everyone's enjoyment of Mrs. Bennet's delicious repast. The gentlemen retired to Mr. Bennet's bookroom for the momentous resolution. No one refused a libation.

Darcy swirled his brandy, knowing every eye was on him. "Gentlemen, it is my opinion that the placement of the girls falls to the younger members of the family. Agreed?" When no one disputed him, he continued. "Brothers, we have spoken to our wives. We have three girls and four couples. Southerland, you are the newlywed of the family. What say you?"

The rector of Kympton Parish set down his port. "Kitty and I would be honored to take any of the girls." His hesitancy was apparent.

"But the repairs on the rectory are not completed."

"No, they are not."

"Would Kitty be distressed if we three took on the responsibility for the children?"

Southerland shook his head, clearly relieved.

Darcy glanced at Bingley, who winked. Elizabeth earlier told him that she had briefly spoken to Jane.

"Tucker, would Mary like an infant?"

Tucker's jaw almost stuck to his chest. "You—you mean Rosanna? The baby?"

"Would she be too much of an encumbrance, or—"

"No!" The young solicitor gathered his thoughts. "You know of our disappointment. Mary—Mary would be overjoyed!" He grinned. "As would I! It would be an answer to our prayers!"

The gentlemen offered vociferous congratulations to their companion. Then, Darcy raised the last matter. "Charles, it is left to you and I to decide where to place Miss Chloe and Miss Phoebe."

"Jane and I will be very happy to take in little Phoebe." Bingley instantly declared.

Darcy was taken aback. "Why not Chloe? Being of an age with Susan, it would be easier on the girls."

"Nonsense! Being older, Susan would be a great help with Phoebe, leaving Jane to give more of her attention to our youngest, Elizabeth. Besides, Chloe is your goddaughter, is she not?"

Caught out, Darcy could only respond, "Why, yes she is."

"There you have it! It is done. Shall we have a toast before we inform the ladies?" Bingley returned with a smile.

ELIZABETH SHOOK HER HEAD. "OUR BROTHER OUTWITTED YOU. I can hardly believe it."

In the privacy of their rooms at Netherfield, Elizabeth and Darcy could finally speak freely of the surprising events of the day.

"You are no more astounded than I. Once he made the argument that Chloe was our goddaughter, anything I said but yes would paint us in a most disagreeable light. And his smile! Charles knew what he was doing. I did not know he had it in him."

Elizabeth snuggled into her husband's embrace. "We are doing a good thing, Fitzwilliam. It does not matter whether it is Chloe or Phoebe. We are caring for my niece."

"*Our* niece, my love." Darcy kissed the top of her head. After a pause, he asked, "Do you think she is *very* much like Lydia?"

Elizabeth could only laugh.

Chapter 3

The nuptials of Lydia Wickham and Colonel Archibald Denny were no different than any other wedding featuring a silly bride and a besotted groom. After a short appearance at the wedding breakfast, the new Mrs. Denny bid a tearful farewell to her children and family before the colonel handed her up into their hired carriage, courtesy of Mr. Darcy. The pair left in a cold late morning breeze, Lydia waving a handkerchief as they disappeared down the road.

The family now turned their attention to the children. Rosanna, only a month old and insensible of the change in her life, was moved with her wet nurse without difficulty to the Tuckers' home within an hour of her mother's departure. Phoebe was aware of her mother's absence, but as this was not an unusual occurrence in her short life, she was soon comforted by Jane Bingley.

Chloe, having just turned three years, was more mindful of the upheaval in her life. She did not care for it in the least.

"I want Mama!"

"I know, I know," crooned Elizabeth, holding the squirming child in her arms, stroking her hair. "Mama has gone on a trip far away, and you must visit with Uncle Darcy and me for a time."

"I want Mama! NOW!"

"Mrs. Darcy," said Mrs. Nivens, "I will take Miss Chloe."

"NO!" screamed the child. "I WANT MAMA!"

Darcy grew exasperated with the child's behavior. He walked over to his wife and took the girl, who was now throwing a proper fit. He held her at arm's-length while she cried and kicked for a good minute before he spoke.

"Miss Wickham. Chloe."

The sniffling little girl slowly stopped swinging her legs about.

"You must not misbehave," said Darcy calmly. "Your mama has gone on a long trip, and she has entrusted your aunt Darcy and me with your care. We are all returning to Netherfield where you will go with Mrs. Nivens to the nursery with your cousin Bennet."

She looked at Darcy. "Where are Phoebe and Baby?"

"Phoebe will stay with your aunt Bingley while the baby goes with your aunt Tucker. They will both be well cared for. You will see them again before we travel to London."

"I want Phoebe!"

"You will see your sister tomorrow. Now, you must be a good girl and mind Mrs. Nivens."

Chloe stared at Darcy for a few moments before her face fell and she howled, "I want Mama!"

Darcy hung his head. "I am sure you do. At this moment, so do I."

It took a few more minutes before Chloe would allow Mrs. Nivens's attentions. The little family took their leave of their relations and traveled the three miles to Netherfield. It was not a quiet trip.

THE NEXT MORNING, DARCY AWOKE TO THE SOUND OF HIS WIFE casting her accounts into a bowl. Shocked, he instantly scrambled out of bed and to her side.

"My dearest, what ails you? You there, Sally! Mrs. Darcy is unwell. Send for the apothecary this instant!"

Elizabeth set down the cloth she used to cleanse her mouth and gave Darcy a long-suffering look. "Fitzwilliam, I am not—"

He heard not a word. "Elizabeth, come and lie down. You are

not well. Was it the dinner last night? I should never allow mutton in the house."

"Fitzwilliam."

"And the fish! I must see to it that Cook has a word with the fish monger today!"

"Fitzwilliam."

"Or perhaps something else? Macmillan! I shall have Mr. Macmillan call!"

"*Fitzwilliam*." Elizabeth firmly grasped his hand. Her firm grip recalled Darcy's attention. "I. Am. Not. Ill," she said, slowly enunciating each word. "I do not require our physician from London. I believe I am with child."

"A child." He stared at her stupidly. "Oh…yes, of course."

Elizabeth smiled.

"A child!" Darcy cried. "Another child! How wonderful!"

Elizabeth laughed at Darcy's foolish grin. "It is well you think so!"

"A girl—it will be a girl this time! Bennet will be such a good brother." Darcy's smile slid suddenly from his lips. He frowned. "Chloe."

"Yes, Chloe is here."

"We will have two children soon. Will not a third be a burden on you?"

An impertinent spark lit Elizabeth's eye. "What do you suggest? Shall we send this one back?"

"No, of course not!"

Elizabeth grew serious. "Surely, you are not thinking of removing Chloe."

"No! I—" Darcy shook his head to settle his thoughts. "I am only surprised we are blessed so soon after taking on—"

Elizabeth's face had turned beet red, triggering Darcy's suspicions.

"Elizabeth, how long have you suspected you were with child again?"

"Not long."

"When were your last courses?"

Elizabeth stared at the ceiling. "November."

"November?"

"You know my courses do not always follow a regular pattern."

Darcy crossed his arms. "You knew you were with child before we went to Longbourn."

She shrugged. "I suspected."

"You *knew* before we assumed the raising of Chloe."

"We could not abandon the poor girl!" she cried.

"Other arrangements can be made." At her stricken look, he added, "She would be well looked after by Bingley or Southerland or…someone."

Elizabeth started to weep. "Forgive me. I did not intend to keep this from you. Do not be angry."

Darcy took her in his arms. "I am not angry, love. I am concerned for you. You and the baby. You must recall how unwell you were with Bennet."

"I was *not* unwell," Elizabeth insisted, her face buried in his nightshirt. "I had to accustom myself to carrying a baby. Now that I know what to expect, it will be far easier with this one." She peeked up at him. "I was going to tell you, Fitzwilliam—truly, once the baby quickened and was out of danger. I did not want you to worry."

"You might as well ask me not to breathe."

"Silly man! You must remember I am a Bennet. My mother had five children in eight years. We country girls are of hardy stock."

"I know, but—"

Elizabeth took his cheeks in her hands. "Dearest, I am not your mother. I am perfectly well, and come July, you will be a father for a second time. *And*, we will take care of Chloe." She kissed him. "I am determined."

Darcy drank in her lovely face. "You know I can deny you nothing."

Oh, but if he could truly explain how much he loved her, needed her, feared for her. She was his life. He could not speak of it; he could only demonstrate his devotion. He kissed her with all the love and passion he had. Her arms slid about his shoulders as she returned his adulation.

"Oh! Beg pardon, madam!" The door to the dressing room slammed shut.

"Fitzwilliam," Elizabeth moaned, "we have shocked Sally again."

"That is not my concern."

"It will be when that door opens again for the apothecary."

He rested his forehead on hers. "You are correct. Let us prepare for him."

THE APOTHECARY'S VISIT WAS BRIEF. HE DECLARED MRS. DARCY perfectly well and directed that the lady perform her duties with an eye to moderation. As Elizabeth had been given this advice before—and ignored it with no consequences—she nodded, smiled, and sent the man on his way.

The Darcys went down for a late breakfast where they shared their news with the Bingleys. After the expected hugs, kisses, and handshakes, Jane asked about Chloe. Elizabeth quickly assured her that nothing had changed, and Lydia's eldest would return with them to London. Darcy reluctantly concurred.

While the carriages were being packed, Chloe had her farewell with Phoebe. The Darcys traveled to Longbourn, while the Bingleys remained one more day at Netherfield before returning to their leased house in London. The interlude at Longbourn was far too short for Mr. and Mrs. Bennet and far too long for Mr. and Mrs. Darcy. Still, the Darcys reached their house in Mayfair well before dark. It was there that Chloe was introduced to her aunt Georgiana.

"An angel!" cried Chloe upon first beholding her.

"No, no," Georgiana said while laughing. "I am not an angel. I am your aunt." She held the girl close.

Chloe grabbed a fistful of her cousin's black tresses. "Blue eyes! Angel!"

"You have blue eyes too."

Chloe considered that. She laid her head on Georgiana's breast. "Angel aunt," she said softly.

"Miss Darcy," said Mrs. Nivens, "allow me to take Miss Chloe to the nursery."

Georgiana stroked the child's hair. "Thank you, no. I shall bear her." With that, Mrs. Nivens took Bennet from Mrs. Darcy's arms, and the pair ascended the stairs.

Elizabeth smiled at her husband. "Apparently, the Darcys have an unusual affinity for Bennet ladies."

Darcy smiled. "Indeed, we do, as you well know."

She kissed his cheek.

The pair went their separate ways, Elizabeth to meet with the housekeeper, Darcy to his study and the pile of letters of business that awaited his attention. He worked for a few hours until it was time to change for dinner. Upon reaching the family wing, he heard a noise from the nursery.

"NO BATH!"

Darcy flinched and braced himself, but no blonde-haired sprite attacked him. With relief, he continued to his chambers.

Chapter 4

The ball hosted by Mr. and Mrs. Arbuthnot in honor of their only daughter, Miss Dorothy Arbuthnot, was hardly the event of the season, though not from lack of trying. Mr. Arbuthnot owned a modest estate in Norfolk of £6,000 a year. Modest would also describe his daughter: modest in looks, modest in deportment, and modest in wit. What was not modest was her fortune of £35,000, safely in trust and invested in the funds. Despite her wealth, a ball was required to favorably launch a nondescript debutante like Miss Arbuthnot into the marriage market that was the Season.

The occasion proved the axiom that the plainer the lady, the grander the event. Surely half the candles in London had been sacrificed to light the ballroom's extravagant decorations. Flowers and greenery were everywhere. The sheer weight of the refreshments threatened the collapse of more than one table. No expense was spared to secure musicians of the highest quality. Undoubtedly, Mr. Arbuthnot had placed his finances in dire straits to promote his daughter.

Sadly, little of the expenditure could be appreciated by the attendees. An extensive guest list assured a packed ballroom, leaving only a minimum of space for dancing.

"Good Lord," grumbled Mr. Darcy, as he, his wife, and his sister slowly made their way through the throng after suffering the reception line, "I believe half of London is here."

"Hush, Fitzwilliam," said Elizabeth good-naturedly. "You would complain—Oh, good evening, Lady Cardwell! Mrs. Wood-Smythe! How good to see you!—you would complain if this were a small card party. Come, I see your aunt and uncle by that great fern on the far wall. Try to smile, my dear."

"Of course. One should always smile in the face of adversity."

Elizabeth rolled her eyes. "Yes, dear. The beatings will commence in ten minutes. Hurry along now."

Georgiana tried unsuccessfully to hold back a giggle.

The Darcys soon joined the Earl and Countess of Matlock. With them were the viscount and viscountess, Lord Fitzwilliam and Lady Eugenie. After initial greetings, the ladies occupied themselves complimenting each other's choice of attire. Georgiana was sparkling in a creation of white with a light gold lace overlay, gold combs, and a pearl necklace. Elizabeth's deep green gown matched the Darcy emeralds at her throat. Lady Matlock was in claret, while Lady Eugenie's navy silk was almost back.

"My word, Darcy," drawled Lord Fitzwilliam as he gestured at his cousin. "A matching waistcoat? You are not a newlywed, you know."

"Harrumph," responded Lord Matlock. "Probably marking his territory if I know Darcy."

"Stop teasing him, both of you," scolded Lady Matlock. "I think he looks very well, very well indeed. You both could take a lesson from him."

Darcy refused to respond, even though his ears were bright red with embarrassment. His uncle was correct. He had selected the green waistcoat not only to please Elizabeth but to ward off any unsavory characters from approaching. Elizabeth hid her smile with a gloved hand.

"I am far too old for such gestures, m'dear," declared Matlock.

She affectionately slapped his arm with her fan. "So you have said, you old goat. Ah! Georgie, I think I spy someone looking for you!"

Sure enough, Viscount Llewellyn soon joined them. While he greeted everyone with the proper decorum, his eyes never left Georgiana. Duty done, he addressed her.

"Miss Darcy, I should be honored for a set."

"The supper set is free," she managed nervously.

Darcy's eyebrows rose.

Young Llewellyn grinned from ear to ear. "Thank you. May I say how lovely you look this evening?"

Georgiana dropped her chin. "Thank you, my lord."

Darcy turned to Elizabeth to see her satisfied smile.

Llewellyn began to speak again but thought better of it. He stood nervously, working his hands.

"Llewellyn," said the earl, "how does your family? Well, I trust?"

He assured him that the Wakefords and Woodhouses were in good health, and then something caught his eye. "Ah, there are my cousins now. May they join us, sir?"

Permission granted, he summoned the couple, Mr. and Mrs. John Knightley. "Wakeford House is closed up at present, so Cousin John was good enough to accommodate me."

Darcy was acquainted with the London solicitor but knew the gentleman's brother better. Once the introductions were done, he asked John Knightley, "Your brother remains at Highbury?"

"Yes, Mr. Darcy," replied Mr. Knightley. "My wife's father prefers the familiar confines of Hartfield, and *his* peace of mind requires George and Emma's agreeable company."

Darcy knew the Knightleys resided at Hartfield even though George Knightley owned the neighboring property, Donwell Abbey. "Remind him he owes me a match when he is next in town." The two were members of the same fencing club.

"I shall."

"Oh, but I do not know when that will be," interrupted his wife. "The London air is so disagreeable! George and Emma are wise to stay away. The winter is tolerable, I grant you, but the summer! I declare, we would remove the children to Surrey in a moment if not for Mr. Knightley's profession!"

Knightley patted his wife's hand. "Of course, my dear."

Lord Matlock and Lord Fitzwilliam shared a glance but said nothing while Lady Matlock politely asked about the Knightley children. Lady Eugenie pretended the couple did not exist.

Throughout the conversation, Elizabeth uttered only the bare minimum of polite discourse. It was unusual for her, but Darcy knew she could not abide the foolish and valetudinary, and Isabella Knightley suffered from the latter. As the conversation subsided, Lord Llewellyn took his relations away, sparing one last tender glance at Georgiana—a look she returned.

An uneasy Darcy pulled Elizabeth a little away. "What is going on?" he whispered.

"A ball, husband." Butter would not melt in Mrs. Darcy's mouth.

"I refer to Georgie, as you well know," he hissed.

Her response was to lightly smile, pat his cheek, and return to Lady Matlock's side, leaving her perplexed husband to ponder the last few minutes.

Lord Llewellyn is a fine young man—intelligent, honorable, and agreeable. Yet tonight, the boy could not put two words together. Except with Georgie.

And Georgie! What was she about? She is acting very strangely. Much like Elizabeth when I returned to Longbourn—

Darcy started.

Oh no!

DARCY DANCED THE OPENING SET WITH GEORGIANA WHILE LORD Matlock, the most prominent gentleman in attendance, led out Miss Arbuthnot. The earl took Georgiana's second set and Lord Fitzwilliam her third.

Darcy and Elizabeth graced the third set as well, and so it was that they both received an unfortunate surprise when they returned to the countess. The unpleasant Mr. Preston lay in wait, and Georgiana could not refuse him the fourth set.

The Matlocks were in conversation with their old friends, Baron and Baroness Higginbottom, and Darcy's notice was divided between watching his sister and attending the Higginbottoms. They were joined by an acquaintance of the baron's, Mr. James Rushworth of Southerton Court. Darcy had met the wealthy and foolish Mr. Rushworth before, finding his conversation particularly dull, even by the low standards of the *ton*. The verbose gentleman was describing in great detail the latest improvements planned for his estate when Mr. Preston returned with Georgiana.

"Miss Darcy!" cried Mr. Rushworth. "Good evening." Georgiana made her curtsey. "I hope I find you well. It has been some time since we all dined together at the Van Horton's—seven or eight months, I believe. I clearly recall your extraordinary performance at the pianoforte."

Darcy recollected that rather large dinner party with pain. While Mr. Rushworth was seated at some distance from him and his relations, after half a year, Darcy could still recall the gentleman's inane conversation.

"I hope," continued Mr. Rushworth, "I may have the honor of claiming the supper set, Miss Darcy."

Darcy's mask of indifference hid his unease, for Mr. Rushworth's reputation was not fully recovered from the scandal of his divorce. Lord Matlock scowled, and Lady Matlock's lips thinned in disapproval. Both the Higginbottoms were noticeably uncomfortable.

"Oh, that set is taken," said Georgiana.

"Indeed, it is, Rushworth," proclaimed Lord Llewellyn as he stepped to Georgiana's side. "How do you do, sir? It has been some time."

Mr. Rushworth grinned foolishly. "Not since that shooting party at Willoughby's. That was good sport, what? Finest hunting dogs I have ever seen."

Llewellyn nodded and turned to glare at Preston, who remained on the opposite side of Georgiana. That gentleman only smirked. The Darcys, Matlocks, and Higginbottoms stood back to watch the three young men demand the attention of Miss Darcy.

It was Georgiana who broke the tension. "Lord Llewellyn, I would like a sip of punch before our dance. Shall we retire to the refreshment table?"

"I would be happy to fetch a glass," offered Mr. Preston,

"No, pray, allow me," cried Mr. Rushworth.

She gave the gentlemen a stone-faced look, her chin rising a fraction. "I thank you kindly, sirs, but as the set will soon begin, it would be best for you both to secure a partner for supper." She nodded to them in dismissal. "Come, milord." She moved directly towards the table, forcing Llewellyn to hurry to join her.

The remaining would-be suitors glanced at each other before taking their leave. A moment later, Lord Matlock laughed aloud.

"Ha! She is my dear sister Anne's daughter all right! Did you see how she handled those three young bucks? A Fitzwilliam through and through!"

"Hugh!" managed Lady Matlock while giggling. "Lower your voice, my dear."

"Very impressive," said the baron. "I am happy I witnessed it. It will be the talk at my club tomorrow, I have no doubt!"

Darcy's pride in Georgiana's actions faded at Higginbottom's claim. He hated gossip about his wife and sister more than he did about himself.

Elizabeth must have sensed his disquiet. "Now, now," she whispered, "do not fret about what cannot be prevented. Georgiana did very well, and *that* will be the subject of talk." Her eyes sparkled. "To quote the finest gentleman I know, 'It could be much worse.'"

Darcy took a breath and chuckled. "Indeed, it could."

DARCY DID NOT ENJOY DINNER THOUGH THE FOOD WAS MORE THAN

passable and the company was excellent. Besides Elizabeth and Georgiana, they dined with the Matlocks, Fitzwilliams, and Lord Llewellyn. However, Darcy paid no attention to the food or conversation. He was too busy studying his sister and her admirer.

It was obvious Llewellyn was smitten with Georgiana. As for his sister, life with Elizabeth the last four years had encouraged her to be less guarded and shy. It was now easy to see she accepted his attentions with restrained but heartfelt pleasure.

Darcy had been blind to it all.

His dinner sat heavily in his stomach as he considered the matter. Was this the man fated to steal away his beloved sibling? Was he truly worthy of her? He glanced at a rather pleased Elizabeth. Had she played matchmaker?

Mr. Arbuthnot began the evening's entertainment by escorting his daughter to the pianoforte. Unfortunately, Miss Arbuthnot's performance was as modest as her other gifts. Other young ladies took turns exhibiting, to mixed results. Some were excellent; others were not. Meanwhile, Georgiana exchanged seats with Darcy and sat next to Elizabeth in an effort to escape notice. Even with her newly developed confidence, she still owned a strong aversion to displaying her talent before strangers.

It was nearing the time for the ball to resume when Mr. Rushworth stood. "I seldom have heard such beautiful music as has been presented tonight! But perfection cannot be complete when there is one more delightful performer of the art here. Might we hear a selection from Miss Darcy?" He gestured towards her.

Darcy could have strangled the buffoon.

For her part, Georgiana blushed but nodded. Lord Llewellyn rose, held out his arm, and gallantly escorted her to the instrument. He whispered something to her once she was seated, stepped around to the front of the pianoforte, took a position where she could see him, and smiled.

Georgiana sat frozen for a moment, her eyes fixed upon the

viscount. She took and released a great breath, placed her fingers on the keys, and began the third movement of Beethoven's *Piano Sonata No. 17 in D minor*.[1] She played the difficult piece, known as *The Tempest*, with exquisite verve and feeling. The dining room was transported to a rocking ship lost in the midst of a great gale on the deep ocean. For several minutes, the assembled were spellbound as Georgiana's music filled the space. Finally, as the last note hung over the crowd, there was absolute silence.

The applause began slowly as the audience recovered their senses. It was polite at first, but then a gentleman rose to his feet. He was followed by another, and another, the applause growing all the time, until all the gentlemen were standing. The ladies were mostly smiling and appreciative, though a few of the maidens were clearly either mortified or jealous.

Georgiana seemed impervious to it all. She simply stared at Lord Llewellyn, a small smile on her lips. For the viscount's part, he grinned as he clapped softly, his gaze locked on hers.

At that moment, Darcy knew he had lost his sister forever.

RETURNING TO THE BALLROOM, GEORGIANA WAS BESIEGED BY gentlemen on every side, full of congratulations and compliments. She was clearly overwhelmed, despite her family's attempts to shield her. Llewellyn could do little to comfort her, but with no under-standing—no *official* understanding, Darcy reminded himself—his lordship could only glower at the interlopers.

Mr. Rushworth made his way through the throng, and Darcy wondered whether he would hang if he struck down the idiot who instigated this commotion.

"Miss Darcy, allow me to congratulate you on your performance. Such music! Such perfection! Why, I could not have heard better in a concert hall in London!"

---

1 https://www.youtube.com/watch?v=hKkR4YFtyJk

Llewellyn stepped between the gentleman and Georgiana. "Rushworth, you have all but referred to a gentle lady as a paid performer! How dare you!"

Darcy and Lord Fitzwilliam stepped in to confront the pair. "My lord, this is not your concern," Darcy advised Llewellyn. "This is a family matter."

Llewellyn reddened. "But I—" He grunted. "Of course, forgive me."

Lord Fitzwilliam looked down his nose at Rushworth. "You will apologize to my cousin at once, sir."

"Of—of course, milord," managed Mr. Rushworth, seemingly more frightened than mortified. "Miss Darcy, I humbly beg your forgiveness for my clumsy— Good God!"

All were taken aback at Mr. Rushworth's angry exclamation. A moment later, the reason revealed himself.

"Crawford! What the devil are *you* doing here?"

A few steps away was Mr. Henry Crawford. Not a particularly handsome man, the charming Mr. Crawford made his way in the world with a lively air and pleasant countenance. He also owned no morals, a fact well known to the gentleman he had cuckolded.

"Ah, Rushworth." Mr. Crawford inclined his head. "I hope you are well. As for the reason I am here, it is a ball, and I mean to dance." He turned to Georgiana. "I beg to be introduced to this lady so I might ask for a set."

Georgiana blanched, Mr. Rushworth sputtered, and Lord Llewellyn glowered. For his part, Darcy knew not whether he should hold back the others or fall on Mr. Crawford himself. Before he could decide, Lord Matlock entered the fray.

"How dare you approach *my* niece without a proper introduction!" Lord Matlock's voice boomed across the room.

Mr. Crawford bowed low. "Forgive me, my lord. I meant no insult. That is why—"

"You have not been introduced to *me*, and yet you presume to speak!" Lord Matlock reminded him. "I require you to leave my presence immediately!"

Mr. Crawford turned white. With another low bow, he quickly retreated. The entire party breathed easier.

Of course, all this attracted considerable attention. Darcy whispered to Georgiana, "Do you have any sets open?"

She glanced at the card at her wrist. "Yes. The one after this."

Just then, her partner for the upcoming dance, the second son of a marquess, approached to claim his set. Meanwhile, the earl and viscount made for the card room. In moments, Darcy found himself standing with his wife, his aunt, his cousin's wife, and his sister's... *something*. Lord Llewellyn shrugged, sketched a bow, and left them.

"Well, *that* was...exciting," drawled Lady Eugenie. "We shall certainly be in tomorrow's papers, I have no doubt."

"Hush, Eugenie," Lady Matlock snapped in a rare episode of correcting the viscountess. "We must find Georgiana a partner for the next set to protect her from rakes like Mr. Crawford."

"Why not you, Darcy?" the viscountess asked.

"I have the closing set," he replied, racking his brain for a solution.

"It would not do to have her dance three times with her brother." The countess scanned the room. "It would reflect badly on Georgiana. She would appear frightened."

"But she is," Lady Eugenie remarked.

"And you would have that confirmed?" Lady Matlock shook her head. "Society's vultures would attack without mercy." She studied the dance floor. "Do you see anyone you would trust for her?"

Darcy suddenly noticed that Elizabeth had slipped away. He looked all about, a slight fear in his breast. Great was his relief to find her at the refreshment table with the Knightleys. She smiled and gestured towards her family party. Darcy watched the Knightleys and Elizabeth approach, laughing and smiling. He nodded at the couple when they arrived.

John Knightley bowed to the ladies before addressing Darcy.

"Mrs. Darcy has informed me of an unfortunate situation and suggests that I might be of service to Miss Darcy.

"Does she have a partner for the next set?"

Darcy turned to Elizabeth, who wore a wide smile. "You are too clever by half, my dear."

Elizabeth laughed as Lady Matlock lightly swatted Darcy's arm. "For shame, Darcy! I believe Elizabeth has displayed exactly the correct amount of cleverness."

"And impertinence," added Lady Eugenie with a raised eyebrow.

"Occasional impertinence in the midst of the *ton* is like water in the desert, Eugenie." The countess turned to Mr. Knightley. "I take it you wish to complete my niece's dance card, sir?"

Mr. Knightley bowed again. "If that meets with her approval and that of her family."

"I have no objection at all. Darcy?"

"If Georgiana agrees, then so do I."

The Darcys and Fitzwilliams spent the next half an hour speaking with the Knightleys. Once Georgiana rejoined them, she happily accepted Mr. Knightley's offer. As they moved to the floor, Mrs. Knightley was able to turn the conversation to her favorite subjects: sickness and disease.

The Darcys were able to move away a few steps. "Have I told you today that you are magnificent, my love?"

"I am far from magnificent, dearest," Elizabeth returned with a soft laugh, "but when it comes to those I love, I have my moments of cleverness." In company, she could risk only a quick stroke along his arm. "I have a handsome and selfless example to inspire me."

He stole a glance at her waist, not yet showing the fruits of their love. "And you inspire me, my dear."

THE END OF THE EVENING WAS NIGH WITH ONLY THE LAST DANCE remaining. The Fitzwilliams had already made their farewells and left. The crowd thinned out. All that remained were the young ladies, their families, the young gentlemen, the serious card players, and the gossips of the *ton*.

Georgiana hid a yawn behind her hand. "Are you too tired to dance the last set, Georgie?" asked Darcy.

"No, no, I am well, Brother."

Her eyes belied her words. Suddenly, they brightened; Darcy turned in the direction she faced and beheld Lord Llewellyn. He noticed, when the viscount was not dancing, that he remained within sight of the Darcy party. He thought for a moment and sighed.

"Pardon me, ladies."

He strode to where the young man stood and began directly. "Milord, if it pleases you, you may take my place in the final dance."

Llewellyn was clearly stunned. "I beg your pardon?"

"Pray do not dissemble, sir. You have been staring at my sister in that mooncalf state all evening. Do you wish to dance again with her?"

The young lord's head swiveled between brother and sister. "Truly? Of course…but the *last* dance?"

"I know full well what it means, and should you accept my offer, I will expect you in my study tomorrow afternoon. Your answer, sir…"

"Yes! That is, if Miss Darcy wishes to—oh yes." His grin split his face.

The two returned to the ladies. "Georgiana, I own a bit of weariness tonight. I feel I cannot do you justice as a dance partner. But here is a young man who might serve." He turned to Llewellyn.

The viscount bowed. "Miss Darcy, I would be greatly honored to partner you in the last set."

Both Elizabeth and Georgiana turned to Darcy—his wife in astonishment, and his sister hopeful and happy. He nodded and, with a soft smile, said, "It is all right, Georgie."

Both ladies understood what was left unsaid. Georgiana curtsied and with a barely level voice replied to Llewellyn, "I am honored, milord."

Darcy and Elizabeth watched the two young people take their

place in the line, the pair completely oblivious to the excited buzzing of the other attendees.

Elizabeth whispered, "Mr. Darcy, this is not the first time you have proven to be one of the finest men I have ever known."

"I thought you said I was *the* finest, madam."

Elizabeth smiled through her happy tears. "Oh, there is always room for improvement. But in time, I suspect you will be a true proficient."

Chapter 5

The following afternoon, the ladies of Darcy House assembled in the front parlor to await the expected callers. Georgiana's maid labored mightily to disguise her mistress's lack of sleep and was only partially successful. Face powder hid the circles under her eyes, but little could be done about the redness in them. Elizabeth tried to comfort her sister.

"You look lovely, Georgiana. You must not fret so."

"But I am certain Lew—I mean Lord Llewellyn will be here soon, and I look a fright! What will he think of me?" She nervously worked her hands.

Elizabeth laughed. "He will think you an angel, as you well know!"

"Will he? He was so kind and thoughtful and handsome! He said something of meeting with Brother. Do you think—? Oh, where is he?"

The clock struck the hour, and almost at the same instant, the knocker was heard. Georgiana took a great breath and assumed her Darcy reserve. For once, Elizabeth had no complaint. She wished at times she could hide her feelings as completely as her husband and sister. Steps approached from the stairs, the door opened, and the butler entered.

"Mr. Preston, madam."

The dratted man must have been waiting outside the front door!

Elizabeth could not completely hide her disappointment and annoyance, but she offered a most correct greeting. For Georgiana's part, the only sign of her distress were the clenched fists at her side.

His usual oily self, Mr. Preston seemed unaware of the tension in the room.

"Mrs. Darcy, good afternoon. I hope I find you well. Miss Darcy! You truly are a vision! I thought nothing could exceed your loveliness last night, but I stand corrected!" He took the closest chair to Georgiana and asked her opinion of the ball.

"It was enjoyable," she allowed. "It is to be hoped that Miss Arbuthnot was well pleased."

"Miss Arbuthnot! Yes, I suppose she did as well as could be expected, given her…charms, but who can speak of Miss Arbuthnot when Miss Darcy is in the room?"

I believe I shall be ill now, thought Elizabeth.

The butler reappeared. "Mr. Rushworth, Mrs. Darcy."

The stunned party rose to their feet as Mr. Rushworth made his way in. Elizabeth wondered how he could show himself after the ball. It was unaccountable—unless he was an idiot.

"Mrs. Darcy," he said as he bowed. "Miss Darcy." He had halfway straightened up when he spied the third person in the room. "Mr. Preston?"

"Rushworth. Have you fully recovered from last night?"

"Recovered? I assure you I am well." He turned to the ladies. "I am seldom ill. Country living is the best, I say. Southerton Court is most delightfully situated." Rushworth claimed a chair.

Mr. Preston smirked. "Then you have not seen today's papers?"

"No. Any reason why I should?"

"No, no reason." Preston sniggered.

Elizabeth inwardly sighed. Mr. Rushworth had confirmed he truly was an idiot. There was an article of the Arbuthnot ball in the papers— a *most* complete one. It spent considerable time describing what was called "a short fracas" involving two gentlemen intimately tangled in a recent scandal and the family of a peer.

As usual in such reports, no names were used, but there were enough hints that most of the *ton* could deduce the participants. The Darcys, jealous of their privacy, were embarrassed but unharmed. Mr. Rushworth, however, would soon learn he was the subject of society's derision once again.

"Lady Matlock, madam."

Everyone jumped to their feet as the countess entered. "Elizabeth, Georgiana, forgive me. I am behind my time." She kissed each lady before turning to the others. "Gentlemen."

Elizabeth ordered that a chair be provided for Lady Matlock. None was ready because her ladyship was not expected, despite her words. In a few moments, things were rearranged so that Georgiana was flanked on one side by her sister and on the other by her aunt. Mr. Preston was obviously put out by the maneuver but could not complain.

Before she took her seat, Lady Matlock whispered in Elizabeth's ear, "Has Lord Llewellyn arrived?"

Elizabeth could only shake her head.

The countess surveyed the room. Aloud, she said, "I am acquainted with Mr. Preston, but I have not been introduced to... *this* gentleman." She looked down her nose at the other occupant.

Elizabeth made the introductions.

"I am honored, milady." Rushworth bowed deeply.

"You have a unique talent for appearing in the newspapers, sir," Lady Matlock said coldly.

The countess then turned her attention to the other gentleman. "Mr. Preston! Tell me, how does your estate fare?"

"Very well, or so my steward tells me." He grinned.

"Tells you! You mean to say you do not know?"

Mr. Preston was clearly puzzled. "I leave such matters to my servants, milady."

"Is that so?" Condescension dripped from her ladyship's voice. "I assure you the earl is intimately engaged in *all* matters at Matlock

Manor. Nothing there escapes his notice." She turned to Elizabeth. "Mr. Darcy is equally occupied with his estate, is he not?"

"You are correct as always, milady."

Lady Matlock set a gimlet eye on a squirming Mr. Preston. "In times like these, with falling prices and rising costs, a gentleman ignores his business at his peril! Would you not agree, sir?"

"Of course, my lady."

"I am engaged in all matters at Southerton Court, milady," injected Mr. Rushworth.

"*Estate* affairs are not what you are known for, Mr. Rushworth," she pointed out.

Silence descended upon the room. Mr. Rushworth, finally aware of the new scandal engulfing him, shakily rose to his feet. "I—I must be going." He bid his farewells to all present.

Before he left, Georgiana moved to him. "Mr. Rushworth, thank you for calling on us. Pray give my regards to Miss Arbuthnot. Did you know she has an interest in topiary?"

"Thank you, Miss Darcy, I— Topiary?" His eyes brightened. "I had no idea."

"Oh yes! It is of all things her delight."

Mr. Rushworth grew distracted. "How interesting. You know, I was just thinking that topiary would be very welcome at Southerton Court. Very welcome, indeed." His attention returned to Miss Darcy. "You are very kind. Thank you."

Georgiana smiled sweetly. "Good day, Mr. Rushworth." The gentleman affected one last bow and quickly quit the room.

As she returned to her chair, her aunt whispered, "Well done."

Mr. Preston chuckled. "Rushworth and Southerton! No improvement is too much there! I wonder he ever has the time to come to town!"

"I believe, sir," said Lady Matlock in an icy tone, "we were just speaking of a gentleman's responsibility to his estate." She looked pointedly at the clock on the fireplace mantle.

Mr. Preston acknowledged he was past his time. "Miss Darcy, may I ask to call again tomorrow?"

Before Georgiana could say anything, Elizabeth interjected, "We shall be occupied all day, I am afraid." She rose. "Thank you for coming, Mr. Preston."

It was an unmistakable dismissal. He made his silky goodbyes and took himself off.

"Thank goodness!" cried Lady Matlock. "I thought he would never leave."

"You were very kind to Mr. Rushworth, Georgiana," observed Elizabeth. "I had no idea of Miss Arbuthnot's devotion to topiary."

Georgiana turned bright red. "I am afraid I was not completely honest," she admitted. "I have no idea of her opinions on gardening." At the other ladies' incredulous expressions, she continued. "Miss Arbuthnot wishes to make a good match, and I know that her ideas and opinions are…flexible. Mr. Rushworth is not right for me, but he might make her happy." She frowned. "Did I do wrong?"

Elizabeth hugged her. "Oh, my dear sister! You did right—very right!"

"He is a fool, but a harmless fool," her aunt proclaimed. "You are a good girl, Georgiana."

"Are we interrupting anything?"

The ladies turned to behold Darcy in the doorway with a smiling Lord Llewellyn.

"My lord, you are welcome. Come in," cried Elizabeth. "You too, of course, Fitzwilliam."

"Ah, I do not think so, my dear." A slight smile played on Darcy's lips. "Lord Llewellyn asks whether our sister is agreeable for a private interview in the library."

Georgiana's hands flew to her lips. "Of—of course. I would be happy…" She almost ran from the room.

Elizabeth was only steps behind her, but her target was her

husband. They watched as the two young people disappeared through the library door.

"Does he mean to—" Elizabeth murmured.

"Yes. Instead of visiting with you ladies, we have been in my study. He requested my leave to propose to Georgiana. I could not disagree. I shall leave it to Georgiana to decide—I doubt not her choice. We waited until the guests left. Which reminds me…" He turned and informed a footman that the family was not at home to visitors. "That should take care of the horde," he told Elizabeth.

By then, Lady Matlock had joined them. "It will not do to stand about in the hall. Come away and sit down."

Darcy eyed the clock. "For ten minutes only. If they are not out of the library by then, I am going in!"

THE JOYFUL COUPLE RETURNED TO THE PARLOR IN GOOD TIME and proclaimed their happy news. After many hugs, happy tears, and handshakes had been exchanged, Darcy requested that the newly betrothed pair retire with him to his study for a discussion of their plans.

"Georgiana, as you know, Richard resigned his guardianship when you came of age," Darcy told the couple after they settled into chairs before his desk. "To marry, you need nothing from either of us, but for your dowry, my permission is required, and you have it, of course."

"I would marry your sister no matter her consequence!" declared Llewellyn. Georgiana gazed at him in adoration.

"Pleasing as those sentiments are, your progeny would certainly regret thirty thousand pounds." Darcy's cutting remark embarrassed the couple, but he pressed on. "Let us be sensible and speak of this, uncomfortable as it may be. Georgie, you are present because I raised you to take an interest in these matters.

"Lord Llewellyn, upon your marriage, these funds will be yours to dispose of as you wish. This, of course, will be covered in the settlement, but a settlement is nothing but a piece of paper. I place enormous trust in your character, milord. I hope you are not offended." Darcy's voice and manner indicated he cared not a whit whether he affronted the young viscount. He wished to make a point.

To his credit, Llewellyn did not answer right away but considered Darcy's words. "What you say is true, sir. Unfortunately, I know of gentlemen who have lost their wives' funds through foolish and reprehensible living, leaving their dependents in desperate straits. I pledge to you that when I take my vows to love and honor Miss Darcy as my wife, I shall also vow to protect and nurture her dowry."

"Well said, milord."

"I trust Lew unreservedly," declared Georgiana.

"*Lew,* is it?" Darcy smiled.

"Yes," said Llewellyn. "I prefer it to my given name, Algernon. My mother has an affinity for uncommon names. My brothers are Cornelius and Thaddeus, and my sister is Penelope."

"I thought the countess was named Catherine."

Llewellyn shrugged. "A name she dislikes. Mother has never forgiven her parents for not giving her the name Cordelia."

Darcy raised an eyebrow. "I see. But her only daughter is—"

"Penelope, I know. My father allows my mother only so much leeway and no more. Besides, my brother is Cornelius. It is close enough, I trust."

Georgiana laughed. "Oh, Brother, your face is a study! Never fear, I do not like uncommon names." She blushed as she turned to Llewellyn. "Should we be blessed."

The viscount took her hand. "We shall have the most boring of names for our children, my dear."

"Ahem," injected Darcy. "Let us not put the cart before the horse. There must be a wedding before we speak of children." He shot a warning glare at Llewellyn.

"Of course, sir." He released Georgiana's hand.

"Excellent. This brings us to the ceremony. Have you given a thought as to the date?"

Georgiana sighed. "I know there will be demands upon us—balls, parties, those sorts of things."

"Indeed. You are the granddaughter of an earl and will be a future countess. I am afraid this will not be a hurried business."

"Like yours?" Georgiana gasped at her own impertinence. "Oh, forgive me!" Llewellyn was clearly taken aback.

"Three months for the progeny of gentlemen is hardly hurried," cried Darcy, "and that was after a year of courtship." *A very unconventional and dramatic courtship*, he reminded himself.

The viscount grimaced. "I am afraid three months would look very bad in our case, Georgie."

"Very true, milord, but I see no trouble with a summer wedding, do you?"

"Not at all." Llewellyn turned to Georgiana. "It is, of course, up to you, my dear. Would July or August suit?"

"July sounds—" She suddenly blanched. "Oh, no! It will not do! Not at all!"

Llewellyn again took her hand while Darcy flew to his feet. Both men tried to calm her to no avail.

"Brother! I cannot marry in July! Lizzy! I cannot!"

The viscount frowned. "Will Mrs. Darcy object to your marrying?"

She whirled on him. "Of course not! But I cannot marry in July! It is unthinkable!"

"But why?"

"LIZZY!" she shouted.

"Lizzy?" Darcy's eyes shot open. "OH!"

"What?" cried Llewellyn.

"My lord, my wife—" Darcy paused. "We are expecting an addition to the family in the early summer."

"Ah, my congratulations, Mr. Darcy. Then, perhaps before Mrs. Darcy's lying-in—"

"NO, not before!" Georgiana squeezed his hand. "Afterwards! I cannot marry at Pemberley until after the baby is here."

"You wish to marry at Pemberley?" asked Llewellyn.

"Of course, Pemberley!" She frowned. "What is wrong with you?"

"Ah, Georgiana," warned Darcy. "Pray forgive her, milord. She has spent too much time with Elizabeth, I am afraid."

Georgiana began to weep. "I am so sorry, Lew! I have always dreamt of marrying from Pemberley. Nowhere else will do."

Llewellyn consoled her, assuring Georgiana that the ceremony would be held at her family's estate.

Meanwhile, Darcy's mind ran through the possible dates. *Assuming the babe is on time, and Bennet certainly was, the birth should be in early July. A few weeks of lying-in and the child should be churched no later than late August. So, October will do—*

"September!" cried Georgiana. "We can marry in September." She looked at Llewellyn. "That is not too long, is it?"

His finger traced the last tear on her cheek. "I would wait a lifetime for you, Georgie, so I suppose I can wait until September."

Georgiana turned to Darcy. "Brother, may I marry in September?"

Any objections faded in the face of his sister's big, dark, wet eyes, so reminiscent of their mother's. "Let us ask Elizabeth."

"SEPTEMBER?" REPEATED ELIZABETH.

"That is not too soon after lying-in, is it Lizzy?" begged Georgiana.

"No, I do not think so." Elizabeth turned to Darcy. "What is your opinion?"

"I do not—"

"That will be no trouble at all, Georgiana," declared Lady Matlock. "I would be happy to assist Elizabeth in hosting your wedding breakfast. After all, I have the experience of Henrietta's nuptials." Her tone left no room for argument.

"The final decision must be left to Mrs. Darcy, Aunt."

To his surprise, Elizabeth capitulated. "It will be as Georgiana desires. Can we *not* make it the event of the year, my dear?"

"Of course, Lizzy," Georgiana promised. "Only the family."

"ARE YOU CERTAIN ABOUT THIS, ELIZABETH?" ASKED DARCY ONCE they had retired for the night. "Say but the word and I will end this straight away."

"Do not concern yourself," she replied. "I do own I was taken aback by the chosen date at first, but you will recall how quickly I recovered after Bennet's birth. My mother too. She was on her feet very quickly after Lydia." She smiled. "We Bennet ladies are made of stern stuff."

Darcy was not amused. "Childbirth is not a joking matter, madam."

"I know. Forgive me." She ran a hand down his cheek. "Truly, Fitzwilliam, all will be well. *I* will be well. There will still be a month to plan everything. Your aunt wishes to help, and it is Georgiana's wish. Mid-September will do admirably."

Chapter 6

"Llewellyn? Oh, Georgiana, could you not have found someone else?" grumbled Lord Matlock.

The Darcys had traveled to Matlock House to receive the blessings of the earl and the rest of the family who had gathered in the drawing room.

"Uncle! Y-You disapprove of Lord Llewellyn?" Georgiana's lip trembled. "Why?"

Darcy shared a quick look with Elizabeth before he declared, "My lord, Llewellyn has received my permission and blessing. Given Georgiana has reached her majority, it is all that is required." Darcy only referred to his uncle as "my lord" when he was upset with him. He was one of the few men who, on occasion, could stare down the Lion of Matlock. "He is an outstanding young man, as you are well aware due to your longstanding association with him. He is an excellent choice. Pray make clear to my sister the reason for this extraordinary statement before you distress her further."

"Hugh. Darcy." Lady Matlock's quiet voice was a subtle reprimand to both gentlemen.

His lordship drew breath and turned to his niece. "Forgive me, Georgiana. Yes, Llewellyn is all that Darcy says he is." He stretched out his arms. "Come to your old uncle." She complied at once and was drawn into his embrace. Matlock kissed her forehead and continued. "I am sorry, my dear. I do like the lad. I like him very well. It is his family—that is all."

"His father, most likely," added Andrew.

"Too true. Wakeford is a bloody idiot, even for a Whig."

"Hugh!" cried his wife. "I will not have such language in my house!" She turned to her sniggering son. "And that goes for you as well, Andrew!"

"What? I did not say anything! Father did!"

"By laughing you encourage him! There will be only gentlemanly behavior in my parlor."

Darcy pinched the bridge of his nose. Sometimes, his family resembled the Bennets far too much.

Georgiana, still in Matlock's embrace, looked up. "You do not like Lord Wakeford?"

"Sweetling, you know I have acquaintances—even friends—in the opposition." The Lion became her loving uncle again. "We disagree politically, but we respect one another. I fear Lord Wakeford is not numbered among them."

"Is he a man of bad character?" She stepped away.

"Oh, he is a character, to be sure," quipped Andrew.

Matlock shot a glare at his son before answering. "I shall say nothing of Wakeford's character. He has not the vices of Fox and that crowd. He is a fool, is all. Not as bad as the pompous Sir Percy Blakeney, but bad enough. I cannot abide a fool."

Lady Matlock took Georgiana's hand. "Do not be distressed, my love. Even your great ox of an uncle knows your Llewellyn is a sensible young man. We are happy to have him join the family." She ended her pronouncement with a kiss on her niece's cheek.

It was done. The matriarch of the family had spoken. Lord Llewellyn was accepted, and all of the Fitzwilliams would fall in line.

"Besides," said Lady Eugenie, "he is a viscount and future earl.

We cannot overlook what connections and prestige he brings to the family. You will be a countess, Georgiana. Congratulations." No one responded to Eugenie's rather cold statement.

Andrew rubbed his hands together. "Well, then! Shall we drink to Georgiana's good news?"

"Wine," declared the countess. "It is far too early in the day for strong spirits." She gave the earl a pointed look.

"Of course, my dear." He sighed.

Taking Darcy's arm, Elizabeth whispered, "Have I said lately how staid and serious our Fitzwilliam relations are?" Her fine eyes glistened with mirth.

Had they been alone, he would have kissed her.

A few days later, Llewellyn was shown into Darcy's study.

"Good day, sir. I have come with the settlement…" His voice died as he took in the others in the room.

Darcy walked over to the young man, his hand outstretched. "Lord Llewellyn, you of course know Lord Matlock and my cousins Lord Fitzwilliam and Sir Richard. Allow me to introduce these other gentlemen. Milord, this is Mr. Gardiner, my wife's uncle, and Mr. Tucker, my solicitor." The gentlemen bowed.

"Forgive me, Mr. Darcy," said Llewellyn. "I was not informed you had visitors. We can discuss our business another time."

"Nonsense, lad," boomed Lord Matlock. "*You* are our business."

Darcy glanced at the older man. "Uncle, we agreed I shall handle this." He returned to Llewellyn. "Pray be seated. Do you care for a drink?"

"The whisky is excellent," offered Sir Richard. "We have sources in Scotland."

"It is about the only good thing about the dratted place," claimed Lord Fitzwilliam.

Darcy poured Llewellyn a glass, and after the usual inquiries about his health and family, they got down to the matter at hand.

"I thank you for your diligence in preparing the settlement for Georgiana. But before we review that, there are things you must know prior to marrying into the family."

Llewellyn looked at the earl before clearing his throat. "My lord, if we are to speak politics, you should know—"

"None of that," cut in Darcy. "All of us are aware of the political differences between your father and my uncle. That is not the subject of this meeting."

"Though it ought to be," grumbled Matlock. "I suppose your club is Brooks's?"

"No, milord. Boodle's."

Matlock rolled his eyes. "Humph. Not much better."

Darcy ignored his uncle. "Let us speak openly of your condition and prospects."

Astonished, Llewellyn looked about. "Mr. Darcy, I must protest!"

"Protest away, boy," thundered the earl, "but if you plan to marry *my* niece, we would know all!"

At this, Tucker spoke up. "It is to your advantage, milord." He waved his hand. "All the gentlemen here are my clients. Indeed, we are all in business together to our mutual benefit."

"Aye," said Sir Richard, "I shall second that!"

Llewellyn turned to Mr. Gardiner. "Pray, sir, what is *your* interest?"

Mr. Gardiner smiled, but it was Darcy who answered. "All will be made clear to you anon. Will you speak, or should I read aloud from these papers?" He held up the settlement.

Llewellyn capitulated. "Very well. My current income is about £4,500 a year, mainly from my estate, Ambervale Lodge. I have no debts. I have a few minor investments, and above Miss Darcy's dowry, I have the ready money to settle an additional £9,000 aside in the funds for any future children. It is my plan to add to this annually."

As the viscount continued to speak, Darcy handed the settlement papers to Tucker.

"I am heir to the earldom and the Wakeford estate. My father has no debts he cannot discharge. The house in London is leased, not owned, but the terms are reasonable. Shall I go on?" The man was clearly aggravated.

Darcy turned to Tucker, who reported, "Everything is complete. A few minor details must be sorted out but nothing significant."

"Excellent. Milord, while it is not part of Georgiana's settlement, you should know my income is somewhat higher than the amount usually bandied about. Last year—not a particularly good one, I must admit—it was nearly £14,000."

"Fourteen!" cried Llewellyn.

"While not as wealthy as my nephew," said Lord Matlock in a self-satisfied tone, "I was very happy with my income last year, as were my sons." Both Lord Fitzwilliam and Sir Richard nodded in agreement.

"I see you are confused, Llewellyn," said Darcy. "Your estate is in Derbyshire, as are both Pemberley and Matlock. You must understand that the secret to our financial success is not in agriculture or mining but in our investments outside of our estates. That is why Mr. Gardiner is here."

Llewellyn stared at the tradesman. "I would know more."

Darcy smiled. "We thought you would."

Mr. Gardiner leaned back, his hands laced over his stomach. "I began as an importer of find goods and fabrics for the *ton*. Over time, I expanded my business by exporting goods overseas. I do not attempt to compete with the East India Company—that would be foolish. Instead, I carved out my own markets. I now own a small fleet of ships that regularly sail to the Continent and America. Tobacco, indigo, and cotton are particularly lucrative. Meanwhile, I fulfill the Americans' desire for fine furniture and other wares.

"My success would not have been possible without the investment of several foresighted individuals." He gestured about the room. "I find it convenient to limit my partners to those I trust, mainly in my family."

Llewellyn nodded. "I see. And Mr. Tucker?"

"He is married to my niece Mary, one of Mrs. Darcy's sisters."

"I assume you are offering me the opportunity to invest in your business."

"Yes, the *opportunity*," said Darcy. "By marrying into the family, you are allowed the privilege of joining us. It is not a requirement. You, of course, will see to your investments as you will. However, I trust you will take advantage of honest potential for securing my sister's future."

"Are you speaking of investing Georgiana's fortune?"

"Absolutely not."

"Lord Llewellyn," said Gardiner, "my ventures carry risk. We have been very fortunate to date, but Madam Chance can be a contrary lady. You should not invest what cannot be lost."

"It would behoove me to remind your lordship," intoned Tucker gravely, "that this conversation is private and must not be shared with anyone outside this room, save your solicitor and steward."

"By that, you mean my father," said Llewellyn wryly.

The earl laughed. "Quite right."

Darcy broke in quickly. "We mean no insult to your father. We have been very cautious about who is invited to these discussions. There are members of our extended families that have been excluded for various reasons." *Bingley, for one*, Darcy recalled.

Llewellyn held up a hand. "Say no more, Mr. Darcy. I know very well my father cannot keep a secret. I shall carefully consider what you have offered."

"Thank you, milord. Your reputation as a trustworthy man precedes you."

Llewellyn laughed. "Or else you would not have allowed me to marry your sister! But, enough of this 'lordship' business. Pray all of you, call me Lew as my family and friends do."

Darcy shook his hand. "I would be pleased to do so."

The other gentlemen welcomed Llewellyn into their fellowship, and as the earl busied himself pouring drinks for all, Darcy whispered one last piece of advice to his future brother.

"Keeping this secret does not necessarily preclude you from sharing this with your wife. Gentlemen usually withhold details of their business dealings from their spouse. I shall not judge them and cannot tell you to bring Georgiana into your confidence. I suggest, however, it would be a poor decision on your part to keep her in ignorance. *Very* poor."

Llewellyn nodded. "Message received."

March

A MEETING WITH THE WAKEFORDS WOULD BE ANOTHER SE'NNIGHT after the earl and countess arrived in London from their seat in Surrey. All the Fitzwilliams in town accompanied the Darcys to the house in Mayfair. It was a goodly space, but it lacked any personal stamp of the Woodhouse family as it was only leased. Elizabeth observed that, except for the family paintings and a few figurines, it could be any house on the street in that part of London.

Upon their announcement by the butler, Lord Wakeford laughed as he chuffed Lord Matlock on the shoulder.

"Hah, Matlock! You never thought you would step foot in here, I would wager! By gad, I shall make a Whig out of you yet!"

"Father, please," begged an apologetic Llewellyn.

Lord Matlock scowled at his counterpart but only said, "Wakeford, I hope I find you well."

The earl only thumbed his waistcoat and chuckled. Lord James Woodhouse, Earl of Wakeford, was a stout gentleman of average height. His hair was so thin he was nearly bald. His pump cheeks hid hazel eyes filled with mirth. A rather slender, aristocratic lady drew to his side.

The earl gestured to her. "I believe you know my wife, Lady

Catherine Wakeford." The Countess of Wakeford curtsied.

"We do," said Lady Matlock. "Good afternoon, Lady Wakeford."

The two countesses could not have been more different. Lady Matlock was the more matronly of the two, only a ghost of her youthful beauty still evident. Yet, her native elegance was evident, both in her carriage and dress—proper for her state but not overly so.

Lady Wakeford, on the other hand, could only be described as overdressed for the occasion, wearing a gown better suited for the ballroom than the parlor. At least four feathers adorned the turban over her light-colored hair.

Darcy and Elizabeth shared a quick look. There would be *two* Lady Catherines in the family by autumn, and which lady would be the more ridiculous only time would tell.

"This young lady is the baby, Lady Penelope. Step up, Penny."

A winsome young lady, not yet twenty, curtsied. She was slim of build, crowned with lovely red hair, and dressed in the light colors of a girl not yet in her first Season. Lady Penelope's open smile bespoke of the same good humor as her brother.

"I have two other sons, Cornelius and Thaddeus. Neil is a captain of artillery in the Regulars here in England, training recruits. You will meet him soon, I trust. It is a good thing those foolish wars are done, eh Matlock?"

Elizabeth could almost hear Lord Matlock grind his teeth. He had been an enthusiastic supporter of the government and the wars against Bonaparte.

"Thad is vicar of our home parish, and his duties keep him there for now," Wakeford concluded.

As Matlock introduced his relations, Elizabeth took time to study the seventeen-year-old Lady Penelope. Redheaded like her brother, her face showed good humor and some sense. It was widely known she was to make her debut next year. Elizabeth liked the girl at once, and it was obvious Georgiana desired to know her better

Lady Wakeford invited everyone to be seated. Tea and

refreshments already awaited them, and Lady Penelope assisted her mother serving.

"Well, Matlock, we shall be relations! Never in my life have I thought it would happen, but there it is! Ha, what a fine joke!" Lord Wakeford began.

"As you say," grumbled Matlock as he accepted his cup. "Lady Wakeford, you have a…lovely house."

Elizabeth well understood her uncle's comment and hoped the countess did not note Lord Matlock's slight pause. The room's furnishings could not be judged as understated or uselessly fine. They were just *there*. There was no inkling of the family residing in the place. They could be in a warehouse.

Elizabeth could not but wonder as to why. Every other family they knew labored to put their imprint on their houses, leased or owned. Why not the Wakefords? She had heard nothing of any reversal of fortune. Fitzwilliam had visited Llewellyn's Ambervale Lodge and reported it as good a house as any. What was the issue with this place?

"Oh, thank you, milord. The house will do tolerably, but it is nothing compared to Wakeford Abbey. Oh, not at all!" Lady Wakeford turned to Lady Matlock. "You must come to visit this summer. I declare our roses are the finest in the kingdom! Nothing else can compare. You must see them."

Elizabeth held her breath. Matlock Manor was cold and impressive—beauty not thought of when it was built—but its well-known rose garden, universally celebrated by all society for its blooms, was Lady Matlock's pride and joy. The guests were clearly taken aback by Lady Wakeford's boasting, and even Lady Eugenie narrowed her eyes.

The Countess of Matlock proved her worth as a true lady. "I am certain you are right, and I shall not be content until I see them for myself."

Lady Wakeford fluttered her hands. "Yes, yes, you must

come—which brings me to the issue before us. The wedding! This talk of Derbyshire—I cannot like it. Surry is so lovely in late summer and much closer to London. No, the wedding *must* be held at Wakeford Abbey so that all of our friends may attend."

Wakeford grinned. "Well said, my dear."

Llewellyn spoke up. "What you say is true, Mother, but the choice of location in these cases falls to the bride. Miss Darcy is particularly attached to Pemberley." Georgiana blushed as her intended straightened his spine. "Pemberley in September it will be."

"But, Algie!" Lady Wakeford whined.

Llewellyn leaned forward in his chair. "Mother, it is Georgiana's choice and mine."

Lady Wakeford threw up her hands in surrender. "Oh, very well. Young people these days! I only hope it is not cold."

"The wedding is to be in September, Mother, not the middle of the winter."

"It has been cool this summer, that is certain," observed Lord Fitzwilliam, which drew a sharp glare from Matlock. Andrew tried to recover. "But…ah…not too cool. No. Quite delightful." He turned to his wife. "Would you not say so, dear?"

Lady Eugenie nodded once.

Lady Penelope changed the subject. "Miss Georgiana, have you begun shopping for your trousseau?"

Georgiana glanced at Elizabeth. "We shall very soon."

"If you would not mind, I would so like to join you." She offered a hopeful smile.

"You, Penny?" Lord Wakeford laughed. "Darcy, watch your pocketbook if my daughter is advising your sister!"

Elizabeth gripped her husband's hand before he could respond. "We shall purchase only items in town that cannot be gotten or made in Derby or Nottingham, as we intend to go to Pemberley in May."

"Why so early?" demanded Lady Wakeford. "The Season will not be over, and most will not flee London until June at the earliest."

Elizabeth's gown well disguised her condition. It had only been a few days since the quickening, and while it was time to announce her pregnancy, she had no desire to do so today in the Wakeford's parlor!

Darcy came to her rescue. "That is so for most of society. As for me, I usually quit London by April so that I may return to my estate for the planting. This year I am foregoing my usual practice in deference to my sister."

"My brother is too kind," added Georgiana, and brother and sister shared a smile.

"But these are her wedding clothes!" cried their hostess. "Surely you can stay into July!"

"Mother, enough," said Llewellyn. "The Darcys' plans are fixed. It just so happens I intend to return to Ambervale Lodge in the late spring as well." He grinned at Georgiana.

"Convenient timing, Lew," Lord Fitzwilliam noted.

"Lady Penelope," said Georgiana, "I would be happy for your company. Perhaps the day after tomorrow would suit?" The younger lady happily agreed.

The ladies fell into a discussion over the shops to visit and current fashion, while the gentlemen debated politics. The sandwiches and biscuits dwindled and a second pot of tea requested when Lady Wakeford exclaimed, "A ball!"

She captured the room's attention.

The countess turned to the earl. "My dear Wakeford! We must have a ball in honor of Algie and Georgiana's betrothal!"

Lord Wakeford slapped his knee. "The very thing, my dear! What say you, Matlock? Shall you dance in my ballroom three weeks from today?"

"Four weeks, my lord," insisted Lady Wakeford. "I cannot think of hosting the ball of the season in less than four weeks!"

"Do you like the idea, Miss Darcy?" asked Lady Penelope, earning a gaze of approval from her brother.

Georgiana, being a Darcy, was by nature reserved, but Elizabeth had labored to free the heiress from extreme reticence. Georgiana confirmed her success by biting her lip while sanctioning the scheme with a nod.

Elizabeth ignored her husband's low groan. The man would just have to steel himself for another ball.

Chapter 7

Fitzwilliam Darcy's idea of a pleasurable outing did not include attending balls. Despite years of gentle correction from Elizabeth, he remained ill at ease when speaking to strangers. Dancing with unfamiliar partners was awkward for him. Standing in the receiving line, expected to make polite conversation to any and all who had been invited by someone other than his wife, was shear torture.

All of which made the Wakefords' ball an excruciating experience.

As the brother and guardian of the bride, Darcy was required to be part of the receiving line. He and Elizabeth were positioned at the end while the Wakefords and the Matlocks flanked the happy couple at the head. Thankfully, the line moved swiftly, for it was decided that the other Fitzwilliams and Woodhouses need not suffer formally greeting the guests. Otherwise, Darcy's agonies would multiply. They were bad enough as it was.

"Fitzwilliam, pray stop fidgeting," whispered Elizabeth at his side.

Darcy managed not to roll his eyes as the next guest was announced.

"Lord Cardwell, Lady Cardwell, thank you." *Good Lord, the Wakefords had managed to outdo the Arbuthnots!*

"Yes, Mrs. Wood-Smythe, I believe they will be very happy." *Will this line never end?*

"Mr. Willoughby, Mrs. Willoughby, may I present my wife, Mrs. Darcy?" *Oh, Elizabeth is rather put out! Of course—I recall something between the Brandons and the Willoughbys. I suppose I should find out what that is.*

"Sir Percival Blakeney and Lady Blakeney," announced the butler.

Darcy's eyes darted to his uncle. If there was a man who could get under Lord Matlock's rather tough skin, it was Sir Percy! He sighed a breath of relief as the baronet and earl greeted each other rather cordially. He then noticed the same gleam in Lady Matlock and Lady Blakeney's eyes. Apparently, both gentlemen were under strict orders to behave themselves.

"Mr. Darcy," Sir Percy drawled upon reaching him, his bright blue eyes peering over the spectacles balanced at the end of his aristocratic nose. Tall and broad-shouldered, he cut a rather dashing figure for a gentleman in his fifties. His dress could put Beau Brummell to shame. "I do not believe you have met me wife. M'dear, this rather tall fellow is Mr. Darcy."

Darcy gave the lovely Lady Blakeney a short bow. "Charmed, milady. Allow me to introduce Mrs. Darcy. My dear, Sir Percy and Lady Blakeney."

After Elizabeth's curtsy, Sir Percy said, "I understand you are acquainted with my daughter's husband, Major Tilney."

"I have that honor. I am sorry he and Mrs. Tilney could not attend."

"Ah, the demands of the King's service! Odd's fish, if the Twelfth Dragoons' bridles do not outdo the sun, York will be right put out!"

"Certainly, dear," remarked Lady Blakeney in a rather long-suffering way. "Mr. Darcy, Mrs. Darcy. Perhaps we may speak later. Congratulations. Come, Percy, I am parched."

As the Blakeneys made their way to a refreshment table an announcement was made. "Mr. and Mrs. Ferrars."

Darcy could not help but roll his eyes.

FINALLY, THEIR DUTY DONE, THE DARCYS WALKED THE BALLROOM searching for their relations. During that time, Elizabeth gave Darcy a hushed précis of Mr. Willoughby's sins. Upon learning of Mr. Willoughby's seduction and abandonment of Colonel Brandon's ward, leaving her with child, he vowed to distance himself from the man. Her husband's acquaintance with John Willoughby was slight, in any case. They were members of the same fencing club, and he had been tempted to buy one of Willoughby's renowned hunting dogs. Elizabeth hinted there was more she could not reveal, but Darcy replied he needed no further proofs. Her word was enough for him. No Pemberley funds would be spent on a Willoughby hound, he swore.

They found Sir Richard and Lady Fitzwilliam in the outer orbit of the combined Woodhouse and Fitzwilliam families. They greeted their cousins warmly, as they had not met since their wedding five months prior.

Their conversation was interrupted by Lord Wakeford's shouted, "There you are! What has kept you?"

Elizabeth turned about to behold two couples approaching. One was Mr. and Mrs. John Knightley. The other was—

"George, Emma! Come meet your future cousin!"

"Forgive us, my lord, but we were unfortunately delayed," said George Knightley. His wife glanced at her sister.

"It could not be helped, my lord," cried a harried Isabella Knightley. "My youngest began coughing, and there was nothing to stop it! I was beside myself with worry!"

"Isabella, it was nothing but his milk going down the wrong way," remarked Emma Knightley. "All is well, my lord."

Emma was a lovely two and twenty, taller than average with light blonde hair, blue eyes, and soft-pink skin. Her pale-blue ball gown with lace overlay complimented her features becomingly. Elizabeth, dark of hair and eyes and owning a slightly sun-kissed complexion, favored warm jewel tones. Indeed, Emma was as different from the four-and-twenty Mrs. Darcy as a young woman could be and still be considered beautiful.

Elizabeth had met Mr. Knightley's young bride during that couple's short wedding tour and had come away unimpressed. Beautiful and graceful, the young lady tended to think a bit too highly of her own opinions and observations for Elizabeth's liking. She owned an intolerably conceited self-sufficiency, reminiscent of the former Caroline Bingley, that Elizabeth found grating. It did not escape her reflections that *she*, at times, could be accused of the same sins, but she was comforted by acknowledging her fault. She doubted Mrs. Knightley did the same.

George Knightley was seventeen years his wife's senior, but one would be hard pressed to guess it for he appeared ten years younger. He was a fine gentleman—in conversation and character, reminiscent of her Darcy. That he held his bride in great affection was unquestioned, and the age difference was not unusual. However, at times, he seemed more of a father than a spouse, gently correcting Emma when she was at her most trying. For her part, she would smile sweetly at her "Mr. Knightley" and carry on politely.

That was another matter that vexed Elizabeth: the way Emma Knightley pronounced "Mr. Knightley." She knew most ladies were formal with their husbands in public—she herself had referred to Fitzwilliam as "Mr. Darcy" in many a ballroom. However, Mrs. Knightley had an irritating habit of lingering over the syllables—*Mis-ter Knight-ley*. It was almost a caress, intimate and private. She wondered whether she called him anything else.

"Darcy!" George cried. "It has been an age. I hope all is well with you."

Darcy took George's outstretched hand. "Never better, Knightley. You owe me a match at our fencing club. You know my wife, of course."

Elizabeth curtseyed as George affirmed Darcy's statement. "And this is my dear wife, Mrs. Knightley. Emma, Mr. and Mrs. Darcy."

Coolly, Emma paid her respects. "My dear Mr. Knightley, I had the honor of meeting the Darcys during our honeymoon tour. I trust I find you both well."

George chuckled. "I would not call a short trip to London a wedding tour, my dear, but you are very right." He turned to the others. "Emma's father is…rather attached to my wife's company. I am in her debt for a proper trip."

"Nonsense! Any pleasure that cannot be found in Highbury holds no attraction for me!" Emma gave him a bright smile as she patted his arm.

Elizabeth kept her own counsel though she found Mrs. Knightley's statement utterly ridiculous. Even a simple country girl could appreciate the art, diversions, and society of London! In small doses, of course.

Colonel and Mrs. Brandon appeared, and after introductions were made, the gentlemen wandered off to discuss politics, which left Elizabeth in the company of her good friend Marianne Brandon, her cousin Anne Fitzwilliam, and the Knightley ladies.

Emma whispered to her sister, "Isabella, you must stop fretting. The nursemaid has everything in hand. All will be well."

"Oh, Emma, I cannot! My child, my lovely child! I should not have come, but John was so insistent." She turned to the others. "You are both mothers, surely. Do you not worry about your children?"

"Mrs. Knightley," said Anne, "I am but five months married."

Isabella gasped. "Forgive me, Lady Fitzwilliam! I hope I have not offended any of you ladies!"

Marianne nodded graciously. "I am a mother twice over, and Mrs. Darcy has a son." Elizabeth saw Marianne's quick glance at her midsection, for Elizabeth had informed her friend that she was in the family way again. "I believe I can speak for her that our children are in the forefront of our thoughts and concerns." She turned to Emma.

That lady tightened her lips. "I have only been married these two years."

Elizabeth did not miss an odd look in Emma's countenance. The lady then changed the subject. "Do you not think the hall looks well tonight?"

"Indeed, it does," offered Marianne. "I particularly like the flowers. They complement the drapes delightfully!"

"I believe you have something to do with that, Emma," said a smiling Isabella.

Emma looked rather pleased with herself. "Yes, well, I do have an eye for color. Speaking of color"—she gestured at Georgiana across the floor on Lord Llewellyn's arm—"Miss Darcy's gown is exquisite."

"For my sister, I thank you," said Elizabeth.

"Was it made in town, Lizzy?" asked Marianne.

"Yes, but the fabric came from my uncle."

Emma blinked. "The earl bought her dress fabric?"

Elizabeth's chin rose a fraction. "No, Mrs. Knightley. My uncle Gardiner is an importer of fine goods, including fabric from faraway places."

Emma blushed. "Ah yes, I recall that now." Whether Emma was embarrassed because Mr. Gardiner was in trade or because she had made a ridiculous supposition would remain a mystery, for Marianne loudly gasped and clutched at Elizabeth's arm.

"Oh no! *He* is here!"

There was only one man who could so discompose her friend. Sure enough, the Willoughbys were strolling by in the company of the Ferrarses and Dashwoods. Now *there* was a trio of trouble for Mrs. Brandon! Perhaps they would continue on if they remained silent.

"Why, there is our sister," cried Mr. Dashwood.

Drat the man! They would not be so lucky.

The five ladies greeted the newcomers, three reluctantly. At least Mr. Willoughby had the good manners to look uncomfortable. His wife was obviously put out by the encounter, as was Mrs. Dashwood. However, both Mr. and Mrs. Ferrars seemed to relish the chance meeting. Mr. Dashwood was oblivious to it all.

"Mrs. Brandon—my dear sister!" was the greeting from Marianne's half-brother. "Fancy seeing you in London. I trust you and the colonel are well. Is he in attendance tonight?"

"We are, and he is," was Marianne's somewhat rude reply. Elizabeth noted that a pale Mr. Willoughby quickly scanned the room. Marianne turned to Fanny Dashwood. "I hope you are all in health. I can report the same for my mother, Edward and Elinor, and the children." She glanced at the Willoughbys. "As are my husband's son, daughter, and ward."

Elizabeth wondered whether Mr. Willoughby was about to be ill. Mrs. Willoughby could have been made of stone.

"Yes, yes, that is good to hear," said Mr. Dashwood. Mrs. Dashwood attempted to look condescending but only succeeded in appearing constipated. Having absolutely nothing else to say to the half-sister he impoverished, John Dashwood fidgeted. There was great hope that the interlude had ended when Mrs. Ferrars decided to have her share of the conversation.

"I say, John, will you introduce us to Mrs. Brandon's party?" There was a glint in her eye Elizabeth did not like.

"Oh, of course." He did the honors between Elizabeth and the others since he had met the Darcys several years prior. It fell to Marianne to make Lady Fitzwilliam and the Knightley ladies known to them.

"And your sister, Mrs. Brandon—Mrs. Edward Ferrars. Are they in attendance tonight.?"

"No," Marianne acknowledged through gritted teeth. "They remain at Delaford."

"Of course. A county vicar has no business in town." Lucy Ferrars was clearly envious of Marianne's companions. "Well, Mrs. Brandon, unlike your sister, *you* have certainly come up in the world." She shifted slightly, all the better to display her expensive gown. "Would you not agree, Sophia?"

Mrs. Willoughby, who appeared to want no part of the conversation, simply nodded.

Mrs. Ferrars continued in a malicious tone. "One must wonder how you accomplished it."

"In the usual manner," Marianne answered without hesitation. "I married a fine gentleman who, through his service to the Crown, has become associated with people of high moral character. I am honored to number among my acquaintance the families of the Earl of Matlock and the Earl of Wakeford—and the Duke of Wellington." She gave an evil smile to her family's nemesis.

"The duke!" cried Dashwood.

"I cannot believe it!" exclaimed Robert Ferrars. Lucy Ferrars simply gaped.

"It is true, sir," she responded. "My husband served on his Grace's staff at Waterloo—at the duke's request."

"I had not known. An excellent connection!" Dashwood turned to his wife. "Would you not say so, my dear?"

Even Mrs. Dashwood could appreciate the stupidity in John Dashwood's statement. "I am happy your husband has returned safely, Mrs. Brandon."

Elizabeth could not tell whether she was sincere or not. "The colonel's friends thank Providence for it. Many did not."

"Indeed," Mr. Willoughby blurted out. It was the first word he had uttered, and he seemed embarrassed over it. Marianne grew angry, and Elizabeth feared she would rail at the man.

"You must excuse us," injected Emma. "The dancing will soon begin, and we have our partners to find"—she turned to the others—"do we not, ladies?"

Mrs. Knightley's statement signaled an end to the confrontation. Insincere wishes were given and received, lies about visiting were delivered, and the two groups went on their separate ways, only one group dissatisfied with the outcome.

Emma summed up the feelings of their party. "Insufferable people! Why my cousin invited them, I do not know. He will hear from me about this." She batted her fan furiously.

"Thank you, Mrs. Knightley," said Marianne, "but it is unnecessary. I am unharmed."

"Of course you are, Mrs. Brandon! *They* are the ones licking their wounds. You quite properly put them in their place. Well done."

THE MUSICIANS TUNING UP WAS DARCY'S INDICATION TO LOCATE his wife for the first set. He found Elizabeth with Marianne, Anne, and the Knightley ladies. He escorted her to their place in the line behind Lord Wakeford with Georgiana and Lord Llewellyn with Lady Matlock.

Elizabeth gave Darcy an impish look. "Am I handsome enough to tempt you, sir?"

"Must you say that every time we dance?" Darcy groaned.

Elizabeth pretended to think. "I believe so—yes."

The music started, and as they worked the figures, they continued their banter.

"I had some little hope you had forgotten my beastly words."

"It was quite a notable statement."

"If you cannot forget, may I be forgiven?"

"Perhaps...someday."

"I believe in the last few years I have amply proved how tempting you are."

"Have you?"

Darcy directed a look at Elizabeth's stomach. "Yes, madam, I have. At least twice."

Two pink spots grew on Elizabeth's cheeks. "You, sir, are not behaving in a gentlemanly manner tonight."

"Indeed? I must ask you to explain yourself."

"You refer to activities not suited for the ballroom."

"I see. You are very right. How may I make amends for my words?"

She offered a wicked smile. "I am certain you can think of something."

The first dance ended, and the pair prepared for the next. Darcy took the opportunity to whisper in his wife's ear, "I shall prove my deep admiration and ardent love later tonight in our chambers, sweet Lizzy."

Elizabeth's eyes shown with love and desire. "I am all anticipation."

Elizabeth enjoyed a dance with Darcy and sets with her uncle and cousin before her condition necessitated a breath of fresh air in a less crowded room. One parlor was given over to Lady Wakeford's collection of large ferns, and accompanied by Marianne, the ladies took their time returning to their husbands as they enjoyed the plants.

One fern in particular required closer inspection. While silently engaged in this activity, Elizabeth and Marianne became aware of a conversation between the two Mrs. Knightleys, who had also sought refuge in the parlor, standing on the other side of the large specimen. Their words stopped the friends from revealing their location.

"I am very surprised at Mrs. Darcy's attendance tonight, Emma," said Isabella.

"I cannot see why. The ball is in honor of her sister's engagement to our cousin. Indeed, it would look very strange if she were not here."

"But her condition! Surely, you know she is enceinte."

"That is my understanding." Emma's voice was level, even cold. "Her condition is not exceedingly revealing; therefore, it should not shock others in attendance."

"True. She appears a stout, healthy-looking lady."

"Her dress is cut very well."

"But the London air is so unhealthy! She should have remained at Darcy House and not endangered her health."

"I cannot disagree about London. Fortunately, I hear the family will soon retire to the Darcy estate in Derbyshire to await the child and prepare for Algie's wedding."

The ladies' voices trailed off as they moved away. A mortified Elizabeth had a difficult time restraining her outraged friend.

"How dare they disparage you!" Marianne cried. "I could tear their hair out!" She turned to Elizabeth. "Stout? What nonsense! Why, there is hardly anything to see! You must not let their words pain you, my dear."

"It is all forgot." Elizabeth hoped Marianne did not hear the tremor in her voice. "Let us return to more excellent company. I am sure Brandon and Darcy are wondering where we have gone."

"You must not let their words pain you, my dear."

It was the early hours of a new day. The ball over and guests departed, the Darcys returned to the privacy of their chambers at the townhouse. Darcy sat on the couch, watching his wife pace the floor, the light from the fire in the grate playing over her nightdress and gown. It was alluring, but Darcy knew Elizabeth was in no humor to appreciate his compliments or engage in the activities he proposed earlier. He had learned *something* in their years of marriage.

"Stout! They called me stout! How could they say such a thing?" cried Elizabeth.

"Obviously, they have poor eyesight, sweetheart."

She continued on as though he had said nothing. "Was it not bad enough I had to endure Lady Wakeford's endless boasting, not to speak of suffering the company of the Dashwoods, Ferrarses, and Willoughbys? No! Those ridiculous, thoughtless—how dare they!"

"The evening was not all bad, dearest."

Elizabeth shot him a death stare before dissolving into tears. "I am not fat, am I, Fitzwilliam?"

Darcy rose to take her trembling form into his arms. "Not at all, my love."

She snuggled deep into his broad chest. "You are just saying that."

"Elizabeth, deception of any kind is my abhorrence." She glanced up at him, one eyebrow cocked. "Very well, it is *mostly* my abhorrence. You have taught me the benefit of the polite falsehood."

Elizabeth sniffed. "It has proven useful, you must admit."

"Particularly with your mother."

She pressed deeper into his embrace. "You are now quite her favorite son."

"I think our son is responsible for that honor."

Elizabeth bit her lip. "You truly do not find me fat and ugly?"

"My darling, you are certainly *not* fat. And as for ugly, did I not dispel that belief when you carried Bennet?"

"Perhaps—" He felt her smile. "Perhaps, you should remind me."

He took Elizabeth's face in his hands. "It would be my pleasure."

Chapter 8

Two days later, a little girl thwarted Darcy's wish of an early departure for Pemberley. Chloe preferred to run up and down the halls rather than prepare for a long carriage ride. Once firmly gathered by the nursemaid, she demanded to ride with Uncle and Aunt Darcy in the lead coach. The train of two carriages and a luggage cart left the city an hour later than planned.

The spacious carriage, with its soft squabs and fine woodwork, was tightly packed; Darcy and Elizabeth faced forward with Bennet between them while opposite sat Georgiana, Chloe, and Mrs. Nivens. They proceeded directly to the Great North Road, bypassing Meryton and the pleasures of Longbourn.

At first, all was well. The children were occupied with talk and games provided by Elizabeth and Georgiana. This did not last.

"Are we there?"

"No, Chloe, we are not," announced Darcy.

"When we get there?"

"When *will* we get there, Chloe. And the answer is not for another two days."

"That a long time!"

"Yes, it is."

Sometime later...

"I got to go."

"We shall reach the posting stop in an hour, Chloe. You must wait."

"I got to go NOW!"

Darcy rapped on the roof with his walking stick. "Ho! We shall stop here, Jonah!"

SOMETIME LATER...

"What is that?"

"That is a tree, Chloe," Elizabeth answered.

"What is that?"

"That is also a tree."

"What is that?"

"That is a cow."

"I like cows. Moo! Moo!"

"Thank you, dear. We all know cows moo."

"Can we stop?"

"No, dear."

"What is that?"

Sigh. "That is a tree."

SOMETIME LATER...

"Chloe, this is the changing station. Come out of the carriage."

"NO! I scared!"

SOMETIME LATER...

"Are we there?"

Thus passed the first day of travel.

Derbyshire

JUST AFTER NOON ON THE THIRD DAY, THE CARRIAGES RUMBLED up the lane from Kympton to Pemberley's front entrance. The house was not in its best looks due to the unseasonable cold and cloudy weather. Most of the adults were in the first coach. The children and nurse had been moved to the second for the benefit of Darcy's peace of mind.

Eschewing any assistance from the attendants, Darcy handed down the ladies from his carriage. Elizabeth was the last to descend, and as her foot touched the gravel drive, there was a loud cry from the other vehicle.

"It is so big!" Chloe Wickham beheld Pemberley for the first time.

Elizabeth moved to take the little girl from the nanny. "Yes, it is, Chloe, and it is your new home."

Darcy closely followed, keeping an eye on his pregnant spouse.

"We going to live here?" She started to squirm. "I want to go in!"

Georgiana laughed delightedly. Meanwhile, a smiling Bennet quietly took a tight grip on his mother's skirts. He was not as impressed with the place, having spent half his life at Pemberley. It was simply home.

Mrs. Nivens took her charge in hand. "Now, now, Miss Chloe, we cannot run about like savages." She held out her other hand to the Darcy heir. "Come along, Master Bennet."

The children were bundled up to the nursery while the adults retired to their rooms and refreshed themselves. Darcy then retreated to his office and the pile of letters awaiting his attention. He had just finished sorting them into three stacks—*immediate, later* and *discard*—when Elizabeth slipped inside. She did not knock, for there was no door in Pemberley closed to the mistress.

"Are you very busy?" she asked.

"Never for you, love," he gallantly replied.

Over the years, Darcy learned to mentally translate his lady's requests. Elizabeth would certainly expect there would be many reports and letters of business requiring her husband's attention after months away in London, although the most important had been regularly forwarded by courier to their townhouse. She would not interrupt and demand his notice for something unimportant.

Elizabeth, smiling at his flirtation, sat in one of a pair of armchairs next to the bookcase. Darcy took the other.

"Is anything the matter, Elizabeth? Are you unwell?"

Her hand dropped to her slightly bulging stomach. "All is well, Fitzwilliam, though I am tired from the journey."

"You should rest," he advised.

"I shall lie down later for a nap."

"Perhaps I should join you." Darcy gave her a roguish grin.

Elizabeth rolled her eyes. "*That* would defeat the purpose of a nap!"

"True," Darcy admitted. "What is it you wish to speak to me about?"

Elizabeth played with the folds of her dress. "I know I should remain at Pemberley until this little one arrives, but I have a request from Baroness Higginbottom for leave to host a dinner in Georgiana and Llewellyn's honor at Bolehill Abbey. We really must agree."

"Must we?" he groaned.

"Fitzwilliam! The Higginbottoms are long-standing friends of the Darcy and Fitzwilliam families. The baroness was one of the first to welcome me to the district."

"Yes, I know." Darcy rubbed his forehead. He liked the Higginbottoms well enough, but a formal dinner with the strangers they were sure to invite held no attraction for him. Suddenly, the phrase *"your selfish disdain of the feelings of others"* rolled through his mind. This dinner was in honor of Georgiana, and he must bear any discomfort as best he could for his sister's sake. "When is this proposed dinner to be held?"

"The second of May."

Darcy frowned. "You are due to give birth in three months, and the second of May is a fortnight from now. That is cutting it rather close!"

"Dear, we *discussed* this when I awaited Bennet," Elizabeth patiently reminded him. "The wives of our tenants work until their pains start, and there are rarely any difficulties. I am a country girl of hardy stock—and *stout*, according to some people."

"Elizabeth—"

She waved her hand. "My mother safely delivered five healthy babies in seven years. In cases such as this, it is well I am Frances Bennet's daughter!"

Darcy slightly shook his head. Their "discussion" when she carried Bennet was more of an argument, and Elizabeth unsurprisingly got her way. Fortunately, her labor was short, and her recovery was swift. However, their sister Mary's disappointment last year was fresh in his mind. He was wise to say nothing of that.

"Very well. I have no objection to a dinner should Georgiana approve. But, I require we spend two nights at Bolehill Abbey." He took her hand. "I would not have you suffer a carriage ride twice in one day."

"Oh, you old fusspot! Very well." She squeezed his hand.

Darcy drew back. "Is this all the reply I should expect?"

She grinned. "You require more recompense, sir?"

"Indeed! My concern for your well-being, my allowance of your intelligence—"

"Allowance?" Elizabeth sputtered.

Darcy continued, hiding a smile. "And my years of devotion surely earns me more recognition from my lady fair."

"After such a tease, do you deserve a reward?" Clearly, Elizabeth's displeasure was feigned.

"Perhaps *appreciation* is a more correct description."

"Hmm. And what expression of appreciation is great enough for such service?"

Darcy gently pulled his wife into his lap. "Fitzwilliam, stop!" she cried. "I am too heavy!"

"Nonsense, my dear. You are but a feather. Now come and give me a proper kiss."

She ran her fingers across his cheek, something he enjoyed. "Would you not like an *improper* kiss instead?"

"Even better. I knew you were intelligent."

"Fitzwilliam!"

"Kiss me, my love."

Thus engaged, they did not hear approaching steps. They *did* hear the crash of the study door slamming open.

"NO BATH!"

"Miss Chloe, stop it this instant—oh! Sir...madam...forgive me!"

Elizabeth would have leapt from Darcy's lap had her husband not tightened his hold upon her. "Mrs. Nivens, it is quite all right." He glanced down at the young girl hiding beside his leg. "Your charge is here, I believe."

Elizabeth carefully disengaged herself and helped gather Chloe. "Now, dear, you must go with Mrs. Nivens."

"No want to!"

"Chloe, stop this at once," calmly demanded Darcy. "Why do you not wish to bathe?"

"Bath is cold!" the child cried.

"Cold? What?" He glanced at Mrs. Nivens who shook her head. "Chloe, the bathwater is not cold, is it?"

The child looked down. "Cold before."

"Before?" Darcy gave her a stern look. "You mean before you lived with us?"

She nodded. Elizabeth bit back a gasp.

He softened his expression. "I promise that the baths at Pemberley will never be cold."

Chloe looked up at him, an adorable pout on her pretty face. "Promise?"

Darcy nodded.

"Here, I shall go with you. Would that not be fun?" Elizabeth gave Darcy a helpless, regretful look before she left with Chloe and Mrs. Nivens.

Darcy threw back his head in frustration. "I really must remember to lock the door," he grumbled. He took a minute to collect himself before returning to his desk and his labors.

THE FOLLOWING DAY, DARCY MET WITH MR. THOMPSON, THE Pemberley steward. After a review of the overall financial condition of the estate, talk moved to the farms. The news was not good.

"The spring planting is in a bad way," Mr. Thompson said. "I have never seen such a stretch of cloudy, cold weather in all my days. It is to be hoped that things will improve as summer approaches. Prices for feedstock are climbing. Our cheese sells well, but what we get for our wool continues to decline."

"With the wars over, that is to be expected," Darcy remarked.

"Indeed, you are right, sir. The government no longer needs to outfit a large standing army. The issue is the manufacturers. They take advantage of the surplus and drive down prices to shocking levels. Also, cotton imports are rising now that the American war is done."

Darcy poured over the figures before him. "If this weather does not improve, an adjustment in the rents may be necessary."

"The needed improvements to the roads will be postponed without those funds," Mr. Thompson warned.

"It is regrettable, but our people's needs are paramount."

"Of course, sir. On a happier note, the mines continue to produce prodigiously. This year's income may recover because of it."

Darcy indicated the papers on his desk. "True, as long as the weather moderates."

Mr. Thompson nodded and returned to his notes. "We should receive the quarterly report from Mr. Gardiner in the next se'nnight. The other investments—"

The gentlemen's discussion was interrupted by a scream from without. Darcy and Mr. Thompson rushed to the door as the shrieks continued. Upon reaching the hall, they learned the commotion was emanating from a nearby parlor, footmen crowding the doorway. Darcy realized it was a girl's voice, and there was only one little girl in Pemberley.

"They so big!" was heard just before another screech.

The footmen made way for their employer, and Darcy beheld Chloe huddled in Georgiana's lap, laughing and screaming at two large greyhounds attempting to sniff her.

"Lysander! Penelope! Heel!" Darcy cried.

Instantly, the two hounds trotted to their master and sat on their haunches by his legs. "Georgiana," he gently began while giving each dog a scratch behind the ear, "what is the meaning of this uproar?"

His sister offered a weak smile. "I thought to introduce Chloe to Lysander and Penelope. She was…very excited to meet them."

"They the biggest doggies ever! I scared!" Chloe cheerfully exclaimed.

The pounding of running feet heralded the arrival of Elizabeth and her sister Kitty Southerland. "What on Earth? Fitzwilliam, we heard the screaming upstairs and—Chloe!"

The child squirmed in Georgiana's lap. "Save me from the big doggies!" There was a note of laughter in her voice.

Georgiana attempted to calm her. "Now, now, Chloe, do not carry on so. Lysander and Penelope are very sweet. See? They wish to meet you." Lysander's sudden bark did not help matters.

"Perhaps a small dog will not frighten you," said Kitty. "I have a very nice Pug dog at the parsonage. Her name is Jade."

"Hairy little beast," muttered Darcy. "Come now, Chloe, stop your exhibition this instant. These dogs will not harm you."

With that, he led the two greyhounds to the child, still in Georgiana's lap. At Darcy's insistence, Chloe tentatively reached out to Penelope, the smaller of the two. The dog reacted happily to her touch, causing the other to jealously whine. "Ah! Lysander wants his share."

Chloe, no longer afraid, giggled as she transferred her attentions to the male. "He so soft!" cried Chloe.

Elizabeth smiled as she shook her head. "That is all well and good, but it is time for you to return to the nursery." At the child's protest, she continued, "Nanny Nivens awaits you, as does Bennet, and Aunt Georgiana must meet with Aunt Kitty and me." She looked at Georgiana. "We have a wedding to plan."

Both Georgiana and Chloe pouted.

"You may play with the greyhounds later," Darcy promised. "You too, Chloe."

His sister stuck her tongue out at Darcy before remembering that Mr. Thompson was there. She colored, handed Chloe over to Mrs. Nivens, and meekly followed the other ladies.

Darcy handed over the dogs' leads to a footman. *Chloe is turning the household upside down.*

He turned to the steward, shrugged, and gestured to his study. "I believe we were speaking of investments, Mr. Thompson."

Chapter 9

May

Mr. Darcy was having a terrible time, Elizabeth knew, but there was nothing for it. There was no escape for them from the Higginbottom estate.

Because of the distance between Pemberley and Bolehill Abbey, as well as Elizabeth's delicate condition, the Darcys came the day before the dinner party in honor of Llewellyn and Georgiana, and they were to stay overnight afterwards. This was the first time the Darcys traveled overnight without the children and the last time Elizabeth would leave home until the babe was birthed and churched.

Their leave-taking was an experience dreadful to Elizabeth's tender maternal feelings. Chloe Wickham cried and cried, clinging to her uncle's leg, begging not to be left behind. Bennet was his father's son, standing stoically on the front steps, holding Mrs. Nivens's hand, trying to be brave as his bottom lip trembled. Elizabeth had tears in her eyes as she snatched up her darling boy and spread kisses over his face.

The trip itself had been without incident—Elizabeth bearing the journey tolerably and Georgiana happy and excited. The Higginbottoms could not be more accommodating and gracious, and the guest rooms were understated and comfortable.

Most of the other guests lived in the immediate area and could return to their homes directly after dinner. Lord and Lady Matlock, whose estate was but an hour's carriage ride, appeared to everyone's delight. The Viscount and Viscountess Fitzwilliam sent their regrets to no one's disappointment.

Lady Higginbottom offered Miss Darcy the honor of approving the menu. After perusing it and viewing the glittering table setting and decorations, Georgiana declared everything absolutely perfect.

In this, Georgiana was sadly proven incorrect.

The preparations started well. Elizabeth chose her gown carefully. It was blue silk with embroidery of the same color about the bodice. The dress was elegant, and it minimized the fact she was with child. Georgiana's gown was gold, the better to set off her dark hair, and adorned with diamond pins inherited from Lady Anne. The gentlemen wore black, and both looked dashing although the two could not be more different. Darcy was half a head taller than his sister's intended, and Llewellyn's slight stature contrasted with Darcy's athletic build.

The main purpose of the meal was to introduce the future Viscountess Llewellyn to the neighborhood. The surrounding gentry were of a kind found in all small English country towns: equal parts ridiculous and impressive, insipid and stimulating, wearisome and charming. Most were strangers, to her husband's abhorrence.

A dozen couples sat in the Higginbottoms' main dining room. Baron Higginbottom had Lady Matlock at his right and Llewellyn at his left while Lady Higginbottom had the earl at her right, across from Georgiana. The Darcys found themselves at the middle of the table, seated across from each other. The elaborate flower arrangement, however, prevented much direct conversation between husband and wife.

Not that Darcy would have heard a word from her, for at his elbow was Ophelia Bartelmount, widow of a prosperous owner of mines. Not only did Mrs. Bartelmount enjoy the sound of her own voice, she had no conversation that did not revolve around her married daughter, her grandchildren, her late parents, or the exorbitant cost of everything.

"This is a lovely dinner," the good lady cried. "When Ernestine gave her first dinner, she wanted to serve roast beef, but the butcher wanted to sell her a joint with yellow fat! I told the man, 'No, no. We must have a joint with white fat. Yellow is quite unsatisfactory.' It was fortunate I had accompanied Ernestine, or she would have certainly purchased that joint.

"Oh, the butcher went on and on about how yellow fat was a sign of aging, and that was the best beef, but I am not so silly! I told him, 'White fat, sir. You will not sell us that old cow. My daughter will not be cheated.' Do you know the butcher started shouting at me, saying I insulted him? Was that not the truth?"

Darcy sat straight in his chair, hardly moving a muscle, except to drink his wine. "I leave such matters to my cook, madam." Elizabeth winced in sympathy.

"And I am certain your cook does a very good job, Mr. Darcy, but one must always watch out for old cow." She waggled her finger, the feathers in her hair moving in concert. "As I told my dear Ernestine, 'Young beef is always best! You must insist on the youngest cut available.' A young bride must have her mother look out for her. Do you not agree, sir?"

"I am certain you are right." With that, Darcy held out his glass for more wine—his third. He gave Elizabeth a long-suffering look.

Elizabeth's pity for her husband's circumstances was slight, for she was having her own difficulties. Knowing Darcy detested these gatherings, she chose to please him by wearing the blue dress with the square neck that he particularly admired. Unfortunately, she did not disguise completely the changes being with child bestowed on her figure. Her bodice was filled to overflowing, and no amount of lace could conceal her abundant charms. Sir Horace Snodgrass, a neighbor of Llewellyn, sat on her right and spent so much time leaning close while speaking to her, blatantly eyeing her bosom, it was a wonder he did not drool soup down her chest.

As a result, Mr. Darcy was either ignoring the vulgar Mrs. Bartelmount or glaring at the loutish baronet. Elizabeth was not the only one to note it. A mortified Georgiana was aware of the tension and was nearly brought to tears. Elizabeth tried to reassure her sister with shrugs and small smiles without success, but it was Lord Matlock who saved the day. The earl loudly commandeered the lecherous baronet's attention towards a discussion of hunting, and the dinner was able to continue in a somewhat tolerable manner until the separation of the sexes after the meal.

The ladies removed to the drawing room where Lady Matlock began the proceedings by properly discussing the upcoming nuptials. This lasted only a few minutes before Mrs. Bartelmount commandeered the discussion with a recounting of her daughter's wedding.

"Lace everywhere, I assure you, but at an excellent price! Those London shops wanted ten pounds—ten pounds, mind you! 'Nonsense,' said I. The shops in Scarborough were far more reasonable, and Ernestine's lace was just as fine, if not better! Five and six, that is what we paid, and not a penny more." She turned to Elizabeth. "It was of a kind like yours, Mrs. Darcy. Pray, what did it cost?"

Elizabeth held a hand to her breast, unconsciously covering her lace. She had promised herself to keep her wit in check, so as not to embarrass her shy sister. "I have no idea, Mrs. Bartelmount. This was Lady Anne's lace."

"And very fine it is," she declared. "I would say she paid more than five and six for it. I know my lace." Returning to the other ladies, she said, "And the food we served! My cook makes an excellent white soup, and she is no French chef." Once again, she inquired of Elizabeth. "How many French chefs does Mr. Darcy employ, pray?"

"Music!" cried Lady Matlock. "It has been so long since I have heard you perform, Elizabeth. Might I trouble you for a demonstration?"

"But, the gentlemen," protested Mrs. Bartelmount. "Should they not be in attendance?"

Elizabeth, seeing her escape, engaged her good humor. "It is of little matter. My aunt knows my talents are more suited for the ladies! I hope my excellent sister, Miss Darcy, will deign to entertain the gentlemen when they join us. It will be a much finer concert!" A smiling Elizabeth held out her hand to Georgiana. "Pray, turn the pages for me."

In between settling themselves and selecting the music, Elizabeth was able to express to Georgiana her appreciation of their aunt's request. "Mrs. Bartelmount is a singular creature," she whispered. "I believe she puts my mother to shame."

"Oh, Lizzy, I am so sorry, but her late husband was a good friend to Lord Wakeford when he was the viscount."

"Take no notice, Georgiana. It is well to remember lonely widows. Now, how like you this piece?"

In the years since Elizabeth relinquished the name Bennet in favor of Darcy, she had labored to improve her musical accomplishments, usually practicing with Georgiana. Most young ladies abandoned their accomplishments upon marriage, having achieved their goal. Elizabeth was not like most ladies. She, like Georgiana, played because she enjoyed music. Elizabeth managed the short Mozart piece without error and earned an enthusiastic response, larger than she could have anticipated. The gentlemen had joined them during her performance, and Darcy's eyes glowed with pride and love. The other ladies demurred, and it was left to Georgiana to entertain those assembled.

With Darcy's assistance, Elizabeth made her way to the sofa. "You are before your time, sir," she observed sotto voce. "Is the baron's port unpalatable?"

"Not at all," he responded in the same fashion. "My uncle wishes to return to Matlock before darkness falls, so we enjoyed a quick toast to Llewellyn and Georgiana and hastened to join you." They then turned their attention to Georgiana's concerto.

Elizabeth smiled as she watched Georgiana. Only in London

had she seen performers become as one with the music as did her sister, and they were all professionals.

Sister. Yes, Georgiana had truly become Elizabeth's sister in her heart. Like Fitzwilliam, she was kind and thoughtful, her reserved bearing hiding deep emotions. She had not her brother's cleverness or dominating presence, but she was just as stubborn when she thought she was in the right. Through Elizabeth's efforts, and Kitty's too, Georgiana had grown livelier and jollier.

Kitty Southerland deserved much credit for that change. Within a few months of Elizabeth's wedding, Kitty Bennet was established at Pemberley. It had been Fitzwilliam's idea. He thought they could do what Mr. and Mrs. Bennet failed to do: make a young lady out of the sullen and insipid fourth Bennet daughter. They expected that Georgiana's example would have a good influence on Kitty.

Thanks to the gentle but insistent efforts of Elizabeth and Mrs. Annesley, they succeeded in improving Kitty. What was not anticipated was Kitty's improvement of Georgiana.

Forming a friendship with a girl close to her own age for the first time in her life, Miss Darcy bloomed. She learned lessons not taught in school. Life was more than preparing to enter society; there was no reason to grow up rapidly. She could simply enjoy her girlhood. In quick order, she and Kitty became boon companions, Georgiana becoming more open, fully recovering from the Wickham near-disaster, while born-follower Kitty parroted her new sister and developed better manners.

Kitty's improvement was vast. When the young Franklin Southerland became the new rector for Kympton Parish, a great achievement for one his age, he became almost instantly captivated by Miss Bennet. As for Kitty, she learned to her surprise that handsome and dashing admirers could wear black coats as well as red. In Mr. Southerland, she found all her requirements in a lover, with the added benefit of residing near Pemberley—a place that had become dear to her heart, having grown close to both Elizabeth and Darcy.

Indeed, Elizabeth loved Kitty almost as much as she loved Jane. But Jane Bingley lived at her husband's estate in Nottinghamshire, and Kitty Southerland resided in a nearby village that was under Elizabeth's patronage. Mrs. Darcy and Mrs. Southerland were a common sight in Kympton, agreeably strolling its streets arm in arm, calling on the poor and infirm.

Elizabeth's affection for Jane did not diminish. Mrs. Bingley remained her particular friend and confidante. But the same could not be said for her sister Mary Tucker. Not that there was any *lessening* of affection between them. They loved each other as well as they should. It was just that, while Elizabeth was close to Jane and Kitty, another filled that place in Mary's life—Caroline Buford, of all people.

The less said about Elizabeth's youngest sister, Lydia Denny, the better.

THE EARL AND COUNTESS ANNOUNCED THEIR DEPARTURE IMME-diately upon the end of Georgiana's concert. All assembled took this as an indication that the evening was over. Elizabeth suspected this was Lord Matlock's purpose, for she espied her uncle giving her a wink when he took his leave. Her perception was confirmed later when Darcy joined her in her bedroom.

"My uncle, for all his bluster, is very attentive to his girls," said Darcy, tightening his robe's sash before sitting upon the bed. "My aunt and Cousin Henrietta taught him that. He knew you were exhausted, so he effectively ran the rabble out the door."

"Fitzwilliam, really! Rabble?"

Darcy's face darkened. "What else would you call them? Mrs. Bartelmount is a rude and boastful chatterbox, and as for Sir Horace—" Darcy rose to his feet. "Fortunately for *him*, my uncle spoke to the baronet before I could."

Elizabeth grew worried, knowing the short tempers of both her husband and the earl. "I *thought* Sir Horace was very subdued when he left. I hope Lord Llewellyn was not upset. They are neighbors."

Darcy paced about the room, hands behind his back, his anger simmering. "Be not concerned about that. As I said, it was fortunate for him it was Lord Matlock who put Sir Horace in his place. My uncle's time in politics has given him the ability to upbraid a man while smiling in his face. Lord Matlock simply handed the baronet a glass of port and told him a short story about his younger days, when a duke paid too much attention to my aunt. The earl was jovial as he explained how he cut the peer's political legs from beneath him, destroying his influence; he recounted the campaign of a mere viscount against a duke in such a manner that we all laughed about it, Snodgrass as much as the rest of us. But the point was made."

"And the point was?"

"Do not trouble a Fitzwilliam lady," he growled.

Elizabeth reddened, her own anger engaged. "While I am happy to be considered a member of that august assembly, I do not require the earl's protection!"

"Would you prefer mine? I would have chosen to call out the baronet."

Elizabeth gasped. "Fitzwilliam, you promised! You promised most strenuously you would never fight!"

Darcy glanced at Elizabeth. "Yes, I did. I would not have called him out—but I still *wish* to. The mere threat of such a meeting would probably serve."

"Men!" Elizabeth exclaimed. "They are all pride and bluster! While you play your games of dominance and conceit, it is the ladies who suffer! I assure you, sir, I can manage a boorish dinner companion!"

Darcy turned away. "Pray forgive my beastly temper, my dear. I cannot bear any disrespect towards you."

Elizabeth sighed. "Of course I forgive you. But surely you know you cannot reprimand the entire world. We must bear the slings and arrows of society as best we can."

"Far easier said than done, dearest. But you are correct. I shall do better."

Elizabeth refrained from raising an eyebrow. Her husband's jealousy over her was part and parcel of his personality. And, to be honest, she found it comforting—until it went too far. *There was that dance two years ago with Mr. Thorpe. I knew what he was about, but Fitzwilliam wanted to murder him.*

"Pray excuse me, my dear. I must prepare for bed," Darcy stated as he made for his room across the hall. Elizabeth extinguished the candles, groaned as she slipped between the sheets, tried to find comfort, and closed her eyes. But sleep would not come until she felt her husband climb into bed beside her, his hand resting comfortably on her belly.

"Rest, love. Hopefully, you will sleep all night tonight."

"From your lips to God's ears." Elizabeth snuggled into his embrace. "Good night, my love."

Chapter 10

"I publish the banns of marriage between the Right Honorable Algernon Woodhouse, Viscount Llewellyn, of St. John Parish, Ambervale, and Miss Georgiana Darcy of this parish. This is the first time of asking. If any of you know cause or just impediment why these two persons should not be joined together in Holy Matrimony, ye are to declare it."

Darcy sat stoically in the family pew in the St. George Parish church in Kympton as the Reverend Mr. Southerland happily called the banns for Georgiana and Llewellyn. Beside him, Elizabeth, Georgiana, and Kitty held hands, their joy clear to all. Lord Llewellyn would have been there had he not decided his presence was required at his own parish to hear the banns called. Undoubtedly, he would be at Kympton next week.

It is official, Darcy thought glumly. *Georgiana will soon leave us.*

He found it impossible to be as easy with the matter as his relations. For over five years, it had been only Georgiana and himself. It had been closer to ten years in fact, for his father lost himself in grief over the death of his beloved Lady Anne. George Darcy was not a proper parent to either of his children until nearly the end. Fitzwilliam Darcy was forced to be both brother and father to Georgiana from six to sixteen years. Then, Elizabeth joined their little family.

Fifteen years! Where had all the time gone?

The light murmur among the congregation at the calling of the banns was not to Darcy's liking. He hated being the center of attention, and this announcement all but guaranteed his family would be first mentioned in any conversation in the district for months.

Duty, however, was foremost inbred in his character. He properly stood at the church door with his wife, sister, and the Southerlands, greeting the families in the parish, accepting their congratulations and well-wishes. Most he acknowledged with a slight nod. To his tenants, he was more animated. The majority of Kympton's populace never set foot in Pemberley, except during his mother's beloved harvest fête, an event Elizabeth had recently restored. His wife was in her element, and her presence made the obligation tolerable, even somewhat enjoyable.

It was with no little relief that Darcy handed his relations into the carriage for their return to Pemberley and Sunday dinner. Darcy made himself comfortable on the seat, only to catch his wife's knowing look. He steeled himself for the tease over his resigned behavior at the church door that surely was on the tip of her tongue.

But the tease did not come. Later, he asked Elizabeth about it.

"I had not the heart for it, dearest," she confessed. "I knew what this day was to you."

Darcy fell that much more in love with her.

ELIZABETH AND GEORGIANA NOW THREW THEIR EFFORTS INTO wedding planning. They spent hours at a time in the mistress's sitting room, sketching out the details and drawing up the invitation list. Seamstresses from Matlock, Derby, and Nottingham traveled to Pemberley to design the wedding dress and trousseau. In these labors, they were often joined by Kitty Southerland and Mrs. Reynolds.

This left Darcy to his own devices. He spent days in the saddle with Mr. Thompson, riding the estate and conferring with each and every one of his tenants. It was an unhappy task, for the news was uniformly bad. The cloudy, unseasonably cold weather had a devastating effect upon the crops. Even the cheese and wool production suffered since feed grain was required to supplement the diet of the sheep and cows. Every day, Darcy dragged himself into his study to pour over his books on agriculture, looking for some possible method to counteract the unfortunate conditions.

The state of the farms was not his only source of vexation. There was another in the shape of a small, blonde-haired whirlwind of a girl. Chloe Wickham proved to be willful, insolent, and loud—quite loud. When she was not demanding her mother, she demanded her sisters, her biscuits, her toys, or just her way. She would not walk when she could run, and she ran quite often. Naps replaced baths as her abhorrence.

Darcy had to admit, however, that there was a native sweetness to the child. She quickly embraced Bennet as a brother, was enchanted by Georgiana, and allowed Elizabeth to mother her.

As for her relationship with him, it was—odd. The child seemed both anxious and fascinated by his presence. Chloe appeared not to know what to make of him. At times, she was drawn to his side, seeking comfort and protection, only to flinch and run away a moment later.

Was this Wickham's fault? What had the blackguard done to her? When asked, Chloe would only say that Papa had gone away to live in Heaven. Then, she would ask again about her mother. Perhaps the issue was Chloe never had a father's influence in her short life.

There was one more distraction. Lord Llewellyn was a frequent visitor to Pemberley given that Ambervale Lodge was but a few hours' ride away. His calls were too frequent for Darcy's peace of mind.

Still, Darcy could not fault the young lord, remembering his own courtship. Though Llewellyn was a friend, it was uncomfortable to watch a besotted young swain pay court to his sister. It did not matter that they were betrothed. Georgiana was and would always be his baby sister, by thunder! Darcy made sure the viscount took rooms in Kympton where Southerland could keep an eye on him.

Elizabeth found his grumpiness over Llewellyn's constant presence particularly amusing. *Blast the woman!* Had he not loved her to the bottom of his soul, he might grow even more cross.

June

DARCY STRODE OUT THE FRONT DOOR OF PEMBERLEY, LOOKING for Elizabeth. She was in the final month of her pregnancy, and this was the third time in the last fortnights she had continued to tramp about the wilds of Derbyshire! Darcy meant to put his foot down.

A cursory glance told him she was not by the lake, so he quickly made his way to Lady Anne's rose garden. Unsuccessful there, Darcy sought out the gardener.

"Aye, master, I saw th' mistress not half an hour ago," the man reported. "She an' Mrs. Southerland were headed down th' walk to th' trout stream."

Darcy spared a moment to offer the gardener a short nod of thanks before hurrying down the path, his anxiety somewhat abated. At least Elizabeth was not alone! The cloudy gray afternoon skies offered little light to penetrate the tree canopy, so he was almost upon the pair before he saw them.

"Elizabeth!"

"Oh, bother," he heard her say to her sister. "Yes, Fitzwilliam?" she called in a louder voice.

He stopped a few paces away, hands on hips. "What are you doing, woman?"

Elizabeth stood as tall as her gravid body would allow. "I am walking. I cannot stay still. You know that."

"Alone?"

"I am hardly alone, as you can see!" She gestured at Kitty. "Have you left your senses behind in the house along with your manners?"

"You know of what I speak! Forgive me, Kitty, but you are hardly able to assist should misfortune befall Elizabeth."

Elizabeth waddled up to her husband, her fine eyes spitting fire. "Fitzwilliam, we discussed this before Bennet was born. I am well! I am not your mother!"

As the two glared at each other, Kitty offered, "Perhaps I should return to the house?"

"No!" both Darcy and Elizabeth answered.

Darcy glowered at his wife. "I requested, if you wanted to continue this mad obsession to endanger yourself by walking out of doors, that a footman accompany you!"

"Requested?" she shot back. "You *ordered* it, as I recall!"

"Lizzy, Fitzwilliam, this is hardly helpful."

The two turned to Kitty.

"It is not my place to interfere, but perhaps you *both* might be right?" At their blank expressions, she continued. "All of her, life Lizzy has sought the outdoors when she was sad or worried or uncomfortable. I believe she is attached to nature as few are. It is who she is. And Lizzy, you know how Fitzwilliam frets over you and how much you depend upon his devotion. It is who *he* is.

"Fitzwilliam, Lizzy needs to walk outside or she will go mad. Lizzy, would it be so bad if a strong footman accompanies you? If you continue to reject this simple precaution, Fitzwilliam will go mad. What say you both?"

Neither responded for a moment.

"Who are you? You cannot be my sister." Elizabeth finally asked.

Kitty pinked. "I have grown up."

"That was a remarkably sensible observation, Kitty," said Darcy. Anger depleted, he asked his wife, "What say you, my dear?"

"I dislike bothering the servants."

"Then ask me. I should be happy to walk out with you."

She brightened. "Anywhere I wish?"

Darcy groaned. "Elizabeth…"

"Just in the garden, then."

Darcy smiled as he took her hand. "Or the lake. Dearest, I cannot help but be worried." He held up his other hand when Elizabeth started to protest. "I know you are far healthier than my mother was, but my fears remain. Please do as I ask."

She sighed. "There are times I wish to be alone."

"When is that?"

She gave him a mock glare. "When I am cross with you."

Darcy smiled. "But that is the time I most need to be by your side, for I know best how to placate your hurt feelings." His fingers stroked her soft cheek.

Elizabeth leaned into his hand. "And you continue to claim you are no romantic."

"Um…I am still here," announced Kitty.

The two broke apart with self-conscious smiles. Darcy tucked Elizabeth's arm into his and offered the other to his sister.

"I take it you were on your way back to the house?"

"Yes, I grew tired. Oh, to have a good ramble, but this little one has other ideas!" She caressed her bulge.

"Perhaps I can read to…" Darcy's voice trailed off. "I say, there is a carriage in the drive."

Sure enough, there was a black coach near the front door.

Elizabeth squinted her eyes. "I wonder who it is?"

"It cannot be Llewellyn again. He rides here," said Darcy. "It is not the earl's carriage. Visitors, perchance?"

"Why, I believe that is Papa's!" cried Kitty.

"No," said Elizabeth. "Papa's carriage is brown."

"He purchased a new one, do you not recall? Mama crowed so over its black exterior. 'Just like Mr. Darcy's,' she said."

Just then, a footman helped a feathered matron out of the vehicle. The lady looked over and waved. "Lizzy! Lizzy! I am here to help!"

Elizabeth paled. "Oh no! The baby is not due for a month at least!"

Darcy closed his eyes. "Heaven help us now."

"OH, MR. DARCY, WHAT A LOVELY HOUSE!" MRS. BENNET'S EVER-present handkerchief fluttered about her face. "But it always is. Just the other day I was speaking of Pemberley with Lady Lucas. 'Lady Lucas,' I told her, 'my Lizzy is mistress of the most magnificent house in all of Derbyshire!'"

"I am all astonishment, my dear. When did Lizzy become mistress of Chatsworth House?"

"Mr. Bennet, how you try my nerves! You know very well Lizzy is firmly established at Pemberley! Not that she could not manage Chatsworth as well as anyone. My daughters are thoroughly trained in their duties! And look, here is Master Bennet! Is he not a fine lad?" She leaned down, arms wide. "Oh, come give your grandmama a kiss!"

The wide-eyed child held back, gripping Elizabeth's skirts while she instructed Mrs. Reynolds to prepare rooms for Mr. and Mrs. Bennet. Chloe, however, did not hesitate to greet her grandparents.

A slightly offended Darcy received his unexpected guests in a somewhat clipped manner. "Welcome to Pemberley. I trust you are well. How was your journey?"

"Oh, just dreadful!" cried Mrs. Bennet, taking no note of her host's disapproval. "Dusty, unkempt roads! The king should do something about them. How I did not suffer an injury I do not know. And the inns! Disgraceful, all of them. Oh, that you lived closer to Longbourn!"

"But then, Darcy would not have Pemberley, my dear."

"And who would give up Pemberley, Mr. Bennet? Such nonsense! Oh my dear, dear Mrs. Darcy!" She hugged her second daughter. "What a fine size you are!"

"Who would, indeed?" Mr. Bennet shook Darcy's hand. "Our trip was uneventful. And quite unanticipated too, I should not wonder. I trust my Lizzy is well?"

Darcy refrained from reminding Mr. Bennet that she was now *his* Lizzy while Elizabeth kissed her father's cheek.

"Papa, this is an unexpected pleasure. We looked for you in *July*," she firmly stated.

"Ah yes. Well…" He looked pointedly at Mrs. Bennet, deep in conversation with Kitty. "With the baby and a wedding to plan, your mother thought you required her early assistance."

"The wedding?" cried Elizabeth. "We need no help with that."

"Your mother is of a different opinion."

Elizabeth turned angrily toward her mother, but Georgiana's arrival prevented the lecture she would without doubt administer. Small talk was exchanged for a short time, then Mrs. Bennet excused herself and retired to her prepared chambers. Mr. Bennet claimed a desire to visit the library, his usual haunt when visiting Pemberley. The Darcys followed him, Kitty and Georgiana taking the children back to the nursery.

"Papa, how could you!" Elizabeth exclaimed after Darcy closed the door behind them.

Mr. Bennet held out his hands as he took a seat in a chair near the window. "Now, Lizzy—"

"Do not 'now Lizzy' me!" Elizabeth stood over her father, hands on hips. "How could you permit this? You must know how busy I am!"

"Yes, I do and so does your mother. She has it set in her mind that you require her assistance. No entreaty would silence her on the subject."

"And for your peace of mind, you capitulated!" Elizabeth threw up her hands and stalked out the door.

Mr. Bennet turned to Darcy. "She is becoming more like you every day." He pointed his chin at the direction his daughter took.

Darcy did not respond to his jest. "This is badly done, sir."

"Be thankful you have a sensible wife." Bennet pouted. "You have no inkling of my burden otherwise."

Having visited both Longbourn and Rosings Park, Darcy knew well the disagreeableness of dealing with an unreasonable lady. He had no sympathy for Bennet, however, as this was a predicament the gentleman chose by marrying a lady such as Frances Gardiner. Bennet's task, therefore, was shielding his daughters by controlling his spouse. This he continually failed to do, earning Darcy's disdain.

Still, for Elizabeth's sake, he treated him with respect, little as he deserved the honor. Darcy learned to tolerate Mr. Bennet's eccentricities and focus on the gentleman's good points. He was a clever conversationalist when speaking of topics that held his interest. He was an excellent chess opponent and generous with his French brandy. Most of all, he was the man who encouraged Elizabeth to read, learn, and debate. Her father helped make his dear Elizabeth into who she was, and for that Darcy would be eternally grateful. He would just have to put up with the gentleman.

It could be worse. At least Llewellyn is not under foot today.

The butler appeared at the door. "Lord Llewellyn is here to see Miss Darcy."

I spoke too soon.

Mr. Bennet chuckled at Darcy's involuntary groan. "I know your pain."

ELIZABETH STORMED TO THE STAIRS, OUTRAGED AT HER FATHER and, if truth be told, still irritated with her husband after their disagreement over her walking out. However, upon reaching the first step, the weariness brought on by her condition defeated her, and she reluctantly accepted the assistance of a footman to continue to the upper floors.

Drat! Fitzwilliam was right.

As she made her way down the hallway, she heard singing and giggling from the rooms usually used by her family when visiting Pemberley. Recognizing Georgiana's voice, Elizabeth did not hesitate to open the door.

There, in the middle of Mrs. Bennet's bedroom, a laughing Chloe was dancing with Kitty to Georgiana's singing. Her smiling mother sat on the bed looking on and cuddling Bennet. Elizabeth stood in the doorway, instantly transported back to her own childhood, remembering doing the same with Jane and Mary.

Bennet spied Elizabeth and spoiled the tableau by squirming in his grandmother's lap, demanding his mother. Elizabeth slowly made her way to her son, and Georgiana offered her the chair.

"Be seated this instant!" cried Mrs. Bennet. "You should not be on your feet in your condition! Upon my word, look at you! You should be abed, taking your ease! You might meet with misfortune, and what would Mr. Darcy then say? Oh, my dear Lizzy, you must take care of yourself!"

"I am well, Mama, truly." Safely in the chair, she kissed Bennet's head and placed him on what remained of her lap. "I hope I did not disturb your ball."

"Not at all," said Kitty. "I told Georgie how we did this when we were little. Oh, what fun that was!"

"I wish I had sisters," Georgiana wistfully replied.

"And now you have five," Elizabeth said, "all full-grown and with their own homes. Never about to 'borrow' a ribbon or a favorite dress. And let us not talk of arguing and mooning over redcoats!"

Kitty pouted. "I was not so very bad, was I?"

Elizabeth took her hand. "Not at all, dearest. And, for the hundredth time, I am so happy you came to live with us. Now that you are married to Mr. Southerland, you will be close by always!"

"All my girls married and so well situated!" Mrs. Bennet declared. "My witty little Lizzy is now Mrs. Darcy and lives like a duchess and was so good to match dear Kitty with a most handsome clergyman! Mrs. Southerland! How well that sounds! My beautiful Jane has her Mr. Bingley. And Mary—oh, what a comfort she is, marrying that clever Mr. Tucker and living in Meryton! If only my other girls did not live so far way. And my poor, dear Lydia—a colonel's lady sailing to India! I have such frights and flutterings when I think of her in that tiny boat in the middle of the ocean!"

"Mama, she and Colonel Denny are on a man-of-war," Kitty pointed out. "They are perfectly safe."

Mrs. Bennet went on. "And now my dear Lizzy is to have another child! You did so well to present Mr. Darcy with his heir. If only I had been so fortunate—and poor Jane too! Two girls! What a shame for her! But Lizzy, you must take care that this one is a boy. Your husband is sure to want a spare."

"I believe that is in God's hands." Elizabeth sighed. There was no turning Mrs. Bennet from this subject.

"Want a *girl* baby to play with!" demanded Chloe.

"She will be far too little to play, dear," said Elizabeth.

"What say you, Bennet?" Kitty tickled the boy. "Do you want a brother or a sister?"

Bennet laughed then hugged his mother. "I want Mama."

Elizabeth hugged him back. "There! My son takes after his father and has no preference on the matter."

"Nonsense, Lizzy," cried Mrs. Bennet, "gentlemen want sons!"

The door opened. "Forgive my interruption," said Darcy, "but there is a visitor for Georgiana."

Seeing Llewellyn standing behind her brother, Georgiana leapt to her feet. "Lew!" She caught herself. "Lord Llewellyn, you are very welcome."

"I am sure," Darcy wryly observed. "My lord, allow me to present my wife's mother, Mrs. Bennet." He gestured to the grinning young man. "This is Viscount Llewellyn, my sister's intended."

Mrs. Bennet struggled to her feet and gave the young lord a proper curtsy. As usual, she was silent in the presence of a member of the peerage. The other ladies were far more casual in their greetings, and Georgiana quickly made her way to Llewellyn's side. Meanwhile, both Chloe and Bennet clambered for Darcy's attention.

"Have you just arrived?" asked Georgiana of Llewellyn as she took his arm. "Would you like tea, or are you amenable to a walk in the gardens? The roses are in full bloom." To Elizabeth's amusement, her sister batted her eyes at her intended.

"I would like a stroll above all things, Miss Darcy," Llewellyn answered in a dangerously low voice.

"We shall not be long," announced a brightly smiling Georgiana to the room.

"Excellent," said Darcy dryly. "Have Clarkston or Winslow accompany you."

Georgiana's face fell, and a disappointed Llewellyn nodded as the pair walked out the door.

"Pray, Mr. Darcy," said Mrs. Bennet, "who are those gentlemen? I am certain the young couple will not be wanting company."

Darcy looked down his aristocratic nose at his wife's mother. "Footmen, Mrs. Bennet, to serve as chaperone." He bent from his waist to kiss Elizabeth's cheek.

"Chaperones, sir?" said Elizabeth sotto voce. "Is that necessary?"

"Absolutely, madam. I well remember our own courtship." A quirk of Darcy's lips was his only reaction to his wife's light blush.

Chloe hugged Darcy's leg. "Dance now?"

Elizabeth hid a giggle as Darcy surveyed the room with an incredulous expression. He gave his wife a helpless look before turning to his ward. "I shall dance, if you will honor me with a set." He held out his hand, as he would at Almack's. They moved to the center of the room. "Maestro, please!" he commanded of Elizabeth with a wink.

Now laughing outright, Elizabeth favored the duo with a light country song. They turned in circles around the space, the other ladies clapping in time. She knew her sensibilities were unregulated due to her condition, but Elizabeth let herself weep with joy anyway.

Chapter 11

For the remainder of June, Georgiana and Elizabeth prepared for the wedding. Plans were discussed, dress fabrics were chosen, measurements were made, and invitations were sent. There was only one problem.

"Mr. Darcy, sir." A worried Mrs. Reynolds stood in the doorway of Darcy's study.

Darcy looked up from his desk in alarm. His study was his refuge, and only Elizabeth would enter it without a knock. That the housekeeper would do so was a serious thing indeed.

"What has happened?" He rose from his chair.

Mrs. Reynolds flushed. "I hate to trouble you, but I do not wish to bother the mistress with this, given her condition."

Darcy sighed and pinched the bridge of his nose. "What has Mrs. Bennet done now?"

"I realize Mrs. Bennet means well, what with the mistress nearing her confinement and planning Miss Darcy's wedding and—"

"Pray tell me the matter."

"Mrs. Bennet insists upon rearranging the furniture in the green parlor."

Darcy looked up. "What on earth for?"

"She claims it is not at all in keeping with Blenheim."

Darcy was dumbfounded for a moment. "Has it been brought to her attention that this is Pemberley House, not Blenheim Palace?"

"I cannot say, sir."

"I imagine you wish for me to speak to her."

The housekeeper offered a nervous smile. "If you would be so kind. The footmen—they know not what to do."

"I shall see to this right away. Thank you, Mrs. Reynolds."

Darcy quickly made his way down to the first floor. The sound of Mrs. Bennet's familiar voice assaulted him well before he reached the entrance to the green parlor. What he beheld was bedlam.

"No, no, no! Next to the window! Not that window, the other window!"

Two footmen were moving a sofa while a third stood by, looking on with a bewildered expression. Mrs. Bennet was directing the men, pointing at one of the windows overlooking the gardens. The carpet was rolled up, and the tables were pushed close to the fireplace.

"Yes!" Mrs. Bennet cried. "Place it down just there. No, no—a bit more to the right. Yes!"

"Might I inquire what is happening in my house?" Darcy worked mightily to keep his voice level and not shout at Elizabeth's mother.

"Ah, Mr. Darcy! Good afternoon. I am rearranging this room for Lizzy."

Mrs. Bennet seemed insensitive to Darcy's mild sarcasm. He realized she had probably grown immune to such, thanks to her husband's continual derision.

"Am I to understand you are doing this at Elizabeth's desire?"

"Oh yes! Every time I come to Pemberley—oh, it is a beautiful place, sir! Simply lovely—the finest house in Derbyshire! Except, perhaps for Blenheim or Chatsworth. But beautiful nevertheless! Yes, well, every time I come, I say to Lizzy, 'Lizzy, this room needs redecoration.' It does, sir, for it is sadly out of fashion!"

"Is it?"

"Oh yes, it is in a sad state! On our journey here, Mr. Bennet was good enough to stop at Blenheim for a day, and I saw the love-liest sitting room! I knew right away that Lizzy must take it as her inspiration for this room!"

"And how is that room different from this one?"

"Why, the couches face each other, with this one near the window, and…chairs would go here, and…a writing desk here and more chairs there. The carpet must be changed—"

"The carpet, madam?"

"It is the wrong color! The one in the music room would do. Of course, the drapes should be replaced."

Darcy looked about. "The music room's carpet could not possibly fit in here."

Mrs. Bennet thought for a moment. "Perhaps if this wall were removed, it would."

"Mrs. Bennet!" Darcy's tone was such that it silenced the woman. He took a deep breath to calm himself and walked amongst the chaos, considering how best to gently end this farce. Mrs. Bennet and the servants watched quietly.

Knowing Elizabeth as he did, he was convinced his wife had not authorized her mother to redecorate anything. Mrs. Bennet was a silly, thoughtless gossip who had taken this undesired task upon herself, but she was not mean or grasping. She meant well, was a decent enough mother to Elizabeth since her marriage, and was a devoted grandmother. Unlike the former Mrs. Wickham, she had not asked for a farthing from her illustrious son-in-law nor demanded to be escorted about in London among the *ton*. There were times he could throttle the foolish woman, but he recalled her loving assistance during Elizabeth's labor with Bennet, and for that alone, he could forgive Mrs. Bennet anything.

He looked out the window and was inspired. "My mother's rose garden," he observed. He looked back at Mrs. Bennet. "You have seen it, of course."

The lady joined him. "Oh yes. Such a lovely garden! One of the finest I have seen—but I must not disparage my own garden. You and Lizzy made good use of it many a time during your courtship!" She winked.

"Yes." He cleared his throat, hoping his ears were not red. "To return to Lady Anne's rose garden, it is a special place at Pemberley. I lost my mother just as I started university, and before that, she was often ill. This garden was one of her joys. I recall her sitting in this very room, overlooking the gardeners at work. You see, a portrait of her hangs over the mantle." He gestured at the painting. "This room has not changed in years, and I must say I prefer it that way. To be in this room is like being in Lady Anne's presence again."

To his surprise, there were tears in Mrs. Bennet's eyes. "I had no idea! How you must have suffered, and Miss Darcy too! She was very young, I take it."

"My sister was not yet seven when our mother died." Darcy grew uncomfortable. He had not intended to upset Mrs. Bennet.

"All these years without a mother! How terrible!" She surveyed the room. "I had not known! This room must be kept in Lady Anne's memory! It must be placed back as it was!

"You men! Quickly! Restore the room as it was before! Make haste! Oh, my nerves!" She fluttered her lace handkerchief. "You must excuse me." With that, she fled out of the room and up the stairs.

Darcy stood dazed. His quickly devised intension was to concoct a kind way of convincing Mrs. Bennet to leave the room as it was. True, the gardens were just outside, and his mother occasionally watched the work from a window, but this was in no way one of her favorite rooms. The green parlor was not a shrine to Lady Anne's memory. Indeed, her portrait was added after his father died and only because the colors of the painting went well with the drapes.

Darcy shrugged. It was not his desire to make Mrs. Bennet feel guilty or unhappy. But if a little dissembling worked...well, it was not *really* disguise. *Of course it was not.*

"Carry on, men," he said as he left the room to return to his study.

He did not get far before he was accosted in the hall by a blonde-haired sprite.

"No want take nap!" Chloe cried as she hid behind Darcy's legs.

A harried Mrs. Nivens approached, Bennet in her arms. "Now Miss Chloe, we must return to the nursery. Forgive us, sir."

Darcy felt Chloe's surprisingly strong grip on his trousers. "Miss Chloe, we should listen to Mrs. Nivens."

"No listen!" Chloe laughed delightfully.

An unhelpful party was heard from. "My dear Chloe, I understand you have a complaint," said Mr. Bennet.

"No want take nap!" Chloe repeated.

"Mrs. Nivens, the child does not wish to nap," he announced with a grin.

Darcy bit back a sigh. "That is obvious, Mr. Bennet."

"Save me, please!" Chloe cried.

"Chloe, that is quite enough." Darcy bent down and picked up the girl. "You are not in danger, but you *will* be in trouble if you do not mind the nurse."

"Not tired!" she bawled.

Mrs. Niven reached for the child. "I am sorry to have bothered you, sir. Miss Chloe can be quite the handful."

Darcy did not surrender the girl. "I could use a bit of fresh air. Would you like to see the stables, Chloe?"

Chloe brightened at once. "Yes, yes!"

Darcy sent a stern look at Chloe. "Afterwards, you *will* take a nap. Agreed?"

Chloe bit her lip, reminiscent of her Aunt Elizabeth. "Yes, Uncle Darcy."

Darcy shifted his ward comfortably in his arms and said to a footman, "Altman, pray fetch the dogs. They could use a stretch of the legs. Mrs. Nivens, if Bennet is not tired, pray bring him to the stables. Will you join us, Mr. Bennet?"

The gentleman lost his smile, as he could no longer tease his daughter's oh-so-proper husband. "Thank you, no. I shall return to the library."

THE CHILDREN SQUEALED WITH LAUGHTER AS THE GREYHOUNDS raced the horses in the pasture. Blurs of tan and brown danced about the stallions and mares, who galloped with seeming delight in their turn. Darcy looked upon the children, immensely enjoying their glee.

Darcy had always expected he would enjoy being a father, but nothing prepared him for the experience of holding his son in his arms for the first time. Affection and love were there, of course, as deep as he had for Elizabeth, yet different. His sense of responsibility and concern for Bennet was ever present.

Unexpected was a feeling of *completion*. This was the meaning of life, his and Elizabeth's, to create and nurture the next generation, to raise and train the next master of Pemberley.

Now that Chloe had joined their family, Darcy had a niggling feeling that the little scamp had worked her way into his heart. And why not? She was a delightful child, bright and happy and inquisitive. She was also mischievous and willful, but Elizabeth claimed to be much the same at her age, so he trusted that Chloe, with firm, loving guidance, would become as remarkable as her aunt was.

Hopefully.

His thoughts were broken by that child tugging on his pants leg. "Ride horsey, Uncle Darcy?"

"I am not dressed for it, Chloe," he explained. At her pout, he called for the stable master. "Mr. Campbell, are any of the stable hands available for a ride about the paddock? For the children, you see."

Mr. Campbell, a middle-aged Scotsman with a full beard, smiled broadly. "Aye, Mr. Darcy, and I think Andromeda would be just the ride. I'll see to it myself." He winked and set off to the barn. A few minutes later, he reappeared with a saddled white horse.

"Oh! She so pretty!" cried Chloe.

Darcy smiled. "Andromeda is very gentle. Your cousin Georgiana used to ride her. Come." Darcy lifted the girl and handed her over to Mr. Campbell, already in Andromeda's saddle. As they began to walk the paddock, Bennet started to complain.

"Me! Me! Me!"

Darcy took his son from Mrs. Nivens. "No, Bennet. A gentleman always gives way to a lady unless there is danger. Your turn will come soon."

Bennet seemed to accept this and put his arms about his father's neck, and together they watched an excited Chloe ride with the stable master.

"Ho, Mr. Darcy!" came a shout as the children changed places. He turned to see Lord Llewellyn descend from his horse.

Darcy bit back a sigh as he waved, Chloe now in his arms. He liked the young viscount. But did he have no business to keep him occupied at Ambervale Lodge—say, until the wedding?

"Good afternoon, Lew."

Llewellyn ambled over, a grin on his face. "Having the children ride?" he observed when he was close enough to speak in a normal tone of voice. "What a capital idea! Miss Wickham, I trust you are well." He offered a small bow that delighted the girl. "And yourself, sir?"

Acknowledging his good health, Darcy was irked when Llewellyn inquired about Georgiana instead of Elizabeth. "Both my wife and sister are well, my lord," he stated in a flat tone.

Llewellyn had the good grace to look embarrassed, and they discussed Elizabeth's health while Bennet finished his turn. With the two children safely in Mrs. Nivens care again, the party moved towards the house.

"Mr. Campbell," Darcy said over his shoulder, "pray have Lysander and Penelope returned to the house once they are winded."

"Aye, Mr. Darcy," the stable master returned.

"Penelope?" Llewellyn stopped dead in his tracks. "You have a dog named *Penelope?*"

"Yes, one of my greyhounds."

Llewellyn started to laugh. "Oh, wait until my sister Penny comes! She will never hear the end of it!"

The party started walking again. "Surely you will not tease your sister over sharing her name with one of my hounds," declared Darcy.

"Perhaps not," said Llewellyn with a grin, "but I cannot speak for my brothers, Neil and Thad!"

Chapter 12

The viscount visited Pemberley for several days. He slept in a guest bedroom at the Kympton parsonage and arrived at Pemberley soon after breakfast. Lord Llewellyn seldom left until just before dinner and sometimes afterwards. He drove his curricle back to Kympton, and the cycle would repeat itself the next day.

Darcy was exasperated by the whole business. Jealous of his privacy, it grated on him to have Llewellyn, for all intents and purposes, invite himself to Pemberley whenever he pleased. Llewellyn was otherwise a fine, upstanding young man, quite besotted with Georgiana, but that was beside the point. Pemberley was Darcy's domain, and he knew he had lost control of it to his sister's desire for her intended's company.

Another issue was Elizabeth. Her confinement was fast approaching, yet she insisted on continuing to perform many of her duties as mistress. She claimed all was well, and she used the example of Bennet's uneventful birth to justify her assertion.

Darcy was a worrier; *he* knew it, *Elizabeth* knew it, and all the *servants* knew it. Bennet had been born in town, and the Darcy physician, the eminent Mr. Macmillan, and a prominent London accoucheur attended her. Now, Elizabeth would labor for their second child with only a midwife and an apothecary present. It had been Elizabeth's choice, but it gnawed at Darcy's soul.

Strangely, Mrs. Bennet's presence was Darcy's only comfort. After five children, the woman knew what she was about when it came to childbirth.

The birth and the wedding. These two monumental events falling close upon the other would drive the sanest man mad. It was a wonder Darcy did not attempt to take comfort in Mr. Gardiner's gift of French cognac.

Work was Darcy's escape, and he spent many hours with Mr. Thompson trying to offset the expected shortfalls in the crops due to the strange, cool, cloudy weather. Darcy's investments in coal proved more profitable than anticipated. If only there were safer ways for the workers to mine it!

About a week later, Darcy and the viscount were in the study perusing a pamphlet describing Sir Humphry Davy's new safe lantern. Darcy was thankful Llewellyn was not always courting his sister and still retained some interest in his investments. Mrs. Reynolds knocked on the door.

"Begging your pardon, Mr. Darcy, Mr. Southerland is here to see Lord Llewellyn."

The gentlemen glanced at one another before rising from their chairs. "Have him come in," said Darcy.

A moment later, Mr. Southerland entered and paid his respects. "I hope I find you both well."

Franklin Southerland was a fit, light-haired man, a habitual smile firmly planted on his fine-looking face. Kitty Bennet's family never supposed that a rector, no matter how handsome, could ever claim the young lady's tender affections. Thanks to his good nature, fine looks, and marked attentions, however, she grew utterly beguiled. Within a half year of meeting, they were engaged, and they had been married now for seventeen months.

"Franklin, have a seat," offered Darcy. "Would you care for any refreshment?"

"Tea would suit me, Brother, but before pleasure, I must

accomplish my mission." He held out an envelope. "My lord, this letter arrived not an hour ago, and given its return, I hastened to present it to you."

"Thank you, Mr. Southerland," said the viscount as he took the offering, "but enough of this 'lordship' business. We shall soon be family, and I should like it if I were Llewellyn or Lew to you."

Southerland nodded as he took a chair. "As you wish. My family calls me Franklin."

Darcy moved towards the door. "I shall have Elizabeth informed you are—"

"Excellent!" cried Llewellyn, holding up the letter.

The other gentlemen stared at the viscount in surprise and curiosity. Llewellyn realized his faux pas. "Forgive me gentlemen, but this is news I have been anxiously awaiting."

Southerland was puzzled. "From Matlock?"

"Yes, it is something of a surprise for Georgiana, but I do not hesitate to tell you," answered Llewellyn. "Lord Matlock has granted permission for me to use the Fitzwilliam hunting lodge."

Darcy was exceedingly puzzled. "The lodge in Scotland?"

Llewellyn was positively giddy. "Yes! It is perfect!"

"It is a very fine place, for a lodge. When do you plan to use it?"

Llewellyn laughed. "Oh, very soon! Very soon, indeed!"

Southerland frowned. "You plan to go shooting now, with your wedding coming on?"

"There will be a bit of shooting and fishing too. But fear not, we shall be otherwise pleasantly occupied, that is for certain."

Darcy sat up. "*We?* Who is going with you?"

"Georgiana, of course."

Darcy bolted out of his chair. "You wish to take my sister to *Scotland* before the wedding? What are you about, sir?"

"No, no! Not before the wedding!" cried Llewellyn. "Afterwards!"

"*What?*" Both Darcy and Southerland exclaimed.

"Georgie and I shall stay at the lodge in Scotland for our

honeymoon! Do you not see? Neither Georgie nor I wish to ride about the country on bumpy roads, shaking our bones to bits, staying with family and acquaintances, all the time answering the same questions and bearing the same knowing looks. London would be unbearable and Bath scarcely better. There are too many people at Brighton. Why not begin our marriage with a few weeks in the midst of the wilderness with only the birds to bother us? It will be perfection!"

Darcy and Southerland were stunned. "Georgiana approved of this?" the rector asked.

Llewellyn rolled his eyes. "Of course not. It is meant to be a surprise. But she will love the idea."

"You understand the lodge is rather rustic," Darcy pointed out.

"That is the best part!"

"How will you eat? You do not expect my sister to cook, do you?"

"No, no. We shall have a handful of servants, and we shall bring Georgie's maid and my man. We are not savages!" He thought for a moment. "But it might be pleasant to have the food delivered from the village. That way, we would have that much more privacy. It is two miles away, I believe."

Darcy meant to object, to have Llewellyn think sensibly, but Southerland stayed him with a hold on his forearm.

"Perhaps," the rector began cautiously, "you may wish to consult Georgiana. It will unfortunately spoil the surprise, but it would be well to have her opinion about the servants." He smiled. "Call it practice for the rest of your life."

Lord Llewellyn bit his lip in thought. "You might be right there, Franklin. Oh well." He jumped to his feet. "No time like the present! Where can I find her?"

"I believe the ladies are in the private sitting room in our quarters," said Darcy. "Have a footman summon her."

"Excellent! May we have the use of the music room?" At Darcy's nod of agreement, the happy viscount made his way out.

Once the door closed, Darcy turned to Southerland. "What was that about? Do you approve of this mad scheme?"

Southerland shook his head. "For myself, not at all, but it is not for me to say. Georgiana will decide. It is possible she will agree, but I think it more likely she will not. She will be shocked for a moment and then let him down gently. Your sister is a sweet, mild girl after all."

THE ARGUMENT IN THE MUSIC ROOM COULD BE HEARD THROUGH-out Pemberley.

"You want to go *shooting* on our *honeymoon*?"

"Not all of the time!"

"And what was *I* to do?"

"I *thought* you might wish to accompany me!"

"And do what? Reload your fowling piece? Flush your game?"

"Of course not! A servant will do that!"

"I *thought* you wished to be alone on our trip! I took it to mean some little cottage for a fortnight!"

"Georgie, that is impractical!"

By then, the residents of Pemberley had gathered outside the music room. Mrs. Bennet's eyes were as big as saucers.

"And why is that?"

"What would we do for a fortnight? I mean—Georgie, we cannot be…you know…we have to do *something* else!"

"Lew, that is vulgar!"

"What *else* would you call it?"

Kitty gasped, while Darcy and Elizabeth exchanged looks.

"Do not take that tone of voice with me!"

"What tone would satisfy you, my lady?"

"I am not your lady yet, sir! And by speaking so, I might never be!"

"Georgie, you must calm down!"

"I AM CALM! DO NOT TELL ME TO CALM DOWN!"

"You are acting like a child!"

"A *child*, am I? Well, this *child* has a mind of her own, and at the present time, I have no wish to see you!"

"Georgiana, I insist you see reason!"

"Get out! Get out, now!"

The next moment, the door flew open as an incensed Georgiana stormed into the hall. Freezing for a moment as she took in the gathered audience, she cried, "I never want to see him again!" She then burst into tears and fled up the stairway.

Shortly afterwards, Llewellyn appeared, angry and distraught. "I suppose you all heard that?"

"My lord," Darcy growled, "you will keep a civil tongue in your head when in the presence of my wife. I suggest we retire to my study to—"

Llewellyn interrupted him, but he spoke in a more moderate tone. "For what purpose? Your sister has ended our betrothal."

"I do not think so. Let us speak on this."

The young viscount waved his hand. "There is nothing more to say. I beg you all to excuse me." He bowed and walked towards the door.

Elizabeth moved to take Darcy's hand. "I must go to Georgie and console her."

"I shall go with you, Lizzy," said her sister.

"And I," declared Mrs. Bennet.

"No, Mother! Your...nerves! You should rest. Papa, will you escort her?"

Mr. Bennet did little to hide a smirk. "Of course. Your mother's nerves and I are old friends. Come along, my dear."

"Shall I go with you, Elizabeth?" Darcy asked.

In their years of marriage, Darcy had learned there were times it was best for his wife to act alone, especially with Georgiana. This was one of those times; she gently shook her head and left for the family wing, Kitty helping her up the stairs, her parents following behind.

"What shall we do, Darcy?" asked Southerland.

"Let us wait to hear from the ladies. Then, perhaps, you may be able to speak to Llewellyn when you return to the parsonage."

HALF AN HOUR LATER, THE GENTLEMEN RECEIVED WORD TO MEET with their wives in the Darcys' private sitting room.

"Georgiana is, by turns, angry, distraught, fearful, and inconsolable," reported a weary Elizabeth. "She is upset with Llewellyn's thoughtlessness and condescension. She feels insulted, her wishes ridiculed. On the other hand, she still loves him."

Darcy gravely asked, "Does she wish to end the betrothal?"

"She would not state it plainly. Instead, she contemplates whether she should go through with the wedding."

"If I may interject," said Kitty, "Georgie is sad and confused. And, in my opinion, she is making too much of this. Bridal nerves are at play here. I agree that his lordship was rather thoughtless, but I am persuaded he meant well." She smiled at her husband. "What young couple has not been fools in love at some time or other?"

Southerland chuckled. "Very true, my dear."

Darcy and Elizabeth shared a smile. *Their* quarrels during their first year had been of epic proportions, yet they still found their way forward, becoming closer, wiser, and more in love than before.

"I believe Kitty is correct," said Elizabeth. "Let us give Georgie a night to cry. All may be made well in the morning as long as Llewellyn apologizes."

Darcy nodded. "I am certain he will." *Or I will wring his neck.*

Southerland rose. "Well, dear, shall we return home so I may speak with the viscount?"

"Will you talk to him alone, or may I join you?" Kitty's eyebrow rose.

Southerland laughed. "We wish to advise him, not kill him!"

"Franklin! I am not so bad."

He gallantly kissed her hand. "In my experience, Bennet ladies are very forthright. Should he prove obstinate, you may feel free to have at him."

Kitty offered a dimpled smile to her husband. "And I shall know how to act!"

ABOUT AN HOUR AFTER THE SOUTHERLANDS LEFT, A NOTE CAME from the parsonage. Lord Llewellyn was not there. He had already left for Ambervale.

Chapter 13

The following morning, Darcy was alone in the breakfast room. Elizabeth had been taking her breakfast in their chambers for the last fortnight. Due to the events of the prior day, she requested that her husband eat downstairs in the hopes that Georgiana would accept her invitation to join her and talk privately. So, the king of Pemberley—banished from his chambers—sat leisurely, sipping a second cup of coffee and awaiting instructions from his queen. It was there he was found by the Bennets.

"Oh, Mr. Darcy, what a terrible occurrence!" cried Mrs. Bennet upon seeing him. "A wedding canceled! The viscount jilted! The scandal! How can it be contained? Miss Darcy might be ruined forever!"

"Mrs. Bennet, please do not—"

"And the dresses!" she continued as she sat down. "Well, they might still be used, I suppose, if—"

"I am certain the dresses will not go to waste. Shall I get you a plate?" asked her husband.

"Oh yes, Mr. Bennet! No kippers, mind you."

"Have no fear. There is not a kipper in sight."

"And plenty of apple butter! Mr. Darcy, the Pemberley apple butter is divine!"

"For my cook, I thank you." Darcy set down his cup. "As for my sister, nothing is decided. Elizabeth is speaking to her now."

"Lizzy—so levelheaded! You certainly picked the wittiest of my girls, sir! Not that Miss Darcy is not clever—she certainly is!"

"My dear," injected Mr. Bennet, "Mr. Darcy is certainly aware of our Lizzy's wit, for he has been married to her these four years."

"Four years in November, Mr. Bennet!"

"I stand corrected. In any case, he certainly knows what he has in Lizzy. Now, may I eat my breakfast in peace?"

"How can you think of eating at a time like this? That poor, motherless child! We must do something! She is ruined! Ruined!"

"More apple butter, dear?"

"Thank you. Mr. Darcy, what shall we do for our poor Georgiana?"

Darcy had just considered that throwing the Bennets out of Pemberley might be a good start when Mrs. Reynolds stepped in.

"Begging your pardon, sir, Mrs. Darcy requests your attendance in her chambers."

"Oh my!" Mrs. Bennet held a hand to her heart. "Is it her time, Mrs. Reynolds?"

"No, ma'am. She is with Miss Darcy."

"Thank you, Mrs. Reynolds." Darcy rose, and as he passed the housekeeper, he whispered, "More apple butter for the table."

Mrs. Reynolds smirked. "Already on the way, sir. And Mrs. Darcy is well."

Darcy smiled and hurried up the stairs. Moments later, he was in the small sitting room that connected their chambers. A tearful Georgiana had been sitting on the sofa, clutching Elizabeth's hands, but when she saw her brother, she launched herself into his arms.

"What have I done?" she wailed. "Lew must surely hate me!"

"No, no, sweetling. Llewellyn adores you, I am certain." Darcy gently rubbed her back. "Go on and have a good cry, and then we shall attend to matters."

Her answer was to shake her head.

"Come, Georgiana," said Elizabeth. "Did we not agree that things are not at all hopeless? Here, sit down before you wet Fitzwilliam's coat. Poor Witherspoon will be beside himself!"

"Poor Witherspoon, indeed," responded Darcy. They all chuckled a bit at the mention of the fastidious valet. Georgiana untangled herself and resumed her place next to Elizabeth. Darcy took a chair and waited.

Elizabeth began. "After a night's sleep, we now see things in a clearer light. We agree they were both at fault." She turned to her sister. "Georgiana?"

Darcy refrained from remarking on his queen's use of the royal "we" and waited.

Georgiana dabbed her tears, her pretty face red and blotchy. "My response to Lew's...*surprise* was unladylike and entirely beneath me. I-I never gave him an opportunity to explain himself. I could have—*should have* handled matters better." She looked at Elizabeth. "I should have acted like you, Lizzy."

Darcy coughed while Elizabeth laughed. "Thank you, but I deserve no such praise! I have acted foolishly in my day, have I not, Fitzwilliam?"

"I have no idea of any such thing," he answered gallantly. "I, however, have been a fool on more than one occasion, as you both well know. Fortunately, I have been forgiven, little as I deserve it." He grew serious. "The matter before us, Georgie, is this: Can *you* forgive Llewellyn?"

Georgiana's throat worked as she slowly nodded.

"Then allow me to suggest that I ride this morning to Ambervale, speak to Llewellyn, and bring him back here. Does that meet with your approval?"

Georgiana bowed her head and looked at her hands. "Will he come, do you think?"

Darcy glanced at his wife before answering. "Llewellyn loves you, sweetling, almost as much as I love Elizabeth." He offered a small smile. "He will come."

With a cry, Georgiana was immediately in Darcy's arms again.

LATER, ELIZABETH JOINED DARCY IN HIS CHAMBERS AS WITHER-spoon packed a few necessities in saddlebags. She took in her husband's change of dress.

"You plan to ride to Ambervale?"

"Apollo will be faster than a carriage," Darcy replied. "Where is Georgiana?"

"She has retired to her rooms." She bit her lip. "Must you take Apollo? He is so…"

"Spirited?"

"Wild, I would say." She could not bear the thought of that beast causing her beloved to lie injured along the road with no help to be found.

Darcy grinned. "Of what use is a stallion if he is not spirited? Never fear, my love. Apollo and I have a good understanding." He stepped closer and took her hand. "Even mounted, I cannot reach Ambervale until the afternoon. I must stay overnight and return tomorrow." His thumb made circles on the back of her hand. "I dislike leaving you at this time."

Her courage rising, she kissed his cheek. "Go. Talk sense into Llewellyn and return with him. I shall be occupied consoling Georgiana while reassuring my mother the wedding will take place as planned. *You* have the easier task."

Darcy's dark eyes bore into hers. "Kitty can assist you."

Elizabeth smiled. "You and I think alike. I have already sent for her."

He touched her swollen abdomen. "I love you."

They were interrupted by a clearing of the throat. "Sir, your bags are packed."

Darcy colored while Elizabeth held back a giggle. It was not the first time Witherspoon had caught them thus.

"Very good," stated Darcy in that impersonal way of his. "Take them to the stables. I shall join you presently."

Once the valet had left the room, Darcy swept Elizabeth into his arms for a torrid kiss. "Let us part here. I do not like you chancing the stairs," he said at last. "I shall farewell Georgiana ere I go. Give my love to the children." Another kiss and he was out the door.

Elizabeth sat down, her emotions finally getting the best of her. She had prevaricated. She hated that Fitzwilliam had to leave, even on such an important errand. But then she recalled something he said that brought joy to her heart.

For the first time, Fitzwilliam had referred to their *children*, not child or son. *Children*. Bennet *and* Chloe.

A tear of pure happiness rolled down her cheek.

FOR ONCE, THE COLD, CLOUDY WEATHER WAS A BOON, FOR DARCY and Apollo made excellent time. It was early afternoon when he surrendered his mount to the stable master, asked that his belongings be delivered to the housekeeper, and entered Ambervale Lodge.

A moderately sized, three-story rectangular house of red brick accented by white columns and trim, it fit in well with the park it dominated. The furnishings were from an earlier time—not surprising for a bachelor's home—and Darcy expected his sister would spend the majority of her first year here refreshing the interior.

Assuming his mission was successful.

"Mr. Darcy to see Lord Llewellyn, Mr. Miller," he informed the butler. "I must beg for a room and valet tonight. My belongings are coming up from the stables." It was not Darcy's first visit to Ambervale, so there was nary a blink or hesitation as the butler escorted Darcy to the study.

"A room will be ready in a half an hour, sir, and his lordship's man will see to your needs," Miller said before knocking on the door. "My lord," the butler announced in a louder voice, "Mr. Darcy to see you." He added sotto voce, "Good luck, sir," and opened the study door.

A questioning response died on Darcy's lips as he took in the state of the study. The pulled drapes had thrown the room into darkness. Papers were scattered on the desk and floor. A half-eaten plate of food rested precariously on a side table next to two bottles of brandy, one empty and the other nearly so. And behind the desk sat Algernon Woodhouse, Viscount Llewellyn, well into his cups.

"Mill—Miller!" he hiccupped. "I said no visitors! Oh, it ish you, Darcy. I shuppose I know why you are here." He waved a hand. "Take a seat and let ush get this over with."

Darcy said nothing but sat down and studied the young peer. Llewellyn was not as fastidious with his dress as Darcy—few men were—but to see him now was a shock. If he was not mistaken, Llewellyn had not changed his clothes since he left Pemberley. His coat stained, his cravat untied, and his person—hair wild, eyes bloodshot, and cheeks unshaven. The man was a disaster.

Good, thought Darcy as he recalled his sister's pain.

"I shuppose you are here for a shettlement," Llewellyn slurred. "F-Fine—whatever you want. I do not care." His elbows on his desk, his head fell into his hands.

"That, my lord, would be far too easy on you."

Bleary eyes surveyed him. "What is your meaning?"

Darcy stood and leaned over the desk on his fists. "My meaning is that you sober up so that you and I may have a *talk*."

Llewellyn blinked, swallowing nervously. "What is there to talk about? Georgiana wants nothing to do with me."

"By my word, Llewellyn, if that is your honest opinion, you are not worthy of my sister, and I should leave you here to wallow in your misery. Stand up, boy!"

"Y-You call me boy, do you?" Llewellyn staggered to his feet. "Mind your mannersh, sir! I am a viscount!"

"So is my cousin, and I shall speak to you as I do to Andrew when he acts the fool."

"F-Fool, am I?" Llewellyn attempted to walk from behind his desk, but only managed to trip and fall on the floor, spilling his brandy. The commotion brought the butler into the study.

"The viscount is indisposed, Miller," Darcy informed him.

"I am not in…in…anything," the young lord protested.

"Except brandy," was Darcy's caustic reply. To the butler, he said, "I imagine a cold bath is called for here. Would you be so kind as to call in a few footmen to assist his lordship to his chambers?"

"I am not leaving," declared Llewellyn.

Miller ignored his employer. "Shall I call for hot coffee afterwards, Mr. Darcy?"

"An excellent idea."

"M-Miller, you work for me, not Darcy!" shouted Llewellyn.

"As you say, milord," replied the butler as he stepped out the door. Moments later, he returned with two burly footmen. "His lordship suffered a mishap. Pray assist him upstairs."

"I am not leaving!"

"Ignore the master," the butler advised. "It seems he struck his head when he fell. Is that not so, Mr. Darcy?"

Darcy hid a grin. "It would appear so."

Llewellyn, complaining all the time, was then gently lifted to his feet by the footmen. By the time the trio reached the stairs, Miller and the footmen had been dismissed from the estate. Miller's only response was an unruffled, "As you wish, sir."

Darcy sidled up to the butler. "I assure all of you: your positions are safe."

Miller nodded, hiding a smile.

HALF AN HOUR LATER, DARCY SOUGHT OUT LORD LLEWELLYN IN his chambers. The young lord, cleaned and dressed, was slouched in a chair facing the fireplace, a cup of tea at his elbow. Darcy bit back a chuckle.

"Are you now in a humor to speak with me?" he asked.

Llewellyn moaned and rubbed his head. "I am in a humor to lie down and die, Darcy. Pray sit down…you are moving far too much for my liking."

Now Darcy did laugh. He had not moved so much as a finger,

but Llewellyn was still in the grip of his brandy-induced state. He bowed to the viscount's request and took a chair.

"I would suggest only bread and broth tonight. Otherwise, you will cast your accounts."

Llewellyn slapped a hand across his mouth. "Thank you for bringing that to my attention." Once in control again, he glared at Darcy. "Will you shay—say what you wish and go away?"

Darcy leaned forward, arms on his knees, all amusement gone. "I would be most happy to leave as my wife is near her confinement, but I am on a mission. I shall deliver the message entrusted to me and go, if that is your desire. Have I your notice?"

Llewellyn turned his blood-shot eyes to him.

"Thank you. My Lord Llewellyn, my sister begs your pardon. If you are agreeable, she will marry you."

Llewellyn immediately brightened.

"I, on the other hand, have objections." Darcy's voice was cold. "Your words during that ridiculous exhibition in my music room are beneath the comportment of a respectable gentleman. I will not have such behavior in my house, and I will not allow anyone to speak to my sister in such a way, no matter his rank.

"Is this your usual conduct? I tell you, sir, if that is so, I fear for Georgiana's future. It is unfortunate that the law gives you the right to rage and storm like a bully once you are married, and there is little I can do about it except to offer my sister sanctuary."

"I—I would never mistreat Georgiana! Never!" Llewellyn cried.

"Indeed? I must doubt your assurances. Just yesterday, you brought her to tears. Let me make clear to you, sir, that at this moment, I would advise my sister to think the better of marrying you. A few thousand pounds added to her dowry would easily repair any damage suffered by jilting you."

Llewellyn sprang to his feet. "J-jilt me?" He almost fell and needed to grasp the back of the chair to steady himself.

Darcy was merciless. "Yes, my lord. Elizabeth and I would be very happy if Georgiana decided to reside with us always."

Llewellyn looked panicked. "You cannot! The banns have been called! You signed the wedding articles! The engagement announcement has been published!"

"Do you truly think anything will prevent me from protecting my sister?"

"You cannot! I need her! *I love her*!" Llewellyn fell back into his chair, his face in his hands. "I love Georgiana," he sobbed.

Darcy said nothing for a full minute. "Then you should prove it."

"How?" the viscount replied into his hands.

"By acting like the gentleman I believe you may become."

Llewellyn slowly turned to him, agony and hope in his expression. "What should I do?"

Darcy shook his head. "Upon my word, milord, you must eat something!" He rose and rang for a footman. "I shall have sandwiches brought up. I am famished. I have not eaten since leaving Pemberley." As he returned to his chair, he said, "We shall talk once you are somewhat sober, but contemplate this in the meantime." He smiled. "Consider what you will say when you grovel before my sister."

Llewellyn groaned.

The two spent several hours in conversation before retiring. The next morning dawned gray but dry—a perfect description of the viscount as he walked through the breakfast room door.

"By gad, you are a sight, milord," remarked Darcy. Lord Llewellyn was in his best traveling clothes, but his face bore a pinched, sickly pallor. "How is your head?"

His young companion took his time gently taking a seat. "If it fell off, I would feel much better." He frowned at Darcy's amusement. "You are painfully cheerful today, Darcy. Is this your typical morning sensibility, or should I congratulate myself on being a source of diversion?"

Darcy ignored his attempt at levity. "Do you recall our agreement last night?"

Llewellyn nodded. "I have thought of nothing else—oh, this head!" He rubbed his forehead.

"Coffee. May I pour you a cup?"

"Will it help?"

"Doubtful, but at least you will be awake."

Llewellyn cracked open one eye. "I see my man was able to do something with your riding clothes."

"Yes, pray give him my thanks." Darcy studied his young friend closely. "Are you certain you wish to travel to Pemberley today?"

"I must," he insisted. "I cannot go another day without begging Georgie's pardon."

"Allow me to deliver a note instead," Darcy offered, "and you can come when you have recovered."

"No. She deserves to hear it from my lips. Nothing less will do." He raised his head. "I am well enough. Any pains I suffer on the way will be my penance."

Darcy nodded approvingly. "Very good. I suggest dry toast with your coffee. You must forgo these excellent eggs." Darcy began eating with gusto as Llewellyn moaned.

Forty-five minutes later, Llewellyn's trunk was secured, Apollo's reins were tied to the back of Llewellyn's curricle, and the two gentlemen climbed aboard.

"Last chance to change your mind, Lew."

"Leave off, Darcy. I am determined."

"Very well. But I strongly suggest I take the reins. You are in no fit state to drive."

Llewellyn waved a hand in submission. Darcy expertly guided the pair of chestnut horses down the lane to the road.

THEY RESTED THE HORSES AT A CHANGING POST ABOUT HALFWAY between the estates. Darcy and Llewellyn took their ease in the public house with tea, bread, and cheese. There were few patrons in attendance, but Darcy, ever desirous for privacy, chose a corner table in the back of the room.

"Eat something, Lew," advised Darcy. "It will help your head." He noticed his companion's color had improved.

"It would feel better if you would *try* to miss the ruts in the road," the viscount complained. Darcy did not reply, and the two ate in silence for a time.

Llewellyn set down his cup of tea. "Have I ruined everything, Darcy?" he quietly asked. "Will Georgiana forgive me?"

Darcy was pleased at the viscount's regret for his part of the argument, but he had to give the man some hope without violating his sister's trust. "Are you familiar with my courtship of Mrs. Darcy?"

Bewildered, Llewellyn said, "I have heard little about that, save something Sir Richard mentioned. That it was not…traditional?"

Darcy laughed. "Traditional, it was not in the least." He paused. "I was a fool—not like you, Lew, but worse. I insulted her when we first met, and I was completely insensible of it." He shook his head. "I 'courted' Elizabeth by engaging in debates. On top of that, I offered the worst—well, *one* of the worst proposals ever given a maiden in the history of England. She refused me with a set down I shall never forget."

"She *refused* you?" Llewellyn was astonished.

"She said I was not a gentleman, and she was right."

"What did you say?"

"I shall not give you the particulars, but it is safe to say I belittled her family and, therefore, herself. She believed some lies about me, but they would have been nothing had I behaved as I ought." He snorted.

"But I have seldom seen a couple so happily wed as you and Mrs. Darcy. How did you manage to secure her affections?"

"It was not easy. I had been a selfish being—in practice, though not in principle. As a child, I was taught what was right but not to correct my temper. I was given good principles but left to follow them in pride and conceit. I was a selfish and overbearing man, caring for none beyond my own family circle, thinking meanly of all the rest of the world. *That* was the man Elizabeth rejected.

"I thought I had lost her and expected never to see her again. However, forgetting her was an impossibility. Therefore, in her honor I made a vow to be that man no longer. I chose to become the gentleman I was raised to be—one that Elizabeth would have been happy to know."

"I cannot imagine the picture you paint, Darcy," claimed Llewellyn. "You are a reserved man, certainly, not given to empty flattery or gossip, but you are not the misanthrope you describe. You are one of the finest gentlemen of my acquaintance,"

"Ah, but you did not know me five years ago. Elizabeth's portrait was accurate, I assure you. I have labored to change it since. That you say so indicates I have made some small success." He chuckled. "I shall never be easy in a ballroom."

"And so, you then courted Mrs. Darcy?"

"Not yet. Recall, I expected never to meet Elizabeth again. But Fate had her own plans, and a few months later we came across each other at the last place imaginable—Pemberley. Elizabeth was visiting the estate with her family."

"She sought you out?"

"No, not at all! She had been told my family was in London. Had she known I had come early, she never would have stepped foot on the grounds."

"She was avoiding you."

"Yes, but not for the reason you may suppose. Elizabeth told me later that she was remorseful over her mistaken trust in some lies spread about me. She was mortified for my sake and hers, and she was shocked when she found me at home. For my part, I was astonished and delighted."

"And you reconciled."

"Yes." *Eventually.* "I tell you this story to share what I have learned. I did not change for Elizabeth; I changed *because* of Elizabeth. She saw me as I truly was, knew I was not the man I should be, and owned the courage to tell me so. She is a strong woman, and you should know that all the women in my family are strong.

"Some are like Lady Catherine, who is rude and overbearing, but others are like Elizabeth, Lady Matlock, and my late mother. Their strength comes from their intelligence and character, their sense of right and wrong. We Darcys and Fitzwilliams seek out strong women and create strong women. And mark it well: Georgiana is strong in her own way.

"Ah, you are frowning! No, Lew, I am not saying that Georgiana is quarrelsome, though you will quarrel in the future, I am certain. All couples do, believe me. I *am* saying she is not a child or a showpiece like so many in the *ton*. If you wish for a wife who has nothing in her head but fashion and gossip yet can host an excellent dinner, then turn back to Ambervale and look for that lady elsewhere. But, if you desire a wife who will be your partner in all things, then you may continue to Pemberley."

Llewellyn shook his head. "What do you mean 'a partner in all things'?"

Darcy looked about the room, making certain no one was eavesdropping. "Elizabeth is not just my wife and the mother of my children. She is my best friend and closest confidante. No major decision is made without her involvement. We discuss *everything*. I know this is unusual, but it is the reason for our success."

"You said something about that when you and the Fitzwilliams informed me of your investments."

"That is only part of it. Our wealth has grown, that is so. But, by including our wives in our business, we are assured of marital happiness.

"You have met my irascible and boisterous uncle, the earl. He is the undisputed master in his family. However, he and the countess routinely discuss politics and strategy in the privacy of his study. As for my parents, the open affection and trust between them was evident to any that knew them. Even Andrew and Eugenie are partners in their own way. Georgiana will settle for nothing less. Are you prepared to give it?"

Llewellyn grew pensive. "Darcy, you have met my parents. I love them, but such a partnership as you describe…that is not possible for them. My mother is too flighty and my father—" He looked away. "He has affection for my mother but little respect. He would never share his business or political dealings with her." He looked down. "Not that she would understand or even desire it."

Darcy looked on as Llewellyn thought. It seemed an age, but upon reflection, it had probably been only a minute or two. Llewellyn raised his head, one side of his mouth quirked up in a half grin. "The difference sounds delightful. Let us go to Pemberley."

Just then the door flew open. "Mr. Darcy!" cried an anxious man.

Darcy's insides turned to ice; the man was a stable hand from Pemberley! He flew to his feet. "Simon, what is amiss?"

The young man babbled, "Oh, Mr. Darcy, I was on my way to Ambervale when I saw Apollo tied to the back of the viscount's curricle. You must come to Pemberley straight away!"

"Is it Mrs. Darcy? Dammit man, what is it?"

Simon took a breath. "Mrs. Darcy's time is upon her! Come quickly!"

Chapter 14

D arcy drove the curricle as hard as he could, Llewellyn hanging on for dear life.

"Damn you, Llewellyn! If anything has happened to Elizabeth, you will regret it all your days! I knew I should not have left! I knew it!"

"For the love of God, take care!" shouted the frightened viscount. "You will overturn the carriage!"

Darcy paid his passenger no heed as they sped through the Derbyshire countryside. Apollo was far behind, returning to Pemberley at a more moderate pace in the care of Simon.

The curricle team, strong and refreshed, responded well to Darcy's hand, yet it was over an hour before they reached the outskirts of Lambton. A frustrated Darcy was forced to slow their progress along the busy, narrow street.

Happy were the gentlemen when the turn to Pemberley appeared! Darcy dashed by the gatekeeper's cottage with a wave and drove the team to make the climb to the great house. When the exquisite manor came into view, both men experienced relief that the jarring, dangerous journey was almost done. Groomsmen rushed to take the exhausted team in hand as the curricle stopped before the main entrance. Darcy spared not a word to them as he leapt from the seat and sprinted to the door, held open by the butler.

"Mr. Darcy!" the old man cried. "Thank heavens you are here!"

Darcy grasped him by the shoulders. "The mistress?" His eyes were wide with fear.

From the top of the stairs he heard Mrs. Reynolds voice. "Mr. Darcy! Mrs. Darcy is well, but she is in the midst of her labors. Come and refresh yourself, sir."

"Not yet! Not until I have seen her!" With that, Darcy took the steps two at a time and brushed past the housekeeper, heading for the family rooms above. He saw Mrs. Bennet leaving the room set aside for Elizabeth's confinement. He hesitated not a moment and was at his mother-in-law's side in an instant.

"Elizabeth! How is she?" panting, he demanded of his wife's mother.

"Fitzwilliam Darcy! You will behave yourself! Lizzy is suffering to bring *your* child into the world, and I will not have you upset her! Upon my word, you are making such a fuss over a trifle! Have you learned nothing from the last time? It is a sad trial, to be sure, but my girls are healthy and strong. Take hold of yourself, sir, before you frighten my dear Lizzy!"

Darcy hung his head for a moment. "I must see her."

Mrs. Bennet tut-tutted. "Oh, very well, but not too long." She took his arm and led him first into a small sitting room and then into the chamber.

The sight before him was disturbingly familiar. The room was dark, lit only by lanterns. The midwife was discussing something with the apothecary while Kitty and a maid stood near the bed, cloths in hand. And in the middle of it was his dear Elizabeth, her lovely hair in a plait.

"Fitzwilliam…" she groaned.

He was at her side in an instant. "I am here, dearest!" He kissed her forehead and grasped her hand.

"Mr. Darcy, I must object!" exclaimed the midwife.

"Oh, be still," demanded Mrs. Bennet. "This is not his first child!

He intends to comfort my poor girl. He will be gone soon enough."

"Your letter," Elizabeth whispered. "It is on the table in your chambers."

Darcy bit back an oath. It was the cursed "last letter" tradition that demanded expectant mothers write to their husbands in case they did not survive childbirth. How he hated the dratted things! "I will never read it," he vowed. "I will never have cause to do so."

Elizabeth smiled. "I used the same one I wrote for Bennet."

Darcy kissed her. "There is my plucky love!"

Suddenly, Elizabeth cried out, writhing in pain. Darcy held her hand, feeling useless, wishing all the time to take her agonies onto himself. Once she settled again, Darcy felt soft hands on his shoulders.

"It is time for you to leave," said Mrs. Bennet. "Lizzy is in good hands here."

Darcy looked over to behold the smiling face of Mrs. Reynolds. "Mrs. Bennet is correct, sir. We shall bring news down when all is done."

"Go, my love," Elizabeth pleaded.

Darcy took a shuddering breath, kissed Elizabeth again, nodded to Kitty, and allowed Mrs. Bennet to escort him from the room. Once in the sitting room, she pointed at the door.

"Get along downstairs where you gentlemen belong! I am certain my husband will keep you company, but pray forgo the brandy! It did you ill last time." She wore a forced smile. "Lizzy will be well, and I shall be with her. Now, go!"

Darcy slowly descended the stairs, musing over Mrs. Bennet. As she was during Bennet's birth, she was a different woman. She had immediately worked to relieve his anxiety and ease Elizabeth's suffering. A center of calmness in a sea of chaos, she had stood by her daughter with the firmest resolve. And why should she not, having faced this trial successfully five times before?

Of course, once the drama was done and his newborn son safely in the arms of his parents, Mrs. Bennet had reverted to her usual silly, ignorant, and thoughtless behavior. Darcy could hardly wait for her volte-face again, for it would be brought about only by the happiest of results.

He was directed by a footman to the parlor where he found Mr. Bennet playing chaperone to Georgiana and Llewellyn. The viscount had obviously wasted no time in reconciling with his betrothed, given that the pair sat close together on the couch, hand in hand. His sister gave out a cry upon his entrance and flew to his side.

"Oh, Brother, thank you for bringing Lew here! How does Lizzy fair?"

Darcy gave Llewellyn a half-hearted glare over Georgiana's shoulder. He was not unhappy with his sister's thanks. After all, he had been successful in ending the couple's estrangement. But he wondered whether he would ever truly resolve himself to Georgiana's eventual marriage and departure from Pemberley, no matter how good a man Llewellyn was.

"I am told Elizabeth is as well as can be expected," Darcy reported. "How long has this been going on?"

"Lizzy complained about pains during breakfast. I knew not what to do, but Mother Bennet did. She demanded that Lizzy be brought to her bed and that the midwife be summoned. I do not know why the apothecary came also."

"My standing orders in case his potions are required."

"Oh." She giggled. "The midwife was not best pleased to see him. Once I sent the rider, Father Bennet and I retreated here."

Darcy's gaze moved to his wife's father, who sat in an armchair with a glass of wine and several books from the library at his elbow. Since his marriage to Elizabeth, Georgiana had taken to referring to the Bennets as father and mother. Darcy rejected such high appellations for his wife's parents but agreed to the more familiar "Bennet" and "Darcy" when conversing with the gentleman. He greeted him in his usual clipped manner.

Georgiana remembered her manners. "Would you care for any refreshment, Brother?"

"Or clean boots?"

Mr. Bennet's sarcastic inquiry drew Darcy's attention to the state of his dress. Oh, he was a disaster! His boots were salvageable, as was his coat, but his vest and cravat were for the fire. Witherspoon would be beside himself.

Darcy stood. "I am for my chambers." He looked over at Llewellyn, who was in a similar state. "My lord, I suggest you do the same."

Knowing he had hours of waiting before him, Darcy acquiesced to a shave before dressing. He was certain his valet was cursing under his breath as he tied a clean cravat at his throat. No doubt Witherspoon took the state of Darcy's traveling clothes as a personal insult. Darcy returned to the parlor to see that Llewellyn had preceded him, again sitting next to Georgiana. Mr. Bennet caught his attention with a wink and nod towards the lovers.

At least they were well chaperoned.

Darcy caught himself pacing. What was he to do? He had no head for business or desire for sport. With a frustrated snort, he walked over to reclaim one of his books next to Mr. Bennet. It was *Lyrical Ballads*—the 1805 fourth edition, a favorite—and Darcy selfishly enjoyed the grumble of dissatisfaction from his wife's father. He reclaimed his chair, and the book ironically fell open to the poem "Anecdote for Fathers," an appropriate selection.

He grew somewhat engrossed in the words of Wordsworth and Coleridge, at times partaking of the tea and biscuits served by Georgiana, his thoughts never truly leaving the momentous events above stairs. Therefore, he was quite surprised to find a small hand upon his knee.

"What is it, Chloe?"

"Where Aunt Lizzy?" The young girl was clearly upset.

Mrs. Nivens hurried in, Bennet in her arms. "I am sorry, sir. She rushed out. The children—they are quite upset."

"Oh, the poor dears!" cried Georgiana.

Darcy picked up his ward. "Can the children hear?"

A pained Mrs. Nivens nodded. "Yes, sir."

"Aunt Lizzy yelling," Chloe said.

"I scared," added Bennet.

As worried and frightened as Darcy was for Elizabeth, he could not bear to have the children suffer in fear. "Let them remain here for now, Mrs. Nivens. We shall entertain them."

"Of course we shall!" Georgiana moved to claim Chloe, allowing Darcy to take his son into his arms.

"Mama is well, Bennet. Chloe, you must not worry over your aunt. She is bringing the new baby into the world. Do you recall speaking with Aunt Lizzy about that?"

Chloe's big eyes gazed at him—eyes that so resembled her father's. Yes, she had George Wickham's eyes, but her hair and face more resembled her mother, Lydia. Truly she was both her parents, yet she was not. She was her own person—a boisterous, happy, stubborn, curious, loving little girl. *One that would be raised as a Darcy*, he vowed.

"Aunt Lizzy says baby in her tummy 'til God says come out. Baby come now?"

"Yes."

"When?"

Darcy sighed. "These things take time. We must wait."

"But *why*?" An adorable pout graced her face. "Not like waiting."

Georgiana and Llewellyn laughed in response, but Darcy could not.

I not like waiting, either.

"I want Mama," Bennet demanded.

So do I, son.

"Let us retire to the music room," Georgiana suggested. All agreed, and soon she was established before the pianoforte. The others took their seats, except for Llewellyn, who insisted on turning the pages.

"Give me my grandson, Darcy," requested Mr. Bennet. The child secure in his lap, he continued. "Now be still, Ben. Your aunt is a true proficient." Chloe then claimed Darcy's lap.

"I believe all know this one. Clap along." Georgiana began to sing. "Sing a song of sixpence, a pocket full of rye…"

AFTER ABOUT AN HOUR OF SONGS AND MUSIC, THE PARTY RETURNED to the parlor. The children enjoyed milk and biscuits while the adults partook of tea or spirits. Darcy settled for tea. Chloe demanded a game of King of the Hill, and a smiling Darcy suffered to be the hill to the surprise of Mr. Bennet and Llewellyn. It was not long before Chloe grew bored with her uncle. This was not the first time she had played this game with him, and she requested the attentions of Lord Llewellyn. To Georgiana's delight, the viscount dutifully submitted.

Darcy brushed himself off and sat next to Mr. Bennet. "I thought I had settled upon your character, Darcy," remarked his wife's father, "but you continue to surprise me. Playing on the floor with your children? I never dreamt of such a thing."

"I played the same games with Georgiana when she was small whenever I was home from school." He glanced at his sister, her pretty face alight with joy, watching the children play with her intended. It was difficult to recall those times in the nursery with her. *Not so small now, are you, Georgie?*

"There is ten years difference between the two of you, is there not?"

"Actually, it is nearly twelve."

"Twelve years! And you came into your inheritance ten years ago." Mr. Bennet mused. "You have all but raised her, Darcy. She is as much daughter as sister. A fine young lady. I congratulate you"

As much daughter as sister. How true that statement was. And in a few weeks, she would be a daughter no more. *But she will always be my sister. She will always be a Darcy.*

Just then, Mrs. Reynolds entered the parlor, all smiles. "Begging the master's pardon, but Mrs. Darcy requests your presence upstairs, sir."

Darcy gripped the arms of his chair, battling between fear and joy, intently studying his longtime servant's happy countenance. At her nod, he all but leapt from his chair. "I…I must go. Pray excuse me."

"Is baby here?"

"Hush now, Chloe," said Georgiana as she embraced the girl. "Uncle Darcy must go up first."

"But *why*? I want see baby *now*!"

"Later," Darcy managed before he bolted from the room. He was up the staircase in a flash and ran to the confinement room. He found a happy Kitty in the sitting room, but he barely paid her any attention. All his thoughts were for those in the bedroom. At the last moment, he seized his self-control and allowed himself in like a gentleman.

The room was still too dark for Darcy's liking, but he could make out Mrs. Bennet fussing with Elizabeth's hair. *Was there something in her arms?* Out of the corner of his eyes, he saw that the midwife and apothecary were preparing to leave. *To the devil with manners!* He gave them a quick nod and proceeded to the bed.

"Did I not tell you there was nothing to fear? Here is our girl and your daughter, sir!" cried Mrs. Bennet.

"Daughter?" Darcy leaned over as a smiling Elizabeth pulled back the swaddling clothes. "We have a daughter?"

Elizabeth, glowing, nodded.

"Oh, I know it is a sad disappointment not to get your spare," Mrs. Bennet continued, "but never you mind. Lizzy knows her duty. There will certainly be better news next time."

"There can be no better news than this," said Darcy as he reached for his child. Newly born, she owned that peculiar egg-shaped head that would disappear in the next few days. Unlike Bennet, she had a full head of dark hair and the most delicate eyelashes.

"Bless me, she is the very image of our Lizzy!"

"She is," Darcy agreed. He pulled his eyes from the little miracle in his arms to the woman he adored. "Are you well?"

"As well as can be expected," she answered with a grin. "You are pleased?"

Darcy laughed. "With you well and our daughter too? I could not be more delighted!" He heard a sniff and saw Mrs. Bennet wiping away a tear. He returned to Elizabeth. "Her name, dearest?"

"Shall we abide by what we decided?" When Darcy nodded, she continued. "Mother, her name will be Anne Frances Darcy."

Mrs. Bennet raised trembling fingers to her lips. "Anne F-Frances?"

"After her grandmothers," stated Darcy. "As for a less formal name, I believe there are too many Annes in the family. What think you, Elizabeth?"

Her eyes sparkled "I say Franny is a perfectly lovely name."

"Franny!" Openly crying, Mrs. Bennet touched her namesake's head. "Thank you." With that, she quickly left the room.

Darcy sat on the bed next to Elizabeth, still holding Franny. "Thank you, Elizabeth. Thank you for our daughter." He kissed her forehead.

Elizabeth gave a low chuckle as she closed her weary eyes. "You say that now. Any daughter of mine will give us trouble—mark my words."

He laughed in return. "I care not. I love you."

"SHE SO LITTLE!" CRIED CHLOE, BEHOLDING THE BUNDLE IN HER uncle's arms.

Georgiana laughed. "So were you, I trust, when you were born,"

"I want play with baby, but she too little!"

"She will grow up faster than you think," Mr. Bennet wryly predicted. "Yes, she looks much like my Lizzy."

"I think she is beautiful," sighed Kitty.

Lord Llewellyn was puzzled. "I cannot see any resemblance to Mrs. Darcy. She looks like every baby I have ever seen."

Mrs. Bennet gasped, and Georgiana cleared her throat. Darcy was amused to see Llewellyn blanch.

"But she is very pretty!" he added weakly. It did little to stop the glares he received from the ladies present.

Mr. Bennet kindly patted the viscount's shoulder. "It takes a father's eyes to see it, I suppose. Your time will come."

Not too soon, thought Darcy darkly.

He carried Franny to the parlor door where Mrs. Reynolds awaited them. "Inform the mistress I shall return soon and sup with her."

"Yes, sir." The housekeeper took the baby. "Ah, I recall carrying Miss Darcy when she was just a wee one. How time flies!"

Darcy turned to watch Llewellyn kiss Georgiana's hand. With a flash of pain he admitted, "Yes, it does."

Chapter 15

It was no surprise to Darcy that Elizabeth grew restless soon after the birth of their daughter. His wife was never one to lie about. She reluctantly followed the midwife's directive that she remain in bed, but she offended the woman by demanding that the drapes be drawn and the windows opened.

Responding to the predictable protest that the room remain dark, Elizabeth declared, "What was good enough for Mr. Macmillan, my physician in London, is good enough for me in Derbyshire."

"A physician? Madam, with all due respect, I have over twenty years' experience," proclaimed the midwife.

"And how many mothers have you lost because they wish to see the sun?" Elizabeth retorted. "The drapes will remain open."

Darcy wisely said nothing. It would do well not to anger Mrs. Darcy. The mistress would not be moved, and the midwife took herself off with a huff. Elizabeth declared they would simply have any future children in London under the watchful eye of the family physician. Darcy blanched, admitting he was in no hurry for her to undergo labor anytime soon. With a laugh, she agreed.

Elizabeth was just as steadfast against Mrs. Bennet's demand that she employ a wet nurse for Franny. She refused, reminding her mother she had nursed her son and planned to do the same with her daughter.

Darcy felt he had to say something. "Dearest," he gently began, "it is well you wish to do this. However, matters are different now than with Bennet. There is a wedding in two months, and you will not be churched for six weeks."

"Nay," she cried. "I was but a month confined with Bennet, and I feel perfectly well. I am determined to be churched in August! You may tell our brother Southerland that today, if you please. Besides, there is much I can do from these rooms."

Darcy withdrew from the battlefield for the time being.

So it was that all planning for the wedding was removed to the confinement sitting room. A small desk now stood against a wall where either Georgiana or Kitty took notes from the discussions. Progress was slow because the room also became a nursery of sorts, for Elizabeth could not be long separated from the other children.

This drew the ire of Mrs. Bennet. She said she feared their presence would impede Elizabeth's recovery. They might also bring illness into the room. At the very least, she found the children's noise at play was bothersome.

Elizabeth dismissed her mother's concerns. She desired the children's presence, so they would stay, and that was an end to the matter. This did not stop Mrs. Bennet's complaints.

Darcy was at a loss on how to deliver his dear wife from Mrs. Bennet's loving, overbearing, and argumentative company. With Bennet's birth, London's distracting delights and Mrs. Gardiner's calming presence did much to engage Elizabeth's mother. There were no such allies at Pemberley. Kitty Southerland was only her second youngest daughter in Mrs. Bennet's mind and easily set aside. The beauties of Derbyshire held no attraction for the good lady. Mr. Bennet was no help as he spent his days hiding in the library. Darcy could not order his wife's mother from the house. He was at his wits end.

Salvation came within a se'nnight of Franny's birth with the unexpected and welcomed arrival of Darcy's favorite aunt, Alexandria Fitzwilliam, Countess of Matlock.

"Darcy, my dear boy! How well you look!" were the grand lady's first words after being announced by the footman. A plump, jolly lady, her agreeable disposition hid a strong will—necessary for any wife of the portentous and intimidating Earl of Matlock. She tilted her cheek for a kiss before doing the same with Georgiana.

Darcy observed a footman bearing a trunk, passing by the parlor's open door. "I take it this is not a short visit," he stated.

"Of course not! We have a wedding to plan, do we not, Georgiana?" Lady Matlock beamed at her niece. "I am here to help. Now, where are Lizzy and the baby?"

Darcy and Georgiana immediately escorted their aunt to Elizabeth's room and to an affectionate greeting between the new mother and the countess.

Four years prior, the family was in an uproar when Darcy had the audacity to marry an unknown country gentleman's daughter instead of a society debutante—as the Fitzwilliams expected—or his cousin Anne, as was Lady Catherine's desire. However, Lady Matlock had been Lady Anne Darcy's good friend, and she knew Darcy's mother wished for her offspring to follow her example and marry with affection if at all possible. So, the countess listened to her son Colonel Fitzwilliam's good reports of the lady and gave Darcy's bride the benefit of the doubt. Within an hour of meeting Elizabeth, Lady Matlock was charmed. She proclaimed Mrs. Darcy her niece, and where the countess led, the rest of the family was wise to follow—even the redoubtable earl.

It was no surprise that Lord Matlock fell in step with his wife; decades ago, he had done the same as his nephew. Miss Alexandria Hamilton's father was a wealthy, untitled gentleman, not one for haunting London or Bath.

That the young Lord Hugh Fitzwilliam even made her acquaintance was pure happenstance as he was with a shooting party at a neighboring estate to the Hamiltons', and Miss Hamilton's horse had frightened away the viscount's target. A startled and angry Lord

Fitzwilliam attempted to take the young lady to task—he had almost shot at her—but Miss Hamilton would have none of it. From atop her steed, the petite, pretty young lady harangued the viscount for not minding his surroundings and for his offensive words.

At that moment, Hugh Fitzwilliam fell in love with the fiery girl.

After the incensed young lady rode off, Lord Fitzwilliam demanded his amused host introduce him to her, and once that had been accomplished, he courted her in earnest. The lovely Miss Hamilton proved to be charming and sweet, no one's fool, and without an avaricious bone in her body.

After only minor resistance, Miss Hamilton realized Lord Fitzwilliam's bark was worse than his bite, at least when it came to *her*. Once assured of his undying love and respect—particularly his respect—she allowed her heart to settle on him, for she was as taken with the handsome viscount as he with her.

It was after their engagement was announced that Alexandria Hamilton learned the full mettle of her intended. The Hamiltons were delighted to be united with the wealthy and powerful Fitzwilliam family. The Fitzwilliams could not but be disappointed that the heir to the earldom had not secured better connections although the most vociferous opposition came from the viscount's sister Lady Catherine Fitzwilliam. The family eventually fell in line, even the reluctant Lady Catherine, for they well knew of Hugh's determination and good judgment. Lady Anne Fitzwilliam was the most welcoming of all, for she loved and trusted her brother.

Society was their largest obstacle. The *ton* was astonished that the promising Lord Hugh Fitzwilliam had been caught by a country girl. Already a force in the House of Commons, great things were expected from the young lion.

"Lion" was an accurate metaphor. The viscount stubbornly defended his bride with a ferocity that was a wonder to behold. He demanded respect and civility for his viscountess from all his acquaintance: family, friend, and foe. He accepted no excuse and gave no quarter. More than one member of Parliament found himself losing allies. In the face of his loving determination, the new Lady Fitzwilliam was a voice of forgiveness and reconciliation. Her grace, steadiness, good humor, and imperturbability soon conquered the *ton*.

Having successfully overcome the initial scorn from society, Lady Matlock would years later see much of herself in her nephew Darcy's young bride. She helped guide Elizabeth through the treacherous maze of her first Season, earning Mrs. Darcy's eternal gratitude and affection.

Lady Matlock was delighted with her new grandniece. "She is absolute perfection, Lizzy!" she declared. "I have seldom seen a prettier child. Darcy, you must be beside yourself."

"She is a pretty enough child, to be sure," remarked Mrs. Bennet, "but surely my son desires a spare."

Georgiana gasped.

Darcy expected nothing else from Elizabeth's foolish mother. "Nay, Mrs. Bennet," he answered. "I could not be happier." It would do no good to scold the woman.

After offering an imposing glare at Mrs. Bennet, Lady Matlock handed the babe to the hovering nurse.

"Have you decided on a name?" Told the child would be Anne Frances and called Franny, she enquired about the christening. "Have you given any thought about godparents?"

"We chose the Bingleys for Bennet," said Darcy. "Perhaps this time we shall look to the Fitzwilliam side of the family."

Lady Matlock raised an eyebrow. "Andrew and Eugenie?"

"Or perhaps Richard and Anne," said Elizabeth.

"The viscount, Lizzy!" cried Mrs. Bennet. "You *must* have the viscount and his wife for Franny! Think of the honor!"

"I find myself in agreement with your mother, Lizzy," a pensive Lady Matlock said. "While you are closer to Richard and Anne, they are newly married and…well, pre-occupied. Not only are Andrew and Eugenie perfectly suitable, they reside nearby at Matlock and can easily travel for the christening. Who knows? Perhaps the honor might...*encourage* things."

Elizabeth and Darcy shared a look. Two months prior, Anne Fitzwilliam suffered a disappointment. She was not far along, well before the quickening, but all the family knew of the tragedy and felt sympathy for the couple. As for the viscount and viscountess, they had yet to produce a child, and Lady Matlock grew impatient. She obviously hoped becoming godparents would spur things along.

"Very well," said Darcy after receiving a nod from his wife. "I shall write to Andrew today."

"Excellent," said his aunt. "There is no time like the present. Be off with you. We ladies have a wedding to plan."

"Oh, my lady," exclaimed Mrs. Bennet, "you must not concern yourself with that! We have everything in hand!"

"*Indeed*?" Lady Matlock's icy response filled the space.

Mrs. Bennet was overbearing and loud, but she owned a healthy deference to the peerage. Blushing, she managed to say, "I beg your pardon. Perhaps you would like to see what has been decided?"

The countess offered a nod. "Yes, I should like to *see* your plans. As for *decided*, that remains to be determined. Darcy, do you not have letters to write?"

Darcy smiled at his dismissal, bowed to the ladies, and escaped to his study.

WHILE THE DARCYS EMPLOYED A COMPETENT SECRETARY, THERE were certain tasks Darcy reserved for himself, such as writing letters to family. He had just sanded a missive in preparation for folding when the study door creaked open.

"Chloe? Why are you here?"

"No let her catch me!" the girl exclaimed as she ran to his leg.

Darcy stood. "Did you slip out of the nursery *again*? We have spoken of this."

"I want see baby."

"She is not here," Darcy pointed out.

"Maybe…you take me see her?" She batted her eyelashes.

Manipulation was clearly a Bennet trait. He picked up the girl and sat her on his lap. "You should have stayed in the nursery with Bennet and Mrs. Nivens."

"She not take me see baby."

"Chloe, I do not wish to be stern with you—" He was interrupted by a knock on the door. "There is Mrs. Nivens." He called out, "Enter!"

It was not the child's nurse. Darcy flew to his feet, Chloe in his arms.

"Goodness, Darcy, you bellow like a bull!" The countess noticed Darcy's burden. "Well! Who do we have here?"

"Allow me to present Miss Chloe to you. Chloe, this is my aunt Lady Matlock."

The lady raised her eyebrows, but nodded in recognition of the girl. "So, this is Wickham's child." Chloe simply stared at the newcomer.

"His eldest."

"A pretty child," she observed. "Is she often in your study?"

"Too often, I must say."

"You lady or aunt?" demanded Chloe.

Lady Matlock laughed aloud. "Both, Miss Chloe."

"*You* take me see baby?"

Darcy sighed. "Chloe, please."

Just then, a harried Mrs. Niven finally made her appearance, full of apologies. "I had just put down Master Bennet when she slipped away! I had no idea where she went!"

"It is quite all right," Darcy assured her. "We are all aware of Chloe's tendency to escape. I shall speak to the carpenter about better securing the door."

"That would be a great help, sir." She gently relieved her master of his ward. "Miss Chloe, whatever shall we do with you?"

"Want see baby!" she wailed.

"I see she is quite insistent upon it," said the countess. "Now, Miss Wickham, you must not carry on so! Miss Franny is *preoccupied* at the moment and will soon be napping. As, I understand, you should as well." She tickled the girl's chin. "Perhaps later you will be able to visit her and your aunt."

Chloe smiled. "I like Aunt Lizzy."

"Everyone likes Aunt Lizzy, sweet child. Now, go with your nurse, and do not fuss. You must act like a lady, and a lady takes her rest in the afternoon."

Chloe yawned and laid her head on Mrs. Nivens shoulder. The nurse smiled, made a curtsey, and left the room with her charge.

Lady Matlock looked on after them. "A very sweet child, Darcy." She turned. "But what are you about? Why have you never presented her to the family?"

Nonplused, Darcy responded, "We did not think the Fitzwilliams would wish to acknowledge her at this time."

"Why on earth not? She is a perfectly darling little girl. A bit wild, to be sure, but I am confident you will have her up to snuff soon enough." She glared at him. "I hope you do not imagine I subscribe to that *bad blood* nonsense Catherine spouts! I know I should not speak ill of the dead, but really, your father was foolish over young Wickham. Old Wickham was a fine man—hard-working, honest, and loyal—but his son was a worthless scoundrel. Godson or not, we have no idea why your father doted so on a rascal like George Wickham. It was the only discord that arose between your mother and father."

"I know they disagreed over him."

"*Disagreed* is putting it mildly. Only their mutual affection and trust kept them from openly fighting over the matter."

Darcy was taken aback, "Trust?"

"Yes. There were whispers that Wickham was George's natural child. Ridiculous, I know. George Darcy was besotted with Anne. He would never look at another woman, much less consort with her. For her part, Anne never believed a word of it, but she openly complained to me about George's favoritism. Hugh tried to counsel your father, but he would not desist. He claimed he owed it to Old Wickham.

"Bah! The boy was useless. That little girl upstairs is far better off without him. As a ward of the august Darcy family, she has every prospect of improving her standing in the world."

Darcy knew better than to ask whether she spoke for the earl. Of course she did. His parents were not the only couple of his acquaintance besotted with each other.

"You will formally present her to the family before the wedding," she commanded, "and you will use her full name. It did not escape my notice that you omitted it earlier. Wickham is a fine name. One scallywag will not ruin it."

Darcy had his orders. "Yes, Lady Matlock. May I now inquire why you sought me out? How can I be of service to you?"

"I came because I require that you have a bottle of sherry brought to my chambers." She shook her head. "Lizzy retired with Franny before I could speak to her about it, and it is not something I would ask Georgiana to do."

The Countess of Matlock would never ask a servant to have spirits placed in her rooms. That office belonged to her hosts. Lady Matlock had been a Fitzwilliam too long not to acquire some of the family's overbearing pride.

"It will be done."

"Thank you. Dealing with Lizzy's mother has given me quite the headache. I shall see you at dinner."

THUS, OVER THE NEXT FORTNIGHT, RELATIVE PEACE REIGNED OVER Pemberley. The calming presence of Lady Matlock eased much of the discourse over the upcoming nuptials, and planning moved forward in an agreeable fashion. Lady Matlock proved successful in checking Mrs. Bennet's more outlandish ideas. Georgiana's bridal nerves calmed. Elizabeth recovered quickly from her lying-in, and little Franny thrived.

Not everything was to Darcy's liking. Lord Llewellyn continued his devoted courtship, always underfoot—so much so that Darcy feared he would take guest chambers at Pemberley. As it was, Mr. Southerland was *almost* put out by the viscount's frequent occupancy in the parsonage's spare bedroom. At any rate, Llewellyn had the good manners to offer to pay for his meals.

Another issue was Mrs. Bennet's repeated attempts to act as mistress of the house. Mrs. Reynolds would only nod and ignore any request that was contrary to Elizabeth's established routine. When Mrs. Bennet complained, a word from Elizabeth or Darcy soon settled the matter—until the next time.

If absence were a sign of good breeding, Mr. Bennet would be proclaimed the ideal guest. That the good man took to hiding from the world—and his wife—by appropriating the Pemberley library was exceedingly vexing.

All these irritations to the master of Pemberley were offset by the health of his wife and children and the happiness of his sister. Indeed, if not for his concern that the harvest would be ruined by bad weather, Darcy would have no worries at all.

These were his thoughts as he stood at his study window, watching Bennet and Chloe outside on the grounds playing with the greyhounds as Mrs. Nivens supervised the romp. Darcy was delighted. What could be more pleasant than the innocent play of his children? His mind recalled himself engaged in play battles on those fields with Richard, Andrew, and George.

George, what happened to you? What caused you to turn against us? Was it simple jealousy or something more? Somewhere, somehow, the boy I knew died and was replaced by what you became. For all the evil you did me and mine, I would have my friend again.

"What a pretty picture, my love."

His musings broken, a startled Darcy whirred around. "Elizabeth! What are you doing out of your rooms?"

His wife stood at his elbow, dressed in his favorite pale-yellow day dress, a tiny excuse of a cap perched upon her lovely tresses. She rolled her eyes at his tone.

"I was bored to death in there. I am perfectly well, as I predicted. Pray, dear, can we not go for a walk?"

"Absolutely not!"

Darcy forgot that Elizabeth did not take kindly to orders. Hands on hips, she growled, "Fitzwilliam Darcy, you will *not* speak to me in that manner!"

After a quick apology, he explained his concerns while clasping her hands. "My love, childbed fever is a real danger. My mother suffered greatly after Georgiana's birth; we thought to lose her then. As it was, she never truly recovered, and her weakness was surely the reason an illness took her six years later. You must rest, if only for Franny's sake."

Elizabeth huffed in defeat. "Oh, fie on you for using the only argument that would persuade me! But, must I remain in the confinement room? Can I not remove to our chambers?" She squeezed his hands. "I have missed you."

Now, *there* was the only argument that would persuade *him*! "Will you remain there, as the midwife urges?"

She smiled happily. "Oh yes! We shall have Franny placed in my bedroom earlier than planned. The ladies and I shall meet in our bright and sunny sitting room, and I promise to take all my meals in our chambers until I am churched. Can it be arranged soon?" she beseeched.

Knowing she had successfully manipulated him into doing exactly what she wanted, he kissed her forehead. "Another week, Elizabeth, and if all is well, we shall have Southerland baptize Franny without delay."

She wrapped her arms about his neck. "You truly are the best of men." There was nothing innocent in the kiss they shared.

"Do you tease me, or do you believe you are ready for such activities as that kiss suggests?"

She smiled impishly. "We shall see in a se'nnight!"

Wicked woman! He gave her a kiss that left her dazed. They then turned their attention to the window, Elizabeth's head on his shoulder, and watched the children play.

"Oh my, what a sweet sight!" she cooed.

"Indeed." It was a joy to watch his son and daughter play.

Daughter? Where had that idea come from?

Before he could more fully consider the notion, there was a knock on the study door. The couple broke apart to a respectable distance before Darcy answered, "Enter."

"Pray excuse me, but there are visitors, sir." The butler held out a salver with three cards on it. Darcy reached out to read them.

"Good heavens! Lady Wakeford, Lady Penelope, and Mrs. George Knightley? Here? Now?"

"Yes, sir." The butler paused. "Their men are unloading trunks at the servants' entrance."

"*What?*" cried Elizabeth.

Chapter 16

Elizabeth, in no fit state to welcome visitors, retreated above stairs to oversee her removal to her usual chambers. Darcy requested the attendance of Lady Matlock and Georgiana to greet the ladies. Mrs. Bennet insisted she attend to represent her daughter. Darcy was not of a mind to oppose her; he trusted Lady Matlock would keep the irrepressible matron in line.

They found the Wakeford party in one of the smaller parlors in Pemberley, a clear sign the servants were unhappy to have surprise guests while the mistress was still recovering from childbirth. They were extremely loyal and protective of their employers.

"Ladies, welcome to Pemberley." Darcy bowed to the Countess of Wakeford, Lady Penelope Woodhouse, and Mrs. George Knightley.

"Thank you, Mr. Darcy," exclaimed Lady Wakeford. "It is always a pleasure to visit Pemberley!" Mrs. Knightley and Lady Penelope curtsied, and Mrs. Knightley offered a polite, "Thank you."

Darcy did the honors. "You know Lady Matlock and Miss Darcy. Allow me to introduce my wife's mother, Mrs. Bennet of Longbourn in Hertfordshire."

"Very happy to make your acquaintance, madam," said Lady Wakeford before she turned her attention to the other women. "Lady Matlock. it has been too long! That dress looks very well on you, I declare. How very fashionable! Do you have a new modiste?"

Before Lady Matlock could respond, the countess moved to take Georgiana's hands. "Oh, my dear girl! How happy we are to find you well! Does she not look well, Emma?"

Mrs. Knightley nodded. "Very well indeed. Ladies, I am happy to meet you."

"Never fear, my dear, dear Georgiana," continued Lady Wakeford. "We are here to make sure everything is ready for your wedding day!"

Georgiana's smile was uncertain. "You are?" She nervously glanced at her aunt and brother.

"Of course. Are we not, Penny? But where is Mrs. Darcy?"

"Lady Wakeford—" Darcy began before he was interrupted by Mrs. Bennet.

"My daughter is above stairs with Franny!" she proclaimed. "As for the wedding, we have everything well in hand. Do we not, Lady Matlock?"

"Are you saying that Mrs. Darcy has had the baby?" Lady Wakeford gasped at Darcy. "Why was there no announcement?"

"An announcement will go to the papers once my wife is churched and my daughter baptized." He fought to keep is voice level. "Lady Wakeford, I must inquire—"

The countess clapped her hands. "She has had a daughter! Did you hear that, Emma? It is well we came! Georgiana needs us more than ever!" Mrs. Knightley shot a look at Lady Penelope, who was clearly mortified.

The butler returned. "Lord Llewellyn, sir," he announced as the sweating viscount, dressed in dirty riding clothes, marched past him into the room. He had clearly ridden hard.

"What are all of you doing here?" he demanded. "You ladies were to remain at Ambervale Lodge until the wedding!"

"What? And leave your intended's wedding to chance?"

Mrs. Bennet's and Lady Penelope's protests overrode each other's.

"I beg your pardon." Lady Matlock's voice instantly stilled the entire room. "I believe Mr. Darcy has a question he desires to pose to Lady Wakeford. Proceed, Nephew."

Darcy thanked his aunt. "Milady, I have been informed that your servants are unloading trunks. Is there any truth to this report?"

"Why, of course. You do not expect us to wear the same gown every day!"

"I take it, then, you plan to stay?" There was a bite to his words.

The countess was insensible to it. "I think that should be obvious. I cannot oversee the planning of the wedding and not be here."

This time, Lord Llewellyn joined Mrs. Bennet's outrage.

"I presume the ladies desire to refresh themselves," Lady Matlock declared, resuming command of the situation. "Darcy, pray have Mrs. Reynolds attend us."

"That is not necessary—" began Lady Wakeford.

"That is a capital suggestion," proclaimed Mrs. Knightley. "Do you not think so, Penny?"

"Oh yes, Emma!" the young lady returned. "I long to divest myself of the dust of the road." She gave Georgiana a beseeching look.

Lady Matlock gave a quick nod at the bell pull. Feeling like a schoolboy again, Darcy dutifully rang for the housekeeper. That she was but a moment in responding proved she was only outside the door.

"Mrs. Reynolds," said Darcy, "pray have rooms made ready for our…visitors. Escort these ladies above stairs if you will be so kind."

"Oh, Georgie, will you not come?" asked Lady Penelope. "It has been so long!"

Georgiana agreed and the four ladies left the room with the housekeeper. All was quiet until the group was well away. Only then did the explosion begin.

"Well, I never!" cried Mrs. Bennet.

For once, Darcy agreed with his wife's mother. He turned to the viscount. "Lord Llewellyn, I demand you account for the outrageous behavior of your relations."

Llewellyn wrung his hands. "I am beside myself! You have every reason to be angry. I understand your indignation—truly I do."

"Understand? I am *beyond* angry, sir," he thundered. "My wife is above stairs, tending to my *newborn daughter* while attempting to prepare for *your nuptials* to my sister! Nuptials you demanded to be held but *two months* after Elizabeth's lying-in! Instead of recuperating from her labors, she now must play hostess to *your relations*, who have the unmitigated gall to invade my house! You have no comprehension of my indignation, my lord!"

"Darcy, that is quite enough of that," Lady Matlock advised.

"Aunt, I would ask you not to interfere," Darcy snapped. "Llewellyn—"

The diminutive lady marched right up to the imposing master of Pemberley. "I will not be spoken to in this rude manner. Sit down, Fitzwilliam."

Years of governesses and masters drilling correct behavior into him came to the fore, and Darcy found himself in a chair before he realized it.

"Good. It is well you can still recall your manners. Now, we must decide how best to take advantage of this turn of events."

"Take advantage?" Darcy sputtered.

Lady Matlock gave him a withering glare. "If you cannot say anything useful, Fitzwilliam, I require that you allow those of us who still have our tempers under good regulation to lead the discussion."

Llewellyn asked, "Discussion?"

"As we cannot toss your relations from the house, we must make use of them. They wish to help with the wedding preparations. Let us be generous and allow them to do so."

Mrs. Bennet gasped. "But my lady! All our plans! They will ruin everything!"

Darcy refrained from saying anything. As far as he understood, Lady Matlock chiefly kept Mrs. Bennet occupied while Georgiana, Elizabeth, and Kitty did the actual planning of the wedding breakfast. If Elizabeth's mother believed she had any contribution, much less responsibility for the event, so much the better if it kept the matron happy—and quiet.

Lady Matlock smiled. "Nonsense, Mrs. Bennet. *Help* does not mean *plan*."

Mr. Bennet stood in the doorway. "I begin to see your point, my lady. I could not but become aware of the fracas in here, even from the library. What assistance may I offer?"

"You will help us?" cried a delighted Mrs. Bennet.

Darcy raised a hand to his forehead. *Mr. Bennet too? I feel a headache coming on.*

DARCY'S HEADACHE DID NOT IMPROVE DURING HIS CONVERSATION with his wife.

"You have allowed those women to stay? Fitzwilliam, what were you thinking?"

"I could not demand that they leave. They will be Georgie's relations. I am not happy they are here, but there is little we can do."

"But, they could remain for the next six weeks!"

"I shall speak again with Llewellyn. He is just as upset with them as we are. Perhaps he can convince them to leave in a few days—certainly after the christening." To his surprise, Elizabeth started for the door. "Dear, where are you going?"

Elizabeth looked at her husband as though he had lost his senses. "I must speak to Mrs. Reynolds about our additional guests."

"Do not bother. Lady Matlock has seen to that."

Elizabeth's stormy face told him it was the wrong thing to say. Her eyes flashed. "So, the Woodhouses invade my home and Lady Matlock assumes my duties. I see I am quite useless here." She had the most adorable pout.

Darcy tried to console Elizabeth, and after a brief resistance, she allowed herself to be easy in his embrace. "You are far from useless, Elizabeth. Franny needs you, Bennet needs you, Chloe needs you, and I need you."

"I am your brood mare, is that it?" At least her voice had softened.

He kissed her. "You are the very heart of Pemberley, my queen."

"The queen is displeased," she murmured into his coat.

"Of that, I am well aware."

She began to pick at Darcy's cravat. "Lady Penelope seems a sweet girl and has made friends with Georgiana. *She* is certainly welcome. I suppose your aunt can contend with Lady Wakeford, but Mrs. Knightley has no business here!"

"I know you do not like her." Darcy was certainly unhappy with George Knightley's wife, given her comments at the Wakefield ball, but he did not have the strong reaction Elizabeth did. To be honest, he did not spare Emma Knightley a thought.

"In her own way, she is as bad as Caroline Buford before her marriage," Elizabeth observed.

Darcy kissed her forehead. "She will not be allowed to trouble you, I promise."

THE CANDLES BURNED LATE INTO THE EVENING IN MR. DARCY'S study.

"These are my final estimates for this year's harvest," said Mr. Thompson. "As you can see, our tenants have fared poorly, and matters are not much better at the home farm. This unseasonable weather has been the very devil. I *could* be mistaken—I have been rather pessimistic—but I cannot see things in any other way. Unless the weather turns radically, things will be bad this winter."

Darcy showed no emotion as he scanned the disappointing figures in the ledger. Without looking up, he asked, "How much grain have we set aside?"

"There is plenty, along with hay for our livestock and horses. If it were only that."

"And if we must divert some for our tenants?"

The steward ran a hand over his face. "It depends, sir, on what they have set aside. Barely enough, assuming they have feedstock 'til spring. If they sold all their grain and the winter is harsh—"

"—then there will be a deficit." Darcy pinched the bridge of his nose. "We had best prepare for any eventuality."

"Yes, sir. I shall meet with each tenant and review their needs, beginning tomorrow. By week's end, I should have a fair idea of where we stand."

"People before livestock, Thompson," Darcy said firmly.

"Yes, sir. The price for more grain and hay will be dear, and we shall be hard pressed to earn much in rents to pay for it."

Darcy drew a deep breath and leaned back. "I suppose you are correct."

"Wool prices are not what they should be."

"That is understandable." Darcy reached for another paper. "Too much wool chasing too few customers."

"Even with this cold weather?"

"Apparently." Darcy found the appropriate sheet and studied it. "Very well, do whatever you deem proper. You have my authority."

Thompson was taken aback. "May I remind you there will be little in rents this year?"

Darcy glanced at his very able steward. "Fortunately, my investments in coal mines should offset some of the discrepancy. The rest shall be covered by economy in the household accounts. We shall get through this winter without Pemberley failing."

"Of course, sir. Shall I take it up with the mistress tomorrow?"

Darcy straightened in his chair. "I shall speak with Mrs. Darcy. Get yourself to bed, man. It has been a long day, and tomorrow will be longer still."

Thompson stood. "I bid you a good night, sir."

Darcy nodded. "My compliments to Mrs. Thompson and the same to you."

LADY MATLOCK PUT HER PLAN INTO ACTION THE FOLLOWING morning. She began by gathering Lady Wakeford, Mrs. Knightley, and Mrs. Bennet in one of the parlors. At the same time, Mr. Bennet and Lord Llewellyn instructed Georgiana and Kitty Southerland to stay above stairs and busy Lady Penelope with talk of Georgiana's trousseau. Darcy's job was to console Elizabeth and carry on with his usual duties.

Lady Matlock discussed the already agreed to plans for the wedding as *suggestions*. She also encouraged Mrs. Bennet to again summon up all her extravagant ideas—notions that had been previously set aside. As Lady Matlock anticipated, Lady Wakeford tended to agree with the countess's more restrained proposals.

The only fly in the ointment, if it could be called that, was Emma Knightley's preoccupation with the details of the wedding breakfast. Colors, flowers, dishes, even the order in which they were served—nothing escaped Mrs. Knightley's notice. Lady Matlock would have found her overbearing were it not that the lady's ideas and observations were well-founded. It was to be hoped that Emma would be satisfied that she had put her stamp on the proceedings. If, however, she wished to be further involved with the breakfast, Lady Matlock foresaw trouble with Mrs. Darcy.

Indeed, Elizabeth was irritated that Emma Knightley was involved at all. Emma and her sister's overheard comments at the Wakefield ball were neither forgotten nor forgiven, and the notion that Emma Knightley was concerned with the wedding planning was quite provoking.

Unfortunately, there was nothing to be done. Elizabeth could not order the relations of Georgiana's intended from the house, no matter how dearly she *wished* to do so. The only recourse acceptable to her was to retreat to her rooms and place her trust in Lady Matlock, Georgiana, and Kitty. That such a withdrawal was Fitzwilliam's desire did not make it easier to accept.

Dratted man!

Elizabeth's opinion hardened when her new guests inspected the newborn Franny. The ladies made all the expected compliments, but only Lady Penelope's sounded sincere. Lady Wakeford's kind words were ruined by wild speculation of the comparative beauty of any potential fruits of Georgiana and Llewellyn's union. Mrs. Knightley said little.

Georgiana correctly read her sister's mood and soon ushered the visitors out, except for Mrs. Knightley who requested a moment of Elizabeth's time.

Emma began once the door closed. The lady, dressed in a fine silk morning dress with not a hair out of place, stood straight and tall, her chin high, her eyes focused on the wall behind the seated Elizabeth.

"It has come to my attention that you overheard a conversation between my sister and me at the Wakeford ball, one that might reasonably have given you pain." Only the nervous working of her hands gave any clue the lady was truly distressed. "Pray allow me to assure you that our object was not to engage in ridicule or disparagement.

"My sister is of a valetudinarian disposition, much like my father. Isabella is not unwell, but fear of illness upsets her sensibilities. Her concerns are both for herself and for others. My great affection for my sister must be my excuse for humoring her when she expresses alarm over trifling issues, particularly when I privately disagree with her, as I did that evening.

"Our conversation was centered on your…condition at the time and my sister's worries for you and your child. She is a mother several times over, and disease is her constant fear. Depend upon it, there was no censure in her thoughts or motives, only sincere concern. As for the words she chose to use, I cannot defend them, but I can comprehend perfectly that they could give offense and my silence taken as agreement. I thought my sister wrong, but you could not know that. Pray accept my sincere and complete apology." With that, she turned her head.

Elizabeth was flabbergasted by Mrs. Knightley's statement. That the lady would beg forgiveness for what was said at the Wakeford ball and in such detail was the last thought on her mind! She was speechless for a moment, attempting to respond to such a declaration.

"Mrs. Knightley," she began, "I, of course, accept your apology, and due to your *very* detailed explanation, I must extend it to your sister as well." She smiled. "Those who eavesdrop seldom hear well of themselves." Emma's pained look indicated that Elizabeth's humor fell flat. "Pray be seated."

"You are very kind." Emma took a chair.

"Not at all. May I ask how you learned I overheard you?"

Emma looked away. "My husband received a letter from your husband."

Elizabeth sighed. *Sir Darcy riding to my rescue again!* How she wished he would stop! "That must have been mortifying. I am sorry you ever became aware of the matter."

"Think nothing of it." Emma smoothed out imaginary creases from her gown.

"I now apologize to you. I have been remiss in thanking you and Lady Wakeford for your assistance in planning the breakfast."

Emma returned her attention to Elizabeth as she waved off her words. "Our only thought was to offer what help we could during your convalescence. We hope you will be satisfied with our efforts. Are you fully recovered?"

Elizabeth nodded. "My daughter is well, and for that I am thankful."

"If—" Emma hesitated. "If it would not be too much to ask, might I trouble you to see the babe again? I could not see her very well given my aunt's exuberance."

Surprised at Mrs. Knightley's request, Elizabeth sent for Franny. It was a moment's work for the nurse to return with the precious bundle.

"Would you care to hold her?" Elizabeth offered.

Emma nodded and carefully accepted Franny in her arms. She

peered closely at the child, the expression in her hazel eyes one of longing. "She is beautiful. Very beautiful." She gently ran her fingers through the babe's hair,

Elizabeth frowned. Was there a tear in Emma's eye? "You have held babies before, I see."

Emma became aloof again. "Yes, my sister's children. Thank you for your consideration." She passed Franny to Elizabeth, and the baby immediately began pawing at her breast. Emma smiled slightly. "You will soon be occupied and will require privacy, I believe. I thank you for your time and kindness," Emma continued. "You are truly blessed. Good afternoon, Mrs. Darcy." She turned to leave.

As she reached the door, Elizabeth said, "I hope you may be so blessed."

Emma stopped short. "I hope so too," she sadly said before letting herself out.

Elizabeth stared at the door, wondering over her last comment.

Chapter 17

Franklin Southerland smiled as he gently poured water over his niece's head. "Anne Frances, I baptize you in the name of the Father, and of the Son, and of the Holy Ghost."

The babe did not particularly care for the gentleman's attentions, despite his profession as a man of God, and she proved her lungs were well developed.

Elizabeth bit back a laugh as she stood next to her husband. Having knelt in thanksgiving for her safe delivery during her short churching ceremony minutes before, she enjoyed watching Lord Fitzwilliam nervously observing Darcy hold Franny over the font. Did he think his cousin would drop the baby?

Elizabeth was not troubled over Lady Eugenie's lack of visible emotion. If the lady had ice-water in her veins, so be it. She would not waste a sigh over it.

After a few prayers, Elizabeth sat in the family pew for the first time in weeks, holding a candle in one hand and Franny in the other. Darcy tried and failed to keep a wiggling Bennet still, for the boy wanted to see his sister. His grandfather came to the rescue, plucking the boy from his father's arms and nestling him between himself and Mrs. Bennet, who in turn had a firm grasp on Chloe.

Soon thereafter, the Darcys, Fitzwilliams, and Bennets stood outside the church doors, accepting well-wishes from the small number of villagers who stopped by to watch the proceedings. Church services were public, after all. Darcy bore it better in Kympton than he did in London when Bennet was born. Here, there were no strangers to tolerate. Still, Elizabeth knew it to be a trial for her husband, so she wasted no time in encouraging the family to depart for Pemberley as soon as it was civil.

Mrs. Reynolds laid out a lovely breakfast of all of Elizabeth's favorites, and in deference to Mrs. Bennet, kippers were nowhere to be found. Those in attendance were family and their guests, including the children, and Chloe made the most of it, running here and there and making a bit of a nuisance of herself. Bennet stood next to his mother, one hand firmly clenching her gown. Lady Eugenie watched the Darcy ward with cool disapproval while her husband ignored the child completely, speaking with Llewellyn and Georgiana. Mr. Bennet laughed while Mrs. Bennet boasted that her grandchildren were the most lively and handsome children in the kingdom.

"Grandchildren are the loveliest creatures, are they not, my lady?" Mrs. Bennet asked Lady Matlock.

"Indeed, they are. Unfortunately, my only grandchild, the son of my daughter, is in Scotland at Lord Montgomery's estate. I cannot see him as often as I like; therefore, I must fill the void with Darcy's children."

"But—" Mrs. Bennet glanced at Lady Eugenie.

The countess sighed. "Not yet."

"Perhaps better news will come from your other son, the colonel."

Elizabeth blanched. The Fitzwilliams and Darcys knew of Anne's recent disappointment. She needed to distract her mother before she said something offensive. "Mama, does not Bennet favor his father?"

"Oh goodness, yes!" Mrs. Bennet snatched up her favorite, the only boy-child in the family. "What a fine young man! *You* will not have to worry about not having a home, Lizzy—not with an heir!" She covered Bennet's face with kisses, to the boy's distress.

Lady Matlock smiled, letting Elizabeth know she was not upset. "I am sorry Mr. Bingley's illness prevented his family's attendance." Bingley suffered from a cold, and Jane would not leave him.

Emma Knightley came forward. "You have more family close by, do you not, Mrs. Darcy?"

"Yes. My sister Jane married my husband's good friend Mr. Bingley. He owns Mayfield in Nottinghamshire, less than half a day's travel."

"Ah," Emma nodded knowingly. "Your sister Mrs. Southerland is in Kympton, and Matlock and Ambervale are all nearby. How very agreeable to be settled within so easy a distance of three sisters and cousins too. It must certainly add to the enticements of Pemberley."

Elizabeth raised an eyebrow. "While it is a fortunate happenstance, I should never have considered distance as a chief advantage of any match."

"Of course, to some," Emma stated. "To others, it is of great importance, second only to the suitability of those involved."

"London is of great attraction to many."

"As can be the country."

"One would own a great attachment to the place."

"Or to family."

Elizabeth studied Mrs. Knightley's heightened color closely and labored to recall what Lord Llewellyn said of her. Mr. and Mrs. Knightley resided near Highbury at Mrs. Knightley's family estate of Hartfield, rather than her husband's Donwell Abbey. In doing so, one must assume Mrs. Knightley owned a strong attachment to her father, Mr. Woodhouse, and that Mr. Knightley, good man that he was, chose to humor his wife rather than have her quit her father's house for his.

Was that the reason George Knightley wed the young Emma Woodhouse—or the reason *she* wed *him*? To marry a man for his proximity to her home was an extraordinary possibility and altogether repugnant to the romantic feelings of the otherwise sensible

Elizabeth Darcy. She loved her family, but she would have had Fitzwilliam Darcy no matter how distant he lived from Longbourn.

"Family can be a great comfort," said Lady Matlock, looking in the direction of the viscount and viscountess, "especially when the children move far away."

"You are so right, my lady!" exclaimed Mrs. Bennet, still holding her grandson. "My poor, dear Lydia is somewhere on a ship, bound for India! When I think of all the dangers of the sea, my nerves—I get such tremblings!"

"India?" inquired Emma.

"My sister's husband is a colonel in the Army, traveling to his new post," explained Elizabeth as she retrieved Bennet from her mother, "and she goes with him."

"Oh, Colonel Denny! So dashing in his red coat," continued Mrs. Bennet. "But India! So far away and filled with all manner of strange people and beasts! Why, Lydia might be eaten by an elephant!"

Understandably, the others were either astonished or amused by Mrs. Bennet's pronouncement.

"Elephants eat plants, Mama," Elizabeth explained.

Lady Matlock patted Mrs. Bennet's arm. "Do not take on so, my dear. Certainly, Colonel Denny will keep your daughter away from…elephants."

Emma bit back a giggle.

"I pray he does. Such a dashing gentleman—but elephants are very large, are they not? Once, my brother Gardiner took Mr. Bennet and me to the Royal Menagerie at the Tower. Awful, fearsome beasts! I was sure to faint! I saw the lions and bears. Is not an elephant larger than a bear?"

"I believe so, Mama, but surely, Colonel Denny will protect Lydia."

"Of course he will! He is a colonel, after all!"

Chloe ran up to the group. "I see bears, Aunt Lizzy? Please?" She yanked on Elizabeth's skirt.

"Chloe, the bears are in London. Perhaps we can visit with them next time we are in town."

"Want see bears NOW!"

The outburst caught the attention of most of the room. Mrs. Nivens rushed to her mistress's side and picked up the complaining child.

"Miss Chloe, what did we say about keeping a quiet voice?"

"Want see bears!" she screamed.

"Chloe, pray stop this at once." Darcy's command silenced the girl immediately. He stepped close to her and spoke softly. "Do as Mrs. Nivens says, go upstairs quietly, and I shall bring you to see these animals when next we are in London. If you are naughty, I shall not."

The girl's lip trembled. "P-Promise?"

A small smile graced Darcy's lips. "Yes, I do."

Chloe laid her head on Mrs. Nivens' shoulder. "He *always* keeps promises," she informed the nursemaid as if this was a settled fact.

"That he does." Mrs. Nivens placed Chloe on her feet and took Bennet in her arms. "I shall have the children rest for now, Mrs. Darcy." Taking the girl's hand, the nursemaid led her out of the room. Chloe looked back and waved.

"You have quite a way with children, Mr. Darcy," observed Emma.

Darcy shrugged, but it was Lady Matlock who answered. "He should. He was both brother and father to our dear Georgiana since she was six years of age. You have done a marvelous job with her, Darcy. You should be proud."

"Oh, indeed so!" cried Mrs. Bennet. "So accomplished, so graceful! She caught—" She stopped mid-sentence at Elizabeth's frown. "Miss Darcy will soon be a viscountess! You have raised her well, and so you will with Franny and Chloe!"

Elizabeth agreed with the other ladies, but her husband would have none of it.

"As proud as I am of Georgiana, all the praise must go to my sister and her former companion, Mrs. Annesley. I deserve no special commendation. I merely did what needed to be done. As for the little ones, Elizabeth and Mrs. Nivens will take them in hand. In that, they and I are very fortunate."

Once again, Elizabeth was struck that a man so proud of his heritage and place in the world could at the same time be humble over his actions. Fitzwilliam was a complicated puzzle that would take a lifetime to unravel.

What a delightful prospect! She looked forward to it.

Emma Knightley wore a wistful expression.

LONG AFTER THE CELEBRATION WAS DONE AND HAVING DISMISSED Witherspoon for the evening, Darcy slipped quietly into his bed-chamber. In the glow of the bedside candle, he saw his wife, eyes closed, snuggled deep into their bed. All that was visible was her dear face and lush hair, but it was enough to warm his heart.

Elizabeth. Darcy still could hardly grasp his good fortune. His pride and her prejudices should have driven them apart forever. Yet, she generously gave him one more underserved chance and allowed him to prove how he had been humbled for the better. By the grace of God, he had made the most of it. He won her affection and her hand. He thought he loved her in Kent, but that was nothing compared to what he felt for her in Derbyshire.

After four years of living with Elizabeth, Darcy realized he had known *nothing* of love in 1812. For four years, she had shared his bed and his concerns—four years of laughter and tears, arguments and apologies, joys and sorrows. They experienced delights, intellectual and physical. They celebrated triumphs and overcame disappointments. Together they saw momentous events and enjoyed quiet afternoons. With the birth of their children, Fitzwilliam Darcy now knew a love and devotion that was larger than himself, greater than Pemberley, something almost incomprehensible.

He removed his robe, draping it over a chair, and quietly slipped into bed. Elizabeth must have sensed his presence, for she blindly reached for him. In moments they assumed her favorite position—she on her side with him embracing her from behind, her head resting on his arm.

With the sweet smell of her hair filling his nostrils, he kissed her cheek while his hand glided across her linen-covered hip. After two children, Elizabeth was now lusciously curvy and utterly irresistible. His hand moved the way she liked, up her torso to lightly hold her breast. Here he had to restrain himself, for she was tender from feeding Franny.

Many nights this would be the extent of their love-making, the pair content to fall asleep in such an intimate aspect. But tonight, Darcy's blood was up, his desire apparent. He wanted his wife, and only waited for a sign she felt the same.

Apparently, she did, for she wiggled her delectable bottom in a manner known to drive him mad. Darcy was a man of action, and he wasted not a moment. Loosening her nightdress, he slipped a hand under and gently massaged her breast while nibbling her earlobe.

"I miss the old days," he rumbled into her ear, "when you came to me in naught but what our Creator graced you."

She turned into his embrace with a wicked smile. "I miss the days when it was warm enough to do so! Blame not your wife, sir, but the unseasonable weather."

"I shall warm you, my love." With that, he moved over her and captured her lips, his hands loosening her plait. Elizabeth responded by clutching the back of his head and drawing him closer, running her fingers through his hair and deepening their kiss. Darcy reached down and grasped her nightdress's hem and pulled it up her thighs. She parted her legs, and Darcy shifted—

The bedroom door opened. "Aunt Lizzy?"

The pair broke apart, Darcy rolling over on his back while Elizabeth sat up, holding the sheet to her neck. "Chloe," she cried while retying her nightdress, "why are you out of bed?"

"Bad dream," the child sniffled.

Elizabeth got out of bed and held out her arms. Chloe scurried into her embrace. "There, there, my dear. All is well." She stroked the girl's hair.

"Speak for yourself," Darcy mumbled, one arm draped over his eyes.

Meanwhile, Elizabeth returned to bed with Chloe in her arms. "Tell me all about it." She gently wiped the girl's tears away with her thumbs.

"I-I saw Mama and Colonel on big boat, far, far away. She wave at me. And…and a big bird, it flew down and took Mama and flew away high in sky, and I screamed and screamed!" Chloe began crying again.

Elizabeth rocked the sobbing child. "It was just a dream, my dear. Your mother and step-father are certainly safe in India by now."

Darcy hoped she was correct. By any reasonable measure, the Dennys should have reached Calcutta, but there had been no letters from Elizabeth's sister attesting to that. In fact, there had been no letters at all. All Lydia Denny's friends could do was exhibit patience, for she was on the other side of the world—if she still lived.

Of course, their fears could be for naught. Like Mr. Bennet, Lydia was a terribly negligent correspondent.

"Want Mama," sniffed Chloe.

"I know," Elizabeth responded. "Come, it is time you were in your bed."

"Wait," Chloe cried. "Uncle Darcy kiss good night." She reached for him.

Darcy sat up and did as he was bade, resisting the impulse of reminding the child he had rendered that service two hours before. A calmed Chloe rested her head on Elizabeth's shoulder as her aunt rose, carrying the child out of the room. Elizabeth gave Darcy a sweet smile as the pair left.

Darcy was displeased as he sat up in bed and waited for his wife's return. "Is she asleep for the night this time?" he asked sourly as Elizabeth closed the door.

"Fitzwilliam, show some charity. Chloe was frightened." Elizabeth gracefully slipped under the sheets.

"This is the third time this month," he grumbled. "And where was Mrs. Nivens?"

"Sound asleep, the poor dear," she answered, returning to his embrace.

"Is it too much for her to keep watch on her charge? For what are we paying her?"

Elizabeth's eyes twinkled. "When she is not minding our ward, she is chasing your heir. Bennet has proven to be very quick for his age." She kissed his cheek. "You are a grumpy one tonight! You know Chloe adores you, and you are not indifferent to her, no matter how much you complain."

Darcy pursed his lips. Elizabeth was right as usual. "She should not bother you. You need your sleep, for Franny will surely have need of you soon."

Just then a thin cry was heard from the direction of Elizabeth's rooms.

"Speak of the devil—"

"Fitzwilliam!"

"Forgive me, my dear." He kissed the top of her head. "I shall bring her to you."

Darcy made his way through the sitting room that divided their chambers into Elizabeth's seldom-used bedroom. A maid had just lifted the complaining baby from the cradle.

"Sir! I was just bringing Miss Franny to the mistress."

Darcy reached for his daughter. "Never mind, Suzanne, I shall do it."

He had to bite the inside of his cheek, amused at how flustered the maid had become. For all Darcy's considerable pride, he consistently underestimated his effect on the fairer sex. No matter how polite or restrained he behaved, his younger maids were nervous or flirtatious in his presence. This bewildered him. He truly had no idea how handsome he appeared to the ladies, disheveled in a robe.

Had Darcy been more like his contemporaries, he could have his way with any of his maids, and there would be little complaint from them. For Fitzwilliam Darcy, such a thought was inconceivable, even before he met Elizabeth. As for what some of his acquaintances practiced, he held such behavior in contempt.

Moments later, the doting father deposited his precious bundle in her mother's arms. By the time Darcy joined them in bed, Franny was contently nursing. He did not watch closely, feeling an irrational need to give the pair privacy. Instead, he contemplated Elizabeth's face as she gazed lovingly at their child. No Madonna in art was more beautiful, he thought.

Twenty minutes later, Franny was satisfied, and Darcy was fast asleep.

An exhausted Elizabeth rose late the next morning, Franny's nighttime feedings disrupting her normal routine. Elizabeth broke her fast in the sitting room upstairs before dressing for the day. After looking in on Franny and greeting the other children in the nursery, she walked down the stairs to her husband's study.

Darcy smiled widely as he rose from his work and walked around his desk to greet her. "How are you faring, my dear? Did you get enough rest?"

A quick kiss and Elizabeth was ensconced in an upholstered chair across from Darcy's desk.

"I am well enough. Franny's demands are much like Bennet's at her age."

Darcy frowned. "Have you eaten? Would you care for coffee?"

Elizabeth, touched by Darcy's constant consideration for her comfort, replied she had eaten but would not refuse a cup. He rang for a servant before returning to his chair.

"I missed you when I awoke," Elizabeth teased.

Darcy overlooked her inflection entirely. "I am sorry, sweetheart! You were sleeping so peacefully I could not bear to disturb you."

"I am only teasing! However, you crept out so quietly, I must wonder at you."

"All in the service of milady. Ah!" The door was opened by Mrs. Reynolds. "A pot of coffee, I pray, Mrs. Reynolds." He turned back to his wife. "Do you care for anything else, my dear?"

Elizabeth declined, and the housekeeper left on her errand. Darcy handed her several letters that had arrived, which she eagerly read. It was their daily custom to review correspondence in each other's presence.

"I noticed our sister Jane writes. What news from Mayfield?"

Elizabeth wore a slight smile as she read. "Nothing of great import. Elizabeth is growing quickly and Susan has become quite attached to little Phoebe. Charles has recovered from his illness."

Darcy only responded with a grunt. Elizabeth noted an uneasiness in his eyes. "Fitzwilliam, what is wrong?"

"I beg your pardon?"

Elizabeth's lips tightened. Darcy remained reluctant to discuss unhappy business with her. That his disposition sprang from a desire to protect her sensibilities rather than a lack of trust did not make this element of his character less irritating.

"Do not put me off. Something is troubling you. Is anything amiss at Mayfield?"

"No, not that I know of."

"You are prevaricating, much as you did during their troubles two years ago. Has Charles fallen foul of another poor investment?"

Darcy waved a hand. "No, no! Our brother has learned his lesson. Indeed, he is more skittish than ever. He will not even look at a proposal outside the attendance of Tucker, Uncle Gardiner, or me."

"Then, what is it?" Elizabeth glanced at her letter again. "It is not...*Phoebe*? She is a child—practically a baby!"

"You misunderstand, Elizabeth. I say nothing against Miss

Phoebe." He rose and walked over to the window. "It is just that she brought something to my mind."

Elizabeth willed herself to be patient. Her husband had his ways, and he would tell her all in his own time.

Darcy stared out the window. "I believe we have discussed that the harvest was not what we hoped for."

The Darcys' relationship was unusual. They discussed and shared the most minute detail of each other's duties. They sought each other's advice and assistance. It increased the intimacy between them.

Darcy looked down. "Thompson reports the situation is more dire than we anticipated. No tenant has done better than we have. In fact, many did worse. The harvest looks to be bad, and we are concerned about the winter."

"Are the grain stores that small?" Elizabeth asked.

"We must be prepared to buy grain for feedstock for the herds and bread for ourselves and our people should the weather worsen. We anticipate little to no rents this year, so we must practice economy."

Elizabeth nodded. "I am not surprised. After our last conversation on this matter, I spoke to Mrs. Reynolds, and we have drawn up plans for just this contingency."

Darcy turned to her, admiration and pride clearly on his face. "I should have expected no less," he said with a smile. "Thank you."

"I would not disappoint you."

Darcy moved close to Elizabeth and took her chin in his hand. "You could never do that."

Elizabeth's lips tingled in anticipation of his kiss, but there was a knock on the door. It was Mrs. Reynolds with the coffee. All conversation ceased until Elizabeth prepared each of them a cup. After a sip, Elizabeth continued.

"Forgive me, but I fail to see what the deficit in our harvest has to do with Phoebe Wickham."

Darcy set down his cup. "Nothing with *Phoebe* Wickham."

It took a moment for her to understand her husband. "Ahh…

are we back to *Chloe*, then? I know last night was a disappointment to you, but—"

Darcy held up a hand. "I hope it was a disappointment for *both* of us, but that was not on my mind." He paused. "You know I planned to begin putting funds aside for Franny."

Elizabeth shook her head at Darcy's apparent change of topic. "I suppose with the new economy that might not be possible."

"Things are not that bad. Our mining investments have done well, and I expect we should have handsome returns from our business with Uncle Gardiner. We should be able to set aside something."

"Then what troubles you?" Elizabeth tried valiantly not to regret her lack of dowry—the usual source of a daughter's fortune.

Darcy turned to the window again. "Elizabeth, it will be many years before the Dennys return to England."

"I imagine so."

"If they do return, do you believe Lydia would want Chloe back?"

Elizabeth thought for a moment. "At this time, I cannot believe it." Indeed, Elizabeth was shocked that Lydia had abandoned her children without a second thought to follow her new husband to his posting on the far side of the world. Elizabeth knew she would never do the same, and Darcy would never ask it of her. The Dennys had been gone only for a few months, yet Elizabeth had already grown to love the little girl.

"I agree," said Darcy. "Therefore, it falls to me to provide for her."

"Of course, you would—" Suddenly Elizabeth saw what he was driving at. "You wish to provide a dowry for Chloe."

Darcy raised his chin. "It is only to be expected."

Elizabeth dashed to her husband, tears in her eyes. "No, it is not, except by you!" she cried as she embraced him. "You wonderful, generous man!"

He kissed the top of her head. "I know you had plans for the green sitting room—"

"Which can wait. Our children come first."

A small smile grew on his lips. "Yes, *all* our children."

Elizabeth rose on her tiptoes and graced him with a passionate kiss. "Another thing, my dearest love. I was disappointed last night too."

He ran a thumb down her cheek. "What an intriguing thing to know!"

One perfect eyebrow rose. "Is it? You seem unwilling to do anything about it."

"Do not tempt me. You know I cannot resist you."

A bawdy grin grew on her face. "You said you liked it when I was bold. But I suppose things change over the years."

"Never that!" Darcy reached down and swooped his giggling wife into his arms. "You doubt me, you vixen?"

"Never in this life." She wrapped her arms around his neck and whispered, "Take me to bed, Fitzwilliam."

The pair made a quick dash up the stairs.

It was a well-satisfied Mrs. Darcy who was called to feed her daughter an hour later.

Chapter 18

Three days later, Darcy could stand by and bear it no longer. To his mind, a hard conversation was necessary, one he knew would displease Elizabeth. His courage up, he knocked on the door of the mistress's parlor. A soft "Enter" was the response, and he let himself in.

Upon his marriage, Darcy insisted on preserving his wife's position and privacy, and would demonstrate it by example. There were two doors in his houses he would never enter without Elizabeth's leave—the mistress's bedroom and her parlor. She, for her part, was amused at his determination to follow the proper forms, for her protests to the contrary fell on deaf ears.

"Oh, Fitzwilliam," said Elizabeth softly with a hint of humor.

"I hope I do not disturb you, my dear."

"Of course not." She indicated the chairs by the fireplace, and soon they were seated. "I know you do not frequent my rooms without purpose. Since we are not in my bedroom, the subject must be of a very dull nature. So, speak on and fear not of scandalizing the help. I shall accommodate you if I can."

He ignored her teasing. Instead, he straightened his spine, took a breath, and stated, "It is time we employed a wet nurse."

Elizabeth blinked. "I beg your pardon?"

"We must find a wet nurse. For Franny." He knew his voice was cold and impersonal as was customary for him when uncomfortable, but he could not help himself.

"Whatever for? I am perfectly capable of nursing my daughter."

"That remains to be seen."

Elizabeth's ire was ignited. "I have cared for our daughter since she was born! She is thriving! I intend to continue to nurse until she is weaned, just as I did with Bennet!"

"That is not my meaning."

"Then what could it be? Is my choice, which you have approved in the past, suddenly abhorrent to you? Embarrassing? For I tell you, Mr. Darcy, you married a proud country girl, and I shall not abandon my child for the benefit of society!"

Darcy realized his misstep. "Elizabeth! Sweetheart! Pray allow me to continue. I doubt not your capabilities but your strength!" He left his chair to kneel before her, taking her hands. "Are you not exhausted?"

"I am a little tired, that is so, but it is to be expected."

Darcy shook his head. "You have not enjoyed a full night's sleep since the birth. There are circles under your eyes. Your walk is unsteady. You suffered the same with Bennet, but then we dedicated all our time to him and you.

"That cannot be the case now, for we must prepare to host a wedding in a few weeks' time, thanks to the thoughtless desires of Georgiana and Llewellyn. Our house is filled with guests, and their number will only grow.

"I know you, my love. You will attempt to manage everything and comport yourself as the mistress of Pemberley, all the while meeting the needs of our precious infant daughter. I would take upon myself those burdens you allow, but you and I know you will not be forthcoming. You will not admit you need help. You will drive yourself to ruin. I know this, my love, for I am the same." He kissed her hands. When he lifted his eyes to hers, he saw Elizabeth struggle with the truth laid before her. She choked back a sob.

"What am I to do? Either I fail my daughter or everyone else!"

"You know you cannot withdraw from your duties any more than I. I understand you would be disappointed to have another nurse Franny, but it will not harm her. She will still love us, for we shall dote upon her." He shrugged. "My mother employed wet nurses, and it has not harmed Georgiana or me."

Elizabeth laughed. "I agree about Georgie."

Darcy smiled. If Elizabeth were teasing him, all would be well. "Thank Heaven you have taken pity on me."

"You left me little choice. Otherwise, I would have to live without my heart."

"And you are mine." He kissed her hands again. "Shall I speak to Mrs. Reynolds?"

She sighed. "I wish to interview the candidates before anyone is employed."

"I expect she can have a few women from Lambton and Kympton come in tomorrow morning for your choice."

"So soon?" Elizabeth frowned. "Have you spoken to Mrs. Reynolds about this already?"

Darcy reddened as he stood. "She was as concerned as I."

"Fitzwilliam Darcy, whatever shall I do with you? Conspiring behind my back!"

"I recall a surprise birthday party two years ago."

"*That* was a *party*!" Elizabeth imperiously waved her hand. "Off with you, traitor! Go meet with your accomplice. I shall endeavor to forgive you this!"

Darcy stood and moved to leave. At the door, he turned back to her. "I love you."

Elizabeth sighed. "Very well—I love you too. Now, go!"

WITHIN A FEW DAYS, ELIZABETH GRUDGINGLY ADMITTED THAT her husband had been correct. She could do far more without having to nurse Franny. Of course, there was a short period of unpleasantness, embarrassment, and discomfort, but it was to be expected. Elizabeth experienced it before with Bennet, so she bore it as best she could. There was a wedding in less than a month!

Now that Elizabeth could bring her whole attention to the wedding breakfast, the presence of her guests became that much more of a burden. Mrs. Bennet would not leave while Lady Matlock was in residence, and the countess would not leave Elizabeth to the tender mercies of Lady Wakeford and Mrs. Knightley. Lady Wakeford would not leave before Lady Matlock, and Llewellyn had little influence on his stubborn mother. Elizabeth had forbidden Darcy from exercising his rights as master of Pemberley.

There was only one solution.

"You asked to see me, Mrs. Darcy?" asked Emma Knightley after she was shown into Elizabeth's parlor.

"Yes. Pray make yourself comfortable. I have called for refreshments." The two sat and awkwardly exchanged pleasantries as they awaited tea and biscuits. The tray arrived soon, and after Elizabeth poured, she got to the purpose of her interview.

"Mrs. Knightley, it would be remiss of me not to again thank you for all your assistance in planning the wedding breakfast while I was otherwise occupied."

"Pray say nothing of that. I am pleased I was of some small help to you."

Elizabeth took a sip of her tea. "I can safely say all things are well in hand now."

"I am happy to hear it."

"You must be anxious to return home."

"Home!" Emma exclaimed. "Oh no, Mrs. Darcy. There can be no thought of returning home before the wedding!" Her tone was that of a governess, slow and explanatory. "Highbury is a great remove from Derbyshire. It is not to be considered. Mr. Knightley will join me once the plans for the harvest are made. I expect him about a fortnight before the ceremony."

Elizabeth gritted her teeth. This was not what she expected! "Am I to understand you not only intend to stay at Pemberley until the wedding, but you plan to have your husband join us—all without an invitation?"

Emma blanched. "Mrs. Darcy, you misapprehend my intentions!"

"I beg that you enlighten me."

"My husband journeys to Ambervale Lodge. I shall join him there."

Elizabeth relaxed somewhat. This news was welcome but less than she required. "You will *join* him or *await* him, Mrs. Knightley?"

Emma reddened. "I am at my aunt's pleasure."

Elizabeth leaned forward. "Forgive me, but I must be blunt. The wedding planning is done, but none of my guests will be the first to leave. Do you see my dilemma?"

"Yes, I do. My aunt—well, the wife of my first-cousin-once-removed, but she requests I refer to her as my aunt—is a lady of strong opinions as I am sure you have noticed."

Elizabeth's inborn impertinence emerged. "It would be difficult not to."

Emma lightly laughed. "It was my desire to know that side of my family better. May I explain?"

Not understanding that this had anything to do with the problem at hand, Elizabeth allowed Emma to continue.

"My great-grandfather, the fourth viscount, had two sons. The elder son, Great-Uncle Thomas, was made Earl of Wakeford by King George. My grandfather thought that, since his brother was now an earl with a new estate, he should surrender the viscountcy. As Great-Uncle Thomas already had a son, he refused."

Elizabeth shook her head. "Of course he should refuse. How could your grandfather believe anything else?"

"Grandfather George was a very stubborn and envious man. He thought he was owed the title and did not appreciate that he was given the lesser but still valuable estate in Surrey—Hartfield—while Ambervale Lodge in Derbyshire was left for the viscountcy when

Great-Uncle Thomas took possession of Wakeford Abbey. Grandfather George refused to speak or correspond with his brother or his family for the rest of his days. My father, therefore, was estranged from the Wakeford Woodhouses and did nothing to heal the breach.

"You must understand: my father is a good and kind soul, but having been raised with the tales of his uncle's perfidy, he had little desire to learn the truth of the matter. If not for my dear brother, John, I would not be in your sitting room this moment. He had made the acquaintance of Lord Wakeford in London and befriended Lord Llewellyn. Through John, my husband met them both, and he has done what he could to reunite the families."

"That was very good of him."

Emma glowed. "There is no better man in the world than Mr. Knightley! But, back to my tale. Fortunately, the Wakefords held no animosity towards my side of the family. Lady Wakeford has been particularly welcoming. She insists that she and the earl are Aunt Catherine and Uncle James to us. I came here at her urging."

Elizabeth sipped her tea to prevent a giggle. *Yes, Lady Wakeford is another Aunt Catherine!*

"So, you see, Mrs. Darcy, I have little wish to upset the tender level of our reconciliation. That said, we have intruded on your hospitality for too long." Emma reached for her cup. "Our task is to convince Lady Wakeford of that."

"Have you any thought as to how it can be accomplished?"

Emma looked over the rim of her cup. "I do not. But let us bring my cousin Penny into our confidence. I trust she will have some idea."

LADY PENELOPE ANSWERED HER SUMMONS WITH GEORGIANA IN tow. The two young ladies were quickly appraised of the issue to be resolved and that their cooperation was required. While Lady Penelope nodded knowingly, a distraught Georgiana protested.

"Must Penny go away? Can she not stay with us until the wedding?" she begged.

Elizabeth turned to Lady Penelope. "Would your mother leave without you?"

"I believe she can be convinced." There was an impish smile on the girl's lips.

Elizabeth and Emma shared a look. "Pray, speak on."

"We shall need the assistance of your charming ward, Miss Chloe."

TWO DAYS LATER, DARCY AND ELIZABETH STOOD IN THE ENTRANCE hall, bidding farewell to Lady Matlock, Lady Wakeford, and Mrs. Knightley. With them were Georgiana and Penny, who was to stay, and Lord Llewellyn, preparing to escort his relations to Ambervale Lodge.

"Mrs. Darcy and Miss Darcy join me in thanking you for your kind assistance. We trust your stay at Pemberley was not unpleasant," proclaimed Darcy formally.

"Not at all," said Lady Wakeford insincerely. "Pemberley is as beautiful as always."

Elizabeth graced her with a nod. "I once again apologize for my ward. Pray allow us to replace your day dress ruined by the spilled scent bottle."

"Think nothing of it. Children will be children, after all. The dress is nothing—nothing at all!" Lady Wakeford paused. "Have you had the room aired out?"

"Mrs. Reynolds is seeing to it as we speak."

"Goodbye, Mother," said Lady Penelope with a kiss. "Thank you for allowing me to remain."

"Of course you must stay and get to know your future sister better!"

Elizabeth was pleased to continue to host Lady Penelope. She had proven to be a delightfully lively and cheerful young lady, not lacking in manners or good sense. She had become fast friends with both Georgiana and Kitty and was a favorite with the children. Even Fitzwilliam voiced no complaint of Lady Penelope's prolonged residency.

Lady Wakeford grasped Georgiana's hands. "My dear, I eagerly await the day I may call you daughter in truth!"

"Ahem," said Emma. "The carriage awaits—does it not, Cousin?"

"Indeed, it does." Llewellyn then took leave of his betrothed. "I shall return in two days' time, dearest."

Darcy rolled his eyes.

The group walked out in the courtyard, the skies cloudy but dry. It would be decent weather for traveling. The Darcys again paid their respects to Lady Wakeford before turning to Mrs. Knightley.

"Thank you for all your help." Elizabeth gave Emma a light kiss on the cheek.

"Thank you for your hospitality, Mrs. Darcy. I look forward to returning for the ceremony"—she lowered her voice—"and not a moment sooner." She glanced at Lady Wakeford in amusement. Elizabeth squeezed Emma's hands before the lady was helped into the carriage by Llewellyn. A moment later, they were on their way to Ambervale.

As soon as the vehicle left the courtyard, both Lady Penelope and Lady Matlock murmured, "Finally!" They laughed together.

"I feel as though there has been some mischief about and not just by Chloe." Darcy studied the ladies with suspicion. "How did Chloe get into Lady Wakeford's chambers?"

Lady Matlock affectionately patted Darcy's cheek. "Do not give it another thought. Ofttimes, it is best to leave such problems to the ladies. But pray be lenient with Miss Chloe."

Darcy's brows creased. "Aunt, what have you done?"

She smiled. "Such a dear boy. Ah—my carriage is here! Let us say goodbye."

Darcy's curiosity would be unsatisfied, for Lady Matlock's farewells were short and quick, and she was soon on the road to Matlock. The remaining ladies moved to reenter Pemberley, but Darcy stopped them short.

"Would someone be so kind as to inform me what has occurred

in my house?" he softly but firmly demanded.

"Nothing very terrible, my dear," answered his wife with a smile. "An infestation has been removed. Are you not happy?"

"Intensely." His frown belied his words. "I would have details, madam, before this hour is done."

"Oh very well," she replied airily as she took his arm. "Come, ladies, let us repair to the parlor and settle this unruly beast."

Needless to say, Chloe's punishment for spilling scent on Lady Wakeford's dress was exceedingly mild.

Chapter 19

Now that most of the troubling visitors had departed Pemberley, a pleasant excitement descended upon the house and its inhabitants. August ended with Elizabeth working hand in hand with Georgiana, Kitty, Lady Penelope, and Mrs. Reynolds, finalizing wedding preparations and ignoring Mrs. Bennet's outlandish ideas. Nothing was overlooked—food ordered, flowers chosen, table linens cleaned, guest rooms aired. The estate shined as never before.

This left Darcy to his usual duties, overseeing the estate and managing his investments. He spent the greater part of the prior week in his study or on his horse. He was in his element. When Lord Llewellyn was not paying court to his betrothed, he occasionally joined him on his tours of the estate.

As for Mr. Bennet, he claimed the library as his private domain. As long as he did not bedevil Darcy, the gentleman was left to his own devices.

Darcy and Elizabeth did not neglect the children. Franny was always in her cradle at her mother's side, and the older children took the air with Darcy and the greyhounds when the weather permitted. A highlight of each day was the gathering of the little family after dinner, augmented by the presence of grandparents and aunts.

Thus, August turned to September. There was but a fortnight before the nuptials—a se'nnight before the expected arrival of their first guests. It was a time of rest and anticipation. Everyone—Mrs. Bennet included—allowed themselves to relax.

They should have known better. Fate is a cruel mistress.

The Darcys and Bennets were in the family parlor, enjoying an afternoon tea before dressing for dinner, when Mrs. Reynolds came in.

"Sir, carriages are approaching."

Darcy rose. "Visitors? It is rather late in the day." Most visitors arrived in the late morning or early afternoon.

"The footmen report one is a luggage cart."

Elizabeth now stood. "Guests already? Who could it be?"

"Did not Lady Matlock say she was returning?" asked Georgiana.

"But next week." Darcy turned to Mrs. Reynolds. "Is it the Matlock carriage?"

"The footmen did not say."

Darcy, Elizabeth, and Georgiana made their way out the front door. The day was cloudy with only a hint of coolness. To their surprise, it was the Rosings Park carriage that approached.

"I thought Richard and Anne were expected just before the ceremony," said Darcy as the coach halted.

An imperious voice from inside the coach cried, "There you are, Darcy! Do not stand about in that stupid manner. Hand me down!"

"Good God," mumbled Darcy.

"Mother, a footman will see to it," said a calmer voice from inside the carriage.

Elizabeth's hands covered her lips. "Oh my!"

Emerging from the carriage was a large woman wielding a walking stick in one hand. Upon exiting, she glared at those assembled.

"Well, Darcy? Is this how you now greet your guests? How polluted have the shades of Pemberley become?"

To Darcy's amazement, for the first time since he married Elizabeth, his aunt Lady Catherine de Bourgh was at Pemberley.

The party quickly descended the steps. "Welcome, Lady Catherine." Darcy bowed, then gestured at Elizabeth beside him. "You recall my wife, of course." Elizabeth curtseyed.

"Yes, yes, of course I do," she responded in a quarrelsome voice. "There is nothing amiss with *my* memory. Well, Mrs. Darcy, I see you have recovered from your trial. How does your daughter?"

"Very well, your ladyship," Elizabeth returned easily.

Meanwhile, two ladies and a gentleman exited the carriage. "Mother, there is no cause to interrogate Lizzy out of doors!" Lady Anne de Bourgh Fitzwilliam scolded. "Allow us to go in, for all love!"

"Succinctly said, m'dear," drawled her husband, Sir Richard Fitzwilliam. "How do you do, Darce?" He held out a hand to his cousin, who gladly shook it. Lady Fitzwilliam greeted Elizabeth and Georgiana with hugs. Behind them, Anne's long-time companion, Mrs. Jenkinson, exited the carriage.

Lady Catherine turned her attention to Georgiana. "You have done your family proud. The Wakefords, while not a particularly prominent family, are suitable connections for the Fitzwilliams. Well done, my dear! It is well *someone* remembers such things." She placed a wrinkled hand on Georgiana's cheek. "You resemble your dear mother more each time I see you. Come, we shall go in. Dawson!"

"Yes, Lady Catherine," responded her personal maid, the fifth member of their party.

Lady Catherine, arm in arm with Georgiana, led the way into the great house, followed by Elizabeth, an irritated Darcy bringing up the rear with the former colonel.

"I assume my usual chambers have been prepared, Mrs. Darcy." Lady Catherine handed her things to a footman.

To Darcy's surprise, his wife answered, "Yes, Lady Catherine, all is in readiness. Anne and Richard, I am certain you wish to refresh yourselves. Mrs. Reynolds will escort you."

Lady Catherine quickly perused the entrance hall. "You have made few changes, I see."

"I saw no reason to change what was perfect, milady," Elizabeth responded.

Lady Catherine eyed Elizabeth for a long moment, and Darcy thought to intervene; instead, his aunt turned her attention to the housekeeper.

"So, Reynolds, you are still here."

"As you see, milady." She curtsied.

"Hmm. And remain as impertinent as before, I expect. Well, what are you waiting for? Come!" With a *thunk* of her walking stick, the grand dame and the Pemberley housekeeper ascended the stairs, trailed by the others. "I expect fresh bedding, Reynolds, and sufficient coal for the fireplace. And sherry—a small decanter of sherry."

"I recall your preferences, milady."

"Good! It is well *someone* does." She threw a dark look over her shoulder at Darcy.

Once they reached the first floor, Darcy requested that his wife and Sir Richard attend him in his study while the rest continued up to the family wing.

Darcy closed the study door. "Why have your arrived early, and what is Lady Catherine doing here?" he demanded of Richard.

Nonplused, the former colonel of Hussars replied, "She was invited, was she not? And as for our early arrival, all fault lies with Lady Catherine." He took a seat. "Apparently, Georgie cannot marry without our aunt's intimate involvement."

"When the invitation was issued, we never dreamt she would actually attend!" Darcy sputtered. "Since my marriage, Lady Catherine has seldom written or spoken to me, much less set a foot in Pemberley."

Richard shrugged. "Lizzy's letter was most insistent."

Stunned, Darcy looked at his blushing wife. "Elizabeth?"

Elizabeth defiantly raised her chin. "Both Georgiana and I wrote Lady Catherine, earnestly requesting her presence."

More puzzled than angry, Darcy asked, "But why? She rebuffed every attempt at reconciliation, she scorned and ignored us, and she treated you quite rudely at Richard and Anne's wedding."

Elizabeth laughed. "If you consider it the height of insolence that Lady Catherine ignored me as I stood beside her, I tremble to think what you would have said four years ago had you witnessed our conversation at the bottom of my father's garden at Longbourn!"

"I received a taste of it when she confronted me a day later in London," Darcy dryly returned. "Never have I been so provoked"— he touched his wife's arm—"though it did give me hope."

Elizabeth's eyes danced as she grew close. "She does so like being useful, my dear."

Richard groaned. "I am here, you know! Can you two not wait to make love?"

The pair took a step away from each other, and Darcy, in a calmer manner, returned to their discussion. "It seems that Lady Catherine is at Pemberley at *your* expressed desire, Elizabeth. I would know why."

"Georgiana wanted her here, as did I."

"I can comprehend Georgie's wishes, but yours I cannot. She has treated you with an unseemly amount of scorn and disrespect."

"Not true—not since Anne married Richard. And indeed, she has recently chosen simply to disregard my existence rather than rant and storm as she did in earlier years." Elizabeth took Darcy's hand. "I hate this estrangement, Fitzwilliam, knowing that I am the cause. A family is meant to be together. I truly believe she finally desires a reconciliation with her dearest sister's children as much as I."

"But to do that, she must accept you, Elizabeth," Darcy demanded.

"And she has!" Elizabeth smiled. "Recall when she greeted me, she referred to me as 'Mrs. Darcy' for the first time. Georgiana's wedding is the perfect excuse to come to Pemberley, despite its *polluted shades*!"

"Lizzy is right, Darce," said Richard from his chair. "Lady Catherine is merely preserving her dignity. Besides, our aunt has not spoken of Lizzy at all in the past year, save satisfaction at her safe deliverance from Franny's birth. In any case, her few complaints are of *you*. Not about failing to marry my Anne—she has given up that notion—but rather, your participation in her overthrow from Rosings."

"I was righting a wrong, Fitz!"

Richard held up a hand. "Save your outbursts for those who deserve it. The chief villain in Lady Catherine's mind is my father. I expect she will not mention anything of the matter to you."

"She will attempt to manage things, depend upon it," Darcy warned Elizabeth.

She lightly laughed. "More than my mother or Lady Wakeford? I am not concerned. If necessary, I shall call on Lady Matlock."

Richard snorted. "Now, *that* would ignite open warfare!"

"True, true," Darcy admitted. "By the way, how are matters at Rosings?"

"We are finding our footing despite Lady Catherine's *advice*. We can deal with her interference." Richard's smile slipped. "You know of our disappointment." At Darcy's nod, he continued. "Anne has been stalwart, by God. I am proud of her. The servants love her, and she is making great strides with the tenants and the villagers.

"But, enough of Rosings. This time is for Georgiana, and it is to her we must turn our minds."

"I would still have Lady Catherine's complete apology to Elizabeth," Darcy stubbornly declared.

"And you will never receive it, Darce," Richard replied.

Elizabeth took her husband's cheek in her hand. "Dearest, should *I* not be one who decides whether I require an apology? Lady Catherine's attendance at Georgiana's wedding is penance enough for me. Consider it an act of contrition. I certainly will be amused with her non-apology apology."

Darcy cared little for his audience as he took his wife in his arms. "You are too good, my love."

"If you kiss her, Darcy, I am out of this room!" cried Richard.

"Do you hear a noise, dear?" asked Elizabeth.

"No." Darcy's lips descended to hers.

They were still engaged so when the study door slammed shut.

"Mrs. Darcy, I must speak to you!"

Darcy and Elizabeth had just climbed the stairs when they were arrested by an angry Lady Catherine, a harried Mrs. Reynolds trailing behind her. She planted herself squarely before the couple.

"I know that you may not be fully familiar with the office of Pemberley's mistress," she disdainfully pronounced, "but such an oversight is not to be borne! I have been placed in the wrong room. You will immediately rectify this mistake."

Confused, Elizabeth inquired, "I do not understand your meaning." She turned her attention to Mrs. Reynolds. "Is she not in the rose room?"

"My room, Mrs. Darcy, is the gold room!" Lady Catherine cried. "You should have been so informed. I blame Reynolds for this!"

"I put her in the best single bedroom, as per your desire, ma'am," reported the housekeeper.

"You see! She admits her fault!" Lady Catherine pointed at her nephew. "Darcy, fix this!"

Elizabeth glanced at her husband, but he only shook his head, clearly indicating this was her office and he would lend her his full support. Pleased, Elizabeth returned to their irate guest.

"As you know, the gold room has two bedrooms. As you will not be sharing your chambers, a single guest bedroom is suitable, and the rose room is the best of those in the family wing. Besides, the gold room is currently occupied."

"By whom?" Lady Catherine demanded.

"By Mr. and Mrs. Bennet," Darcy interjected. "And before you say anything, they are family."

"This is outrageous! I am almost your nearest relation!"

"I must remind you, milady, that the position of 'nearest relation' now falls to Elizabeth, and *she* is mistress of this house."

Darcy's smile warmed her; however, it was not the time to contemplate how much she adored her husband. There was a dragon to conquer.

"Milady, you must pardon me, but I will not ask my parents to change rooms. That they would, should I request it, indicates their excellent manners. However, it would insult my character. The rose room was especially prepared in anticipation of your hoped-for arrival. In fact, certain items belonging to Lady Anne were placed in the room for your pleasure. Have you, perchance, noticed them?"

Lady Catherine was clearly taken aback. "No. What items?"

"Allow me to show you."

The quartet walked down the hall to the rose room. There Elizabeth gestured to the table by the window.

"Milady, there you will find a pair of miniatures of you and Lady Anne. They were done, I am told, prior to your marriages. Is that so?"

Lady Catherine studied the miniatures. "Yes. I just turned fifteen and Anne was seventeen, just before her come-out." She lightly drew a finger over the image of Lady Anne. "I had forgotten she had them."

Elizabeth continued. "On the wall is a painting of Matlock House, and by the bedside is Lady Anne's prayer book."

"Mother made notes inside," added Darcy.

Lady Catherine, her face expressionless, looked about the room. "Roses were Anne's favorite flowers," she said softly. She coughed, and Elizabeth was certain it was to hide a sob. "These rooms will do," she declared, the imperious lady back on full display. "Dinner will be promptly at four o'clock, I assume?"

"Of course," Elizabeth answered.

"Excellent. It is well that someone of your unfortunate background is versed in such matters. I shall take my rest now, as all ladies of good breeding should." She shot a look at Elizabeth.

Elizabeth grasped Darcy's hand firmly, indicating that he should not express the anger he surely felt at his aunt's dismissal. "You are quite correct. Pray excuse us."

With that, the couple and Mrs. Reynolds left the room. The housekeeper shared a smile with her mistress and continued downstairs, while Darcy and Elizabeth made for their chambers.

"Rest, Elizabeth?"

"Eventually."

The entire party gathered before dinner in the family parlor rather than the formal drawing room, a choice that clearly displeased Lady Catherine. There, Darcy introduced Lady Penelope and Elizabeth's parents.

Lady Catherine paid the barest of civilities to Lady Penelope and none to Mrs. Bennet, as that lady's roots were stained from the stench of trade. She peered closely at Mr. Bennet.

"I understand the vicar of Hunsford, Mr. Collins, is your heir. You seem to be in good health. How fortunate for your family."

Darcy was not surprised his aunt now referred to Collins as "the" vicar and not "her" vicar as the good reverend had transferred his allegiance from Lady Catherine to Sir Richard and Lady Fitzwilliam.

"Mr. Bennet's health was a great worry, your ladyship," injected Mrs. Bennet, "but now that all my girls are married—and so advantageously, I must say—why, I sleep very well at night, I assure you! Very well, indeed!"

Even Lady Catherine blanched at that remark.

"You are very welcome, my dear," replied Mr. Bennet sarcastically. "It remains my most earnest wish to see to your every comfort by my continued existence."

Flustered, Mrs. Bennet swatted his arm. "Oh, how you enjoy teasing me!"

Elizabeth quickly changed the subject. "Lady Catherine, you of course remember my son, Bennet George." The boy held his mother's hand, quietly taking in the strangers. "And this," she gestured to the infant in Mrs. Nivens's arms, "is Anne Francis, named for her grandmothers."

"A pretty-enough baby. Her looks will not come in for some time, I suspect." Dismissing the babe, she turned her attention to her grand-nephew. "Your future responsibilities increase, young Darcy. You have a sister to look after. It is hoped you may grow equal to your duties."

"Mother, they are babies!" exclaimed Anne. "Oh, let me see Franny! She is lovely, simply lovely."

"Aye," agreed a smiling Richard, who bent to pick up Bennet. "How are you, my little man? Giving your father trouble, I trust?"

Bennet had no response but a short giggle.

"And this," Darcy added, "is my ward, Chloe Wickham." Holding her hand, they took a step forward, Darcy wondering how his aunt would react. Tension descended about the room.

"Harumph," was Lady Catherine's response.

"You have wiggles on your face," Chloe observed. "Do they hurt?"

Lady Catherine flushed while the rest erupted with laughter. "Children," the matron declared, "should be seen and not heard."

Fortunately, Mrs. Reynolds announced the dinner was ready, so the children were gathered up by the nursemaids to return to the nursery while the adults proceeded in to dine. They did not go into the grand dining room but to the more intimate space reserved for family—something Lady Catherine remarked upon with distaste.

As host and hostess, Darcy and Elizabeth sat at the foot and head. Elizabeth had Sir Richard on her right and her father on her left. Lady Catherine was on Darcy's right, and Mrs. Bennet on his left. This was by design, for there were three ladies left, and Elizabeth had Georgiana seated next to Richard, and Lady Penelope on her other side, next to Mrs. Bennet. Anne was beside Lady Catherine. It allowed her to be best placed to control her quarrelsome mother, something she was fated to do throughout the meal. Georgiana was as far removed from her aunt as possible.

Lady Catherine did not hesitate to express at length her opinions of the wedding preparations. She began by regretting it was far too late to change the location of the nuptials from Pemberley to London.

"Georgiana, as the granddaughter and niece of earls, should be married from Matlock House. I myself was married in St. George's Hanover Square, as was Lady Anne. I cannot be happy with a mere country parish chapel!"

"That 'mere country chapel,' as you so quaintly put it, was the place of Georgiana's baptism," Darcy calmly responded. "St. George Parish in Kympton holds a special place in our family. It was there Georgiana learned what it is to be a dutiful Christian. It is a bedrock of our faith, and a place of peace and comfort in good times and bad."

Georgiana spoke up. "That is so, Brother. I will be married nowhere else." She showed a firmness that must have seemed unfamiliar to her aunt. It was clear the bride would brook no change.

Thwarted for the moment, Lady Catherine tried a new tack. "But a country parson? Darcy, surely he would be amenable to have your uncle the bishop preside over the ceremony!"

"I am certain Mr. Southerland would step aside, good man that he is, but I would not so insult him." Darcy held up his hand to forestall Lady Catherine's complaint. "Mr. Southerland is family—my wife's brother by marriage. He is my expressed choice for the living, an excellent shepherd for the congregation, and a dear friend. In any case, my uncle is in poor health, which is the reason that the couple will call on him in Westminster during their wedding tour. Let us speak no more of it."

"Mother, your soup is getting cold," pointed out Anne.

A pouting Lady Catherine attended to her soup while the remaining attendants engaged in more pleasant conversation. It only lasted until the fish course.

"Mrs. Darcy, we shall draw up the menu for the wedding breakfast tomorrow morning," Lady Catherine announced.

"Oh, do not be concerned over that!" Mrs. Bennet responded. "All has been decided."

Lady Catherine glared. "That remains to be seen."

"Lady Matlock was quite pleased with the selections. Such a gracious lady!"

Darcy watched his aunt turn beet red at the mention of her brother's wife. "*Lady Matlock* was here and planned the wedding?" she demanded of Elizabeth.

Unruffled, Elizabeth replied, "She visited prior to the christening. I dare say she only reviewed what Georgiana had already decided upon. Is that not right, dear?"

"Oh yes!" Georgiana declared. "Lady Matlock did nothing at all!" She bit her lip.

Darcy hoped his relations' prevarication would mitigate the situation. Lady Catherine's loathing of Lady Matlock was well known in the family, a circumstance with which the Bennets were unaware.

"Shall we review the menu tomorrow, Lady Catherine?" Elizabeth offered. "I believe Georgiana and I shall be available in the early afternoon. Perhaps Anne will join us."

"It would be a pleasure," Anne responded.

A brilliant stroke, my love! thought Darcy. Both Darcy and Elizabeth knew no one could better control Lady Catherine than Anne. The grand dame was forced to concede. However, as the dishes were removed, Darcy expected Lady Catherine was considering a new avenue of attack.

He was right.

"The dress!" Lady Catherine proclaimed as Darcy was carving the roast. "I must see the dress!"

PEACE REIGNED ABOUT THE BREAKFAST TABLE THE NEXT MORNING. As both Lady Catherine and Mrs. Bennet were late risers, those partaking of the superb offerings of the Pemberley kitchen were in high spirits. The exuberant conversation between Georgiana,

Elizabeth, Anne, and Penelope centered on wedding matters. They were practically talking over each other, while the gentleman quietly spoke of current events and sport. Without his wife present, Mr. Bennet was pleasant and insightful, foregoing his habitual derision. Richard displayed his usual jocular disposition, which never failed to draw out Darcy's more engaging nature.

Once Mrs. Bennet made her appearance, Darcy believed it the better part of valor to retreat to his study. The other gentlemen thought likewise. Richard declared an intention to ride, while Mr. Bennet slipped away to the library. A mock glare from his Elizabeth was Darcy's reward for his escape.

Several productive hours passed, and after conferring with Thompson, Darcy recorded instructions for his secretary. His concentration was abruptly destroyed by a loud, demanding Lady Catherine. Obviously *seriously displeased*, as she so often claimed, her voice carried throughout the house.

Darcy set down his pen with a huff. Such vulgar behavior at Pemberley was not to be borne! His aunt's conduct at times made Mrs. Bennet appear a saint!

Steeling himself for a confrontation with his irascible aunt, he went looking for her, all the time pondering this defect in her character. Did Lady Catherine truly believe bellowing at the top of her lungs made her discourteous opinions and confusing directions respectable?

He found his aunt in the kitchen, of all places, berating the cooks. "Madam, you will stop this rude display at once!" he ordered.

Lady Catherine had the effrontery to appear offended. "How dare you take that tone of voice with me! What would your mother say?"

"She would say that a guest scolding their hosts' servants is the height of ill-manners," Darcy shot back.

"Thank you, my dear," came an aggravated voice over his shoulder. "I have been attempting to convince Lady Catherine of that for no little time."

Darcy turned. Elizabeth stood scowling, arms crossed over her chest, near the pantry beside Mrs. Reynolds. "I did not notice you in the corner there. What is Lady Catherine's business with our cook?"

Elizabeth rolled her eyes. "She has an objection to the menu."

"It will not do!" cried Lady Catherine. "It will not do at all! I must taste each and every dish proposed, and *this person*"—she gestured at the head cook—"refuses to oblige me!"

"She demands that Cook cease preparing dinner and do as she requires," Elizabeth angrily reported.

Incredulous, Darcy asked the cook the number of dishes in question. He could not hold his temper at the answer.

"*Dozens*? You demand to shut down my estate's kitchen so that they may prepare dozens of dishes for *your* personal inspection?"

"Again, you raise your voice! Have you forgotten what you owe me as your nearest relation?"

"*That* office falls to my wife, madam, as I have said." Darcy struggled to moderate his voice. "There is but one mistress of Pemberley, and that is Elizabeth."

"Of course, Elizabeth is mistress! I am not lacking in understanding," she declared, surprising everyone. "Sadly, she has not benefited from my experience. I am attempting to be of help to her."

Confounded, Darcy sought to make sense of his aunt's words. It seemed she accepted Elizabeth while still trying to manage things. Lady Catherine's confusing behavior had not diminished with age.

Elizabeth stepped forward. "I appreciate your efforts, my lady. Allow me to assure you: everything that will be served has been enjoyed at Pemberley for many years. Is that not so, Cook?" Darcy could tell she held her annoyance under tight regulation.

"Indeed, ma'am," that good woman responded.

"Perhaps samples of the cakes might be prepared for tea tomorrow?" Elizabeth proposed as a peace offering.

"Aye ma'am, as *you* wish." The cook gave Lady Catherine a dark look.

Just then, a harried Lady Fitzwilliam burst into the kitchen. "Mother! What have you been doing? Pray you are not bothering Cook!"

"I am not bothering anyone," Lady Catherine protested. "I am assisting Elizabeth."

Elizabeth looped an arm around the grand dame's. "We have an understanding, do we not, my lady?"

One would think she was perfectly calm if the fire in her eyes was ignored. With very little effort, she guided Lady Catherine out of the kitchen, Anne lightly scolding her mother as they left. Darcy apologized before leaving with Mrs. Reynolds.

"Do not fret, sir," the housekeeper advised. "The mistress and I can handle Lady Catherine." She lightly chuckled. "*That one* is much the same as when your mother was mistress. I know what Lady Catherine is about, and we shall allow nothing to spoil Miss Georgiana's wedding."

"I shall depend upon that, Mrs. Reynolds."

A loud scream interrupted their conversation. At once, master and housekeeper rushed to the newest disturbance.

"Have I mentioned I am weary of all this shouting in my house, Mrs. Reynolds?" Darcy growled.

Near the staircase to the first floor, they found Lady Catherine in a temper, flat against the wall, as two footmen attempted to hold back the greyhounds from jumping on her. Lysander and Penelope were joyfully barking, dodging Lady Catherine's stick, while Elizabeth and Anne tried to calm everyone.

"Nephew, what are those *creatures* doing in the house?" shrieked Lady Catherine.

"Those are my greyhounds, and they should not be in here at this time," Darcy retorted. To Elizabeth, he said, "Need I ask how this happened?"

She rolled her eyes. "Chloe, I am certain."

"Remove those monsters at once! At once, do you hear!" Lady Catherine demanded.

"They are hardly monsters." Darcy took a now-calm Lysander in hand. "They are excited to meet a new person. They are friendly and *usually* well-behaved. That is, when they are not threatened." He glared at Lady Catherine's walking stick.

Sure enough, Lysander sat on his haunches, panting, happy to accept a pat on the head from his master.

"Pray calm yourself, madam. These footmen will remove the dogs to their kennel." The servants took that as their cue to escort the hounds away.

"I am sorry you took a fright, Lady Catherine," Elizabeth apologized. "Do you require a chair?"

"Of course not! I have ever been celebrated for my equanimity and mettle. I was simply concerned for the damage such creatures might commit in my dear late sister's house!"

"Those dogs are well-trained," said Anne tiredly. "They will cause no more trouble to Pemberley than my Romeo does to Rosings."

"And that is *another* thing—"

"Mother!" cried Anne in her best *de Bourgh* voice. "That issue is settled!"

Lady Catherine glowered. "You see how it is, Darcy? I am constantly ignored! Why I continue to share my advice I do not know. Come, Anne, I shall return to my room." She frowned. "I trust those creatures will be removed before dinner."

Darcy stood with Elizabeth as his troublesome aunt was escorted above stairs. "Need I put locks on every door in Pemberley?" he sighed.

Elizabeth lightly laughed. "I shall speak to Chloe. It will not happen again. But I must say she reminds me of another mischievous young girl."

"Indeed?" Darcy lifted Elizabeth's chin with his hand. "Dare I hope Chloe will turn out as well as that child?"

"Hope springs eternal."

Chapter 20

D arcy stood at the entrance to Pemberley in his customary attitude—back straight, head level, arms clasped behind his back. The family gathered outside to greet the arrival of the Matlock carriage. Darcy's only sign of nervousness was the workings of his fingers, something Elizabeth must have noted right away.

"My goodness, Fitzwilliam, 'tis only your uncle and aunt," she whispered.

"Yes, and Andrew and Eugenie, but pray recall Lady Catherine is here."

"She is a rather unforgettable presence. But surely, she would not make a scene."

"We should be so fortunate. Ah, there is the coach." Darcy stood straighter as the Matlock carriage stopped before them. A footman opened the coach door, and the ponderous voice of the earl was heard.

"Finally! I believe we struck every rut in the road! These old bones can hardly take such mistreatment anymore."

Lord Matlock emerged, followed by the viscount who then handed down the ladies while the earl accepted an affectionate welcome from Darcy and Elizabeth.

"Lizzy, you are looking as lovely as ever!" He kissed her cheek and shook Darcy's hand. "Good day, Darcy. Now, where is the lady of the hour?"

"Here, my lord," said Georgiana, giving him a proper curtsey.

"None of that, my girl! Give your old uncle a hug!"

Georgiana gladly did so while the rest of the Matlock party was greeted by the Darcys. For all his gruff demeanor, Lord Matlock clearly took a particular delight in what he called "his girls"—not only his daughter, Lady Henrietta, but also his nieces and the wives of his sons and nephew. Soon, everyone moved into the vestibule and handed off their traveling coats.

"I trust we are the first to arrive?" inquired Lady Matlock hopefully.

"I am afraid not," Darcy admitted.

"Is that my brother?" The quarrelsome voice of Lady Catherine came down from the drawing room on the first floor.

"*Catherine* is here?" exclaimed an astonished Lord Matlock.

"Oh dear!" the countess remarked. Andrew bit back a chuckle, while Eugenie had nothing to say—as usual.

The earl shook his head. "I cannot believe she deigned to attend. Cathy has not stepped foot in Pemberley since George's death." He glared at his nephew. "You should have warned me."

"What, and spoil the surprise?" Andrew teased as the party made their way to the first story.

"Andrew, please," implored Darcy. "Uncle, I know Lady Catherine can be tiresome, but I remind you that we are gathered here for Georgiana's wedding."

Lord Matlock held up a hand. "Say no more. I shall not let her bait me."

"Best of luck with that," muttered Andrew.

Lord Matlock ignored the jibe. "Are there any other unexpected guests? What of your uncles: the judge and the bishop?"

"Sir Edward remains in London and has requested that Georgiana and Llewellyn call upon him when next in town. My lord bishop is in poor health and remains at Westminster."

"I am looking forward to seeing him," remarked Georgiana. "We shall visit Westminster on our tour. I must say the judge quite frightens me!"

"He frightens me too," claimed Andrew.

Elizabeth laughed. "Oh, Sir Edward appears a bit dour at first, to be sure, but it is all pretense. I found him very amusing!"

"*Amusing?* Sir Edward Darcy?" Lord Matlock chuckled. "You have a singular power over Darcy men, Lizzy. But I suppose if anyone can charm that old misanthrope, it is you, lass!"

The banter had everyone in high spirits, until they stepped into the drawing room. There, standing by a chair with a possessive attitude more suited for Rosings than Pemberley, was Lady Catherine de Bourgh.

"So, Brother, you have presumed to show your face here," was her quarrelsome greeting. "What do you have to say for yourself?"

Darcy noticed that Elizabeth slipped her hand about Lord Matlock's arm in an effort to calm the earl.

"Good morning, Sister," he gruffly returned. "I see I find you well." He then promptly ignored her. "Richard, Annie, good morning! Mr. Bennet, Mrs. Bennet, it is good to see you. Lady Penelope, I hope you have enjoyed yourself."

"Is that all you have to say to me?" demanded Lady Catherine, interrupting the others.

"Yes, Cathy." He then kissed Anne's cheek. "How are you faring, Annie?"

Lady Catherine slammed her walking stick on the floor. "I will not be dismissed! And I despise pet names!"

"Oh, Mother," cried Anne, "pray stop this unseemly display!"

"I am never unseemly," the grand dame insisted.

"Of course not, Lady Catherine," stated the countess, not meaning a word of it. Her sarcasm did not go unnoticed. Andrew laughed aloud.

Lady Catherine searched the room. "Lord and Lady Montgomery did not travel with you?"

Lord Matlock snorted. "If you had bothered to read the letter my wife sent to you, Cathy, you would know my daughter and Lord Montgomery are even now crossing the Channel on their long-delayed trip to the Continent! By the way, Georgie, they send you their heartful congratulations."

"Hugh, you WILL stop calling—"

Before Lady Catherine could finish, Georgiana spoke up. "Please, everyone! I wish for my family to be here for my wedding, and I would ask that we not argue." She stepped closer to Lady Catherine. "Can we not set aside all disagreements? I wish this to be a happy time."

"Well said, Georgiana," declared Darcy proudly. "My wife and I second my sister's request." The glare he sent his uncle and aunt clearly stated he would enforce Georgiana's desire.

"Pray all of you be seated," announced Elizabeth. "Refreshments will be here momentarily. Your rooms have been prepared. Dinner will be at four."

No sooner had everyone been settled than the butler entered. "Mr. and Mrs. Tucker have arrived with Mr. and Mrs. Southerland, sir."

Darcy, Elizabeth, and Georgiana immediately left to welcome the newcomers in the entrance hall.

"Mary, Tucker! I thought you were to come with the Bingleys." said Darcy.

"Change of plans," returned Tucker. "Lord Matlock wished to meet with me on a small issue. We arrived last evening and are staying with the Southerlands."

"Did you bring Rosanna?" asked Elizabeth of Mary.

"Yes, she is at the parsonage with the nurse." Mary and Georgiana exchanged greetings.

"Nonsense!" cried Elizabeth. "You must stay here! Tucker, pray send for Rosanna and your things."

Of course, both the Southerlands and the Tuckers protested, but Mrs. Darcy would not hear any disagreement. A Pemberley footman was soon dispatched to Kympton in the Tucker carriage to fetch the baby, the nursemaid, and the trunks. Meanwhile, Elizabeth notified Mrs. Reynolds of the Tuckers' arrival and the additional guests for dinner.

When the Southerlands and the Tuckers were shown into the drawing room, Lady Catherine waved her stick at the solicitor.

"What is *he* doing here?" She glared at the man who helped orchestrate her removal to the Rosings dower house a year prior.

"He is married to my wife's sister, which makes him *family*," Darcy said dangerously. "Mine and Georgiana's."

"You made excellent time, Tucker. Excellent!" exclaimed the earl. "Shall we meet in an hour? The viscount will join us. Darcy, may I use your study?"

Meanwhile, Lady Matlock and Anne greeted Kitty and Mary with great fondness. Watching her family accept such people of inferior birth as their own, Lady Catherine's response was a snort and a sneering silence. It was the best that could be expected.

DARCY, ANDREW, AND RICHARD ATTENDED LORD MATLOCK's meeting with Tucker. A border dispute between his estate and a neighbor that had been brewing for three decades had arisen again, and Lord Matlock wanted the matter settled forever. Tucker, for all his youth, had proven to be a wizard when it came to stubborn, arcane problems as had been shown with the battle over Rosings. This issue was no different. His solution was comprehensive, ingenious, and only slightly expensive. Darcy approved of his brother's proposal at once though Andrew and Richard required additional persuasion as to the cost. Finally, the earl gave his solicitor permission to proceed.

Over a celebratory brandy, Darcy decided to take his uncle to task. "My lord, must you argue with Lady Catherine? It is upsetting to the ladies, particularly Georgiana. And you know my aunt hates being referred to as 'Cathy.' You and Andrew are inciting her wrath."

"You promised to behave, Father," added Richard.

The Lion of Matlock harrumphed. "Good intentions, my boy, often fail when in company with my sister. And, if you wish to reproach me, Darcy, then I will scold *you* for not sending word of her presence!"

"We were all surprised at Aunt Cathy's attendance," quipped Andrew. "I wondered whether pigs had taken flight."

"She has only been here for two days," Darcy explained. "I did not feel it was worthy of an express."

"I shall defend Darcy. Anne and I were astonished when Lady Catherine, at the very last moment, announced her intention of traveling with us to Pemberley," said Richard. "We were loading the trunks at Rosings when she presented herself, her maid, and her luggage. I saw the letters from Lizzy and Georgie myself, imploring her attendance. I still cannot account for it."

Darcy shook his head. "Can you not? There is no one more forgiving than Elizabeth. I should know."

"Oh!" cried Andrew. "There is a tale there! You must tell all!"

"Just the worst proposal in English history," reported Richard with a smile.

Darcy drew a hand over his face. "I knew I should not have told you."

"Too late now, boy," demanded a smiling Lord Matlock. "Talk!"

SURPRISINGLY, DINNER WAS RELATIVELY PEACEFUL. DARCY expected Lady Catherine would complain about the seating arrangements. Elizabeth placed Lady Catherine at her left, with Lady Matlock at her right. Lady Catherine should have sat opposite the earl, but that would have encouraged disaster with the siblings sniping at each other. For additional harmony, Sir Richard was next to his wife's mother with Lord Fitzwilliam next to the countess. Having no one but Elizabeth at whom to rail, Lady Catherine kept her comments to a single slight over "country manners" and then remained silent. Lady Eugenie, Lady Penelope, Anne, Georgiana, the Tuckers, the Southerlands, and the Bennets made up the rest of the party. Elizabeth took great care to seat her mother as far from both Lady Catherine and Lady Eugenie as possible.

There was no table in the kingdom that the Earl of Matlock did not lord over. He was his usual bombastic self, full of advice, stories, and humor. He demanded his say in any and all conversation in a loving, paternal way. It was obvious that Lord Matlock was proud and pleased with his relations, and among that number he counted Elizabeth's sisters and spouses. All received his approbation, except the troublesome Lady Catherine, whom he ignored.

Matters became different with the separation of the sexes. The gentlemen had hardly finished their first glass of port when raised voices from the drawing room drew their attention. With a sense of foreboding, Darcy led his relations to the ladies, their steps quickening as they grew closer.

"Cathy is at it again," growled Lord Matlock

Darcy held up his hand in a vain attempt to calm the earl. An embarrassed footman opened the door, and upon entering, Darcy witnessed Lady Catherine holding court as though she were at Rosings while Elizabeth and Mrs. Southerland consoled a shaken Georgiana.

"There is still time to have the bishop conduct the wedding!" she declared. "To have a country parson bless the union of a Darcy and a Wakeford is preposterous!"

"Mother, the wedding is in two days," Anne pointed out.

"Are you saying *my son* is not worthy of marrying Miss Darcy to Lord Llewellyn?" Mrs. Bennet was deeply offended.

Darcy knew he needed to speak now. "Ladies, your voices are carrying and—"

Lady Catherine overrode him. "Mrs. Bennet, it is clear you have not been a part of society. This wedding will not have the proper elegance expected of my family."

"Pray recall *I* was part of the planning, and I assure you all is perfectly lovely," injected Lady Matlock with forced composure.

"Lacking elegance!" cried Mrs. Bennet. "I will have you know I have held *five* weddings! Five—including Lizzy's to Mr. Darcy! And all were the talk of Hertfordshire! How many weddings have *you* planned?"

"You dare cast aspersions on Anne's wedding to Sir Richard?"

"ENOUGH, I SAY!" thundered Lord Matlock. He strode over to his sister. "Cathy, I demand you cease this outrageous display of bad manners!"

"Stop calling me that!" she screamed in return. "My name is *Catherine*!"

"Everyone, please!"

To Darcy's astonishment, Elizabeth's plea somehow silenced the room. She rose from the couch.

"I know you all want the best for Georgiana on her wedding day. We want it to be perfect. But no wedding is ever perfect. Mother, recall how Charles and Jane slipped and nearly fell in the snow by their carriage as they were leaving? Or how the pianoforte was out of tune for Mary's?" She turned to Darcy with a smile. "I recall the heated bricks for our carriage were forgotten, and we suffered quite a cold ride to London!"

Most of the room chuckled at that. Even Lady Catherine nearly smiled.

"You are right, Elizabeth. I recall several of Andrew's friends becoming quite foxed at his and Eugenie's breakfast." Lady Matlock gave her eldest son a glare.

"Yes, because Richard put brandy in the punch," Andrew claimed.

"Only after you did the same," Richard good-naturedly shot back.

Mary laughed. "Remember, Kitty, how Franklin was so nervous he almost forgot his vows?"

"His nerves were nothing to yours," Kitty teased back.

Elizabeth smiled. "We all remember those little amusing things that happen at weddings, but what we warmly recall is who was there—our friends, and most importantly, our relations." Elizabeth walked over and took Lady Catherine's hand. "I speak for Georgiana when I say the greatest gift we can give her is attending her wedding."

A calmer Georgiana joined Elizabeth. "Yes! I am so happy we are all here together. It means the world to me."

Lady Catherine glared at the earl. "You will cease referring to me by that horrid name?" Lord Matlock answered with a nod.

Light conversation filled the time until everyone retired to their chambers for the night.

Chapter 21

The morning before the wedding, the Woodhouse and Llewellyn carriages arrived. Emerging from the elaborate Wakeford coach were the earl and countess with Mr. and Mrs. George Knightley. Lord Llewellyn, along with two other gentlemen, bounded out of his more modest carriage.

Darcy, Elizabeth, and Georgiana would have welcomed them on the steps, but a light rain forced everyone inside. After kisses and handshakes, Lord Wakeford did the honors for the pair of newcomers.

"Allow me to introduce my younger sons, Captain Woodhouse of the King's Army and the Reverend Mr. Woodhouse. Neil is in the artillery corps, while Thad is rector of our home parish."

Captain Cornelius Woodhouse resembled his father, and not just in looks. There was a slight haughty air about him. Darcy wondered whether the captain had earned his swagger in battle or simply inherited it from his parents. Sir Richard, a combat veteran of many engagements, would be able to tell.

Mr. Thaddeus Woodhouse was a shorter version of Llewellyn but not as sociable. He appeared nervous, almost shy, and Lord Llewellyn took pains to draw him out in conversation.

The Darcys escorted the party to the drawing room where the rest of Pemberley's guests awaited them. The Wakefords affectionately greeted their daughter while delivering insincere happy replies to all other salutations. Darcy noted a look shared between Lord Matlock and Mr. Bennet, indicating that neither were deceived by Lord Wakeford's false affability.

"Well, Matlock," boomed Lord Wakeford, "tomorrow we shall be related! Never thought that, did you?" He laughed. "Better than trade, what?"

All seem to know that Wakeford was referring to Mrs. Darcy's relations. Llewellyn blushed at his family's poor manners, and Darcy gritted his teeth. However, Lord Matlock rose to the occasion.

"As you say, Wakeford. By the way, here is the coming man. Tucker!" He beckoned the solicitor. "We must talk once we return to town. I believe you have a new venture to discuss with me, eh?"

Darcy was unaware of any new investments, so he concluded the earl was amusing himself by deceiving Lord Wakeford. Apparently, Tucker assumed the same.

"Of course, my lord," he responded in a dry, emotionless manner, giving the other peer a sidelong glance. "I believe I shall have all the details once I return to London. Shall we meet in a fortnight?"

Matlock rubbed his hands together. "Excellent! I believe it will be very profitable."

"My lord, we should refrain from discussion of the particulars *here*," Tucker warned, again glancing at Wakeford.

"Of course." He patted Tucker on the shoulder with a wink. "Mum's the word."

"I say," cried Wakeford, "what *are* you talking about, Matlock? It sounds very lucrative."

The earl waved his hand in dismissal. "Nothing that would interest *you*. It would not do for you to muddy your hands in trade, what?" He slipped an arm about Tucker's shoulders. "I see our wives are conversing by the window. Let us join them, my boy." With that, they left Lord Wakeford to sputter in frustration.

Darcy had witnessed the entire exchange along with Llewellyn and George Knightley. He was not happy with either peer. "Lew, I must apologize for my uncle. That was rather rude of him."

"Say nothing of it. My father behaved no better. I am certain he deserved it."

"Still, it was badly done." He turned to Knightley. "I must beg your pardon for my relations."

"It seems we all have relations to blush over. How is the fishing, Darcy? I regret we shall not have the time to find out for ourselves."

With that, the conversation turned to more pleasant subjects.

IN THE AFTERNOON, ELIZABETH WAS ABLE TO STEAL AWAY INTO her parlor to review the menu for the wedding breakfast. All was ready despite the repeated attempts of interference from Lady Catherine. The food had been ordered, the flowers gathered, and the ballroom set for the breakfast.

The last item was most important. Lady Catherine's favorite chair was to be placed in a far corner, the better to keep her away from her brother.

Oh, what a bother it is, Elizabeth thought. The two of them were as bad as Kitty and Lydia had been when young.

The flowers for the church were Kitty's charge, of course, and Elizabeth had no doubt of her sister's competence now. She prayed it would not rain.

A footman knocked. "Mrs. Knightley wishes to see you, madam."

Drat! What did the woman want?

Elizabeth had strived to be more civil to Mrs. Knightley during her late visit, but could the lady not leave her in peace? "Show her in."

Emma Knightley was beautifully dressed and coiffed, as usual, even after several hours in a crowded carriage. If Elizabeth had liked her better, she would have inquired as to how she accomplished it.

"Mrs. Knightley, I hope you have recovered from your travels."

"Oh yes. My cousin's carriage is well-sprung, and the roads were in a good state, despite the inclement weather."

Mrs. Knightley seemed a bit nervous as the ladies took their seats. Due to the small size of Elizabeth's study, she remained at her desk while Mrs. Knightley sat in a chair placed nearby. Elizabeth waited for Emma to begin.

She glanced at the papers on Elizabeth's desk. "I trust I am not disturbing your work."

"Not at all. Everything is ready for tomorrow." Graciously, Elizabeth added, "Your kind suggestions have proved very helpful. Thank you."

Emma dismissed her expression of gratitude with a wave. "Not at all. I am only happy to have been of service during your, ah, convalescence. I have an eye for such things." She blushed a bit and fiddled with her dress. "Your daughter—she is well?"

Perplexed, Elizabeth returned, "Yes, very well, as are all the children. It is kind of you to inquire." She wondered why Emma Knightley would care about the children.

She raised pleading eyes to her. "If it would be…" Emma bit her lip and sighed. "Mrs. Darcy, might I visit her…with them?"

"You wish to see the children?" Elizabeth was astonished.

"Yes, if it would be no trouble."

"Now?"

Emma nodded.

There was little that pleased Elizabeth more than interest in her children. "I am quite finished here. Let us remove to the nursery directly."

FRANNY RAISED NO OBJECTION TO BEING HELD BY MRS. KNIGHTLEY, but then the babe hardly cared who held her as long as someone did. Chloe was openly curious about their visitor, while Bennet, the shyest of the trio, preferred to seek solace in his mother's arms.

"She is lovely, Mrs. Darcy," remarked Emma as she allowed the baby to suckle her finger.

"What baby doing?" Chloe, her hands on Emma's thigh, strained to see.

"Come here, my dear," said Elizabeth. "There is no need to trouble Mrs. Knightley."

"It is no trouble at all. My sister has five children, and while I do not see them as often as I should like, I have grown quite immune to sticky fingers and blunt questions."

Chloe went to Elizabeth's side. "Yes, the John Knightleys live in London, I recall. Five children!" Elizabeth laughed. "I hope they are not all girls."

"Isabella has produced the required heir and spare. The rest are girls." Emma frowned. "Do you favor sons, Mrs. Darcy?"

"Not at all, although I would never give up my darling Ben here for anything!" Elizabeth assured her. "I fear my jest has failed miserably. I come from a family of five daughters, you see, and I am aware of the consternation a parent may experience over concerns of seeing the girls well settled when the time comes. You have met my mother."

After a moment, Emma smiled. "I begin to see. Was it so very bad?"

Elizabeth shrugged. "Not really, seen from this side of it." She thought of Lydia's scandal with Wickham and shuddered. "We survived." She stroked Chloe's hair.

Emma was thoughtful. "Your mother wanted you married. My father…" She paused. "My father is not so sanguine. He is very attached to Isabella and me and fears being alone."

Elizabeth immediately understood Mrs. Knightley's unusual living arrangements. "So, you and Mr. Knightley live with him."

Emma nodded. "There is no gentleman more thoughtful than Mr. Knightley. His Donwell Abbey is but a mile away, but even that distance was too far for Father's comfort."

"Will he not be jealous of his peace when the children come?"

It was not Elizabeth's best day for her celebrated wit. Emma paled and then burst into tears. Elizabeth, of course, attempted to console her companion, apologizing profusely.

"No, no, the fault is not yours," Emma eventually managed. "It is mine! Two years married and I have yet to be blessed!"

"Two years is not so very long."

Emma shook her head in distress. "It is, it is! When my dear Miss Taylor married Mr. Weston, she fell with child almost from the off! Isabella had her John within a twelvemonth of her wedding! I fear I am barren!"

Elizabeth was caught between sympathy and vexation. "Had your mother not explained things to you?"

"She has been gone these fourteen years, but Isabella talked to me prior to my marriage."

Elizabeth silently sighed. It was up to her to comfort Mrs. Knightley. "Pray forgive me, but your sister may not have been the best mentor if things were as easy for her as you say. Allow me to speak from my own experience. My sister Jane and I were both married by a joint ceremony in November of 1812. Four months later, Jane fell with child. Her daughter Susan was born in 1813. My son Bennet did not come until late 1814. Franny, as you see, came almost two years later.

"You must not lose hope, Mrs. Knightley. Two years is not long to wait. Children come in God's own time, and we must trust in Him. Meanwhile, be patient and enjoy this time." She ruffled Chloe's hair. "You will miss it when you are dealing with a fussy baby!"

"I not fussy!" Chloe asserted.

Emma dabbed her eyes with a handkerchief. "And if they never come?"

Elizabeth took her hand. "Have you spoken to your husband?"

"No, I do not wish to trouble him." She shook her head. "Lord, I am so silly these days! I do not know what has come over me. You are right. What will happen will happen. I must have faith."

"I shall not tell you what you should do, but I have found great comfort in sharing my hopes and fears with my husband."

Emma tenderly gazed at Franny. "Perhaps, perhaps. I wish him to be proud of me."

"You know him far better than I, but I cannot believe any friend of my husband to be less than a kind and caring gentleman."

Emma's smile returned. "You have named Mr. Knightley exactly! Thank you, Mrs. Darcy. You have eased my fears considerably." She returned her attention to Franny. "You have beautiful children."

Elizabeth bent down to first kiss Bennet's head then Chloe's. "Thank you. I do."

AFTER A LIGHT SUPPER, THE GENTLEMEN JOURNEYED TO NEARBY Kympton for the traditional bacchanal for the groom the night before the wedding. They gathered in the sitting room of the parsonage. Darcy, Andrew, and Lord Matlock stood in a corner while Richard conversed with the Woodhouses and Knightley. Southerland, being the host, oversaw the distribution of wine and spirits. Once everyone was served, Lord Matlock raised his glass.

"A toast, gentlemen, to Lord Llewellyn and Miss Darcy! May Lew and Georgiana have peace and prosperity all of their days."

"And procreation!" Captain Woodhouse laughed at his own witticism.

"There will be none of that!" The stern master of Pemberley set down his glass and stepped forth. "I shall remind you gentlemen that I am Georgiana's brother and guardian. I know the usual conduct tonight is to have sport at the groom's expense, but I will tolerate no disparagement or jibes at my sister's. None whatsoever." His mask fully in place, he glared at the captain.

"Come, Darcy, we are only having a bit of fun!" complained Lord Wakeford.

"My cousin spoke before me," declared Richard. "I, too, am Georgiana's guardian, and I stand with Darcy on this."

"Here, here," grumbled Matlock.

"Gentlemen, please," injected Mr. Southerland. "We are gathered here in fellowship. Tomorrow, we join our families. Let us show respect for all our ladies."

"Well said, Southerland." Llewellyn turned to his relations. "Can we not agree, for friendship's sake?"

"You always were a spoilsport, Algie." Captain Woodhouse said as he punched his brother's shoulder.

"What shall we talk about, then?" asked the Rev. Mr. Woodhouse.

Llewellyn grinned. "I heard something about an awful marriage proposal. What do you say to that, Darcy?"

"It could not be all that bad, as the lady did marry the gentleman," Darcy retorted, thinking fast. Lord Wakeford was as big a gossip as any matron of the *ton*. It would not do for him to know of the Hunsford disaster. "Far more interesting is a certain gentleman who wished to spend his wedding trip at a hunting lodge."

"A hunting lodge?" said Mr. Knightley as Llewellyn paled.

"Yes." Darcy took a sip. "In Scotland."

"*Scotland*?" boomed Lord Matlock. "Llewellyn, was *this* the reason you asked leave to use my lodge?"

"That old pile?" added Andrew. "It is in the middle of the wilderness! No servants and the closest village is miles away! By God, man, what were you thinking?"

"Hold," cried Lord Wakeford. "Algie, you wanted to bring Miss Darcy to a Scottish hunting lodge? On your wedding trip?"

"Er…" Llewellyn looked about the room, trying to explain. "It was not my best idea."

"I should say not, Algie!" Captain Woodhouse cackled.

Matlock was not finished with the viscount. "You wished to drag *my niece* to a hunting lodge deep in the wilds of *Scotland?* Have you gone bereft of your senses?" The scowl the earl wore would have chilled Napoleon himself.

Even Lord Wakeford was taken aback. "Algie, explain yourself!"

Hiding a smirk as the others berated a defensive Llewellyn, Darcy sipped his drink, relishing the fact that vengeance was indeed a dish best served cold.

ELIZABETH GAVE THE LADIES WITH HER A SLIGHT, UNCOMFORTABLE smile as she knocked on the door before her. "Georgiana, may we come in?"

Permission granted, Lady Matlock and Lady Wakeford followed Elizabeth into her chambers. Georgiana, blushing, stood by the bedroom doorway in her nightclothes. Clearly taken aback by the number of guests, she nervously asked that they be seated in the small sitting room.

Lady Matlock then began in a kind and soothing voice. "My dear, you can be in no doubt of the subject we wish to discuss with you."

Georgiana nodded, curious eyes on Lady Wakeford.

"Is Penny within?" that lady asked.

"No, milady. She left for her chambers a few minutes ago."

"Excellent. I asked her to allow us this private interview with you. My Penny is a very good girl."

Georgiana's color deepened. "She mentioned a meeting was to be expected, but she failed to say that you were to attend."

"As Algie's mother, it is my duty to inform you about your marital duties, in the absence of your dear departed mother."

Georgiana cringed.

Elizabeth immediately spoke up. "We comprehend your embarrassment, dearest," she assured the girl, giving a quelling glance to Lady Wakeford. "Our purpose tonight is to prepare you for your married life and to answer any questions you may have." She smiled. "I assure you, we are all uncomfortable."

"I am a silly goose." Georgiana picked at her robe.

"Nonsense," said Lady Matlock. "Now let us begin. Soonest said is soonest over." At Georgiana's nod, the countess explained what a bride should expect on the wedding night. The mechanics were glossed over. Georgiana had grown up in the country and had *some* idea of how things progressed. Instead, Lady Matlock spoke of tenderness, patience, and trust. "There will be discomfort, particularly at first, but it should fade in time—especially if your husband is gentle."

"Of course Algie will be gentle!" Lady Wakeford asserted. Georgiana turned beet red.

"Pray allow me to continue." Lady Matlock smiled at her niece. "The most important thing to remember is to talk to your husband. Tell him how you feel. Do not be ashamed to let him know what you like."

"Oh, I could not!" Georgiana declared.

"You must, my dear. Men are quite dense, you will learn, especially in this. The marriage bed is no place for maidenly decorum. You must speak." The countess laughed. "I expect he will rather like it."

"Like? Talking about...*that*?" Georgiana appeared flabbergasted.

Elizabeth could not help sharing a grin with Lady Matlock. "I am afraid so," she admitted.

"Not Fitzwilliam!"

Elizabeth only raised her eyebrows.

Georgiana buried her face in her hands. "I am so embarrassed! How will I ever look at Brother again?"

Lady Matlock patted her knee. "Do you have any questions, Georgiana?"

She slowly lowered her hands. "Could I..." She looked at the others. "Could I speak just with Lady Matlock, please? I appreciate you both coming—truly I do. It is just—"

"Of course, we understand," said Elizabeth, forestalling any comment from Lady Wakeford. Indeed, she did. Listening to the wife of her brother and the mother of her groom discussing marital relations? Elizabeth hugged the mortified girl. "All will be well, dearest. Listen to your aunt, and sleep well tonight. We shall see you in the morning."

ELIZABETH WAS NEARLY ASLEEP WHEN DARCY EMERGED FROM HIS dressing room. "Has your merrymaking at the parsonage already ended?" she softly asked.

"Did I wake you?"

"No, I was waiting for you."

He slipped under the sheets. "My uncle and I retired early from the field. We left Llewellyn to the tender mercies of his relations and Richard."

"Oh dear!"

He kissed her temple. "Do not worry. Southerland is there. He will make certain Llewellyn does not overindulge. Our groom will be fit for the ceremony tomorrow."

Elizabeth snuggled close. "Unlike Richard last year."

Darcy snorted. "He stood no chance with his fellow officers in attendance! In any case, he made it through his vows without casting his accounts. Quite an achievement, I believe. Has Anne forgiven him yet?"

"She claims she has, but rest assured, she will remind him of it in future when necessary. I must say I do not understand this need for gentlemen to carouse the night before a wedding."

"I did not."

"Yes. It was only you, Papa, Bingley, Hurst, and Richard. We had none of your other family at our wedding, save Georgiana." Elizabeth turned to him. "Do you wish it was different—that more of the family and your friends from London and Cambridge came to Meryton to celebrate the end of your bachelorhood?"

"Knowing who awaited me at the altar the next morning? No." He kissed her. "Besides, you are wholly accepted by the family now—even by Lady Catherine."

"Oh, how hard she labored not to!" Elizabeth laughed. "But even she could not forever maintain her disappointment, not with Anne well married and witnessing our happiness."

Darcy adoringly gazed at her. "Have I said I am in awe of you?"

Elizabeth gave a throaty chuckle. "Perhaps, but I am quite at leisure to hear you expound upon the subject."

Chapter 22

At last, the wedding day was upon them—a day Darcy dreaded. Still, he would do his duty by his sister.

He and Elizabeth shared a light repast in their chamber's sitting room before he retired to dress. Meanwhile, Elizabeth put on a heavy wrap over her night rail and hurried downstairs.

She had just overseen the arrangement of light refreshments for their guests and was returning to her chambers when she heard quick steps approach down the hall. Turning, she beheld an extremely happy Emma Knightley, hair in a braid and in a dressing gown, dashing in her direction.

"Mrs. Darcy, I must speak to you for a moment!"

Elizabeth hid a sigh and led Emma into her bedroom, now no longer used as a nursery for Franny. "How may I be of service to you?"

An ecstatic Emma grasped Elizabeth's hands, smiling widely. "I was sick to my stomach this morning!"

Elizabeth, baffled, took a half-step back. "I am sorry to hear it." *This* was the reason Mrs. Knightley interrupted her extremely busy morning—to complain about the previous night's dinner? Had the lady lost her senses?

Emma's face dropped. "But, is that not a good thing?"

A good thing? It was a moment before Elizabeth took Emma's meaning. "It *can* be," she carefully said in a kindlier voice.

"But it *must* be!" Emma insisted. "I am *never* ill!"

"Indeed?" Elizabeth raised an eyebrow.

Emma shook her head rapidly, her grin returning.

Elizabeth's lips quirked. She could not truly like Emma Knightley. She found her immature, frivolous, nosey, interfering, and at times overbearing. Yet, Mrs. Knightley helped with the wedding planning while Elizabeth recovered from Franny's birth, rid Pemberley of Lady Wakeford's obnoxious presence, and was kind to the children. Mrs. Knightley's fears and hopes over having children of her own recalled to Elizabeth's mind her own struggles in the first year of her marriage. This touched Elizabeth's tender heart, and she could do nothing but give the lady comfort.

"Then I shall hope that your discomfort is for the happiest of reasons." She grew serious. "Have you told your husband?"

"No!" Emma assured her. "I do not wish to raise his expectations. Is that the right thing to do?"

"My advice is this: it is customary and right to delay any general announcement until the baby quickens. However, if your hoped-for condition advances and the signs become more evident, I recommend that you share your happy news with your husband. He can be of great comfort during that time."

"Oh yes! Mr. Knightley is the best of men, and he so wants to be a father." She glanced at her attire. "I must get dressed."

"As must I." Impulsively, Elizabeth kissed Emma's cheek. "You will be in my prayers, Mrs. Knightley."

"And you will be in mine." With that, a happy Emma showed herself out.

ELIZABETH HAD ONE FINAL DUTY TO GEORGIANA. SHE ENTERED her sister's chambers to find her nervously sitting on her bed, her maid dismissed, hands clasped.

"Bridal nerves, my love?" Elizabeth kissed her cheek.

"Was it the same for you?"

Elizabeth laughed. "Oh yes! Ask Kitty. I was beside myself, worrying that something would happen and put things off!"

"You did not doubt Fitzwilliam?"

"Not then and not now." She frowned. "Do you doubt Llewellyn?"

"Oh no! I doubt myself. I am only a country girl at heart. How can I be a viscountess? How can I be worthy of Lew?"

"Take heart. I, too, am but a country girl, a gentleman's daughter. But I am also Mrs. Darcy, married to the best man I know.

"Sometimes I wonder at my good fortune. Yes, I still have worries and doubts. At those times, Fitzwilliam comforts me. Not as the great Mr. Darcy, master of Pemberley, but as my loving husband and friend." She grew close and whispered, "For you see, dear sister, all things considered, your brother is but a gentleman farmer. So, we are equals, as I once told Lady Catherine."

"I recall that story! I wish I could have seen you set down my aunt!"

"It was quite the event!" Elizabeth paused. "Georgiana, Llewellyn will be your husband. Tell him of your struggles and doubts as I do with Fitzwilliam. If you are fortunate, he will share his troubles with you. It is the way to build a strong marriage. Now, have you any concerns over tonight?"

Georgiana shook her head. "No. You, Lady Matlock, and Kitty eased my fears." She kissed Elizabeth's cheek. "Thank you for being my sister, Lizzy."

Elizabeth handed her a letter. "My last task for you today. Pray read it before the others arrive to help you dress. I love you, Georgiana."

Elizabeth then left the room so Georgiana could read in private.

Bath

My dear Miss Darcy,
 I hope this letter finds you and all your family in good health. All is well here in Bath, so I turn my attention to you. I requested

that Mrs. Darcy give this to you on your wedding day.

My dear girl, allow me to wish you joy. Entering the marriage state is expected of all ladies, but it is a serious business. Happiness is oft dependent on the parties involved. In this case, I have no fears for you.

Lord Llewellyn's family has an admirable reputation, and you have an excellent example in yours. Mr. Darcy was very kind to allow me to remain with you during the first half-year of his marriage. During those months, it became my decided opinion that Mrs. Darcy was an excellent choice for wife and sister. I left Pemberley knowing you were in good hands.

Miss Darcy, pray allow me one last lesson for you. The romance in the beginning of a loving marriage is all that is delightful, but soon arrives the responsibilities that come from the state. Accept this, embrace this, for this is the root of true happiness. We all must bear the slings and arrows of daily life. Doing so with a supportive spouse brings a sense of peace and satisfaction like no other.

My own marriage was such a one. My time with my dear Mr. Annesley was short, but my reward was two wonderful daughters. It is with my eldest, her husband, and children I now reside.

I was your companion for not quite two years. During that time, I observed your recovery from the harm done you. Do not thank me, for all the labor was yours. I could not be prouder if you were my own kin.

Welcome this moment, commit yourself to your future life as a wife, a mistress of a house, and—as God decrees—a mother. The rewards are above counting.

Health and happiness to you and your viscount.

Yours ever,
Matilda Annesley

WHILE ELIZABETH AND MRS. REYNOLDS OVERSAW THE FINAL touches of the wedding breakfast, Darcy labored to assemble the majority of their guests and escort them to their various carriages. Both Lady Catherine and Mrs. Bennet demurred, for both thought it their duty to assist the bride. Neither would leave if the other did not. Fortunately, Mr. Bennet took his wife in hand, while Lady Anne Fitzwilliam scolded her mother into reluctant compliance. Meanwhile, Lady Matlock, Mrs. Southerland, and Lady Penelope remained to help Georgiana dress.

Darcy paced about at the foot of the stairs, his watch in hand, to the amusement of his wife.

"Fitzwilliam, really! I doubt you were this nervous on our own wedding day."

"There you are mistaken, my dear. Until you appeared at the church door, I feared your father would change his mind and forbid…"

Darcy's voice died away at the sound of a door closing from above. Mrs. Southerland and Lady Penelope, both giggling, descended the stairs, Kitty in blue and Lady Penelope in green.

"Georgie looks so beautiful!" effused Kitty.

Lady Penelope proclaimed, "Lew will not be able to take his eyes off her!"

Everyone looked up to behold Georgiana and Lady Matlock. The bride was lovely, gold, silk gown with a white lace overlay. Her dark curls peeped out from under a golden bonnet adorned with the same lace. Darcy quite lost his breath.

Slowly the pair made their way down the steps, continuing in silence until brother and sister were face-to-face. Lady Matlock kissed her niece's cheek and left the house with Lady Penelope and Kitty. Elizabeth paused to compliment Georgiana's dress, bestowing her own kiss and hug before joining the ladies in the waiting carriage.

Darcy and Georgiana had yet to say a word—they only joined hands and stared at each other. Through watery eyes, Darcy took her in. Just yesterday, it seemed, he held his six-year-old sister in his arms, trying to console her while grieving their mother's passing. It had always been the two of them. Now, here she was—a young lady of one-and-twenty, preparing to marry. Where had all the years gone?

"Oh sweetling," he gasped, "how can I let you go?"

Georgiana began to cry. "Fitzwilliam—"

"I love you, Georgie."

"I love you, Brother."

Darcy smiled as he released one hand to draw his handkerchief. "No tears today. This is a good day." He handed the square to her. "Llewellyn is a fine man, a good man, and he loves you. He may even deserve you."

They shared a chuckle.

"Georgiana, you go to make your own home and your own family. This is how it should be. But remember, you will always be a Darcy and a part of Pemberley. A part of me."

Brother and sister briefly embraced before Georgiana drew back, and with a brilliant smile said, "I shall remember, I promise. Now, pray take me to my husband."

THE PAIR REMINISCED DURING THE RIDE TO KYMPTON. ON THIS cloudy, gray day, Darcy and Georgiana were bright and cheerful. No unhappy memories were recalled. They spoke of childhood romps and being snowbound. Of horseback rides and dance lessons. Of Christmases at Pemberley and concerts in London.

Of their parents, Darcy would only say, "Mother and Father are looking down at us and smiling. They would be as proud of you as I am. They loved you so."

Once they reached the church, everything became a muddle to Darcy. No sooner had he handed down Georgiana than Lady Matlock and Lady Penelope swept her away. They primped her dress and produced the bouquet. The doors opened, Lady Matlock scurried down the aisle, Lady Penelope followed at a more sedate pace, and then it was the Darcys' turn.

He gazed at his sister, so grown-up, so lovely. Struggling with an enormous sense of loss, Darcy donned his armor of stoicism to hide his sorrow. Georgiana slipped her arm around his, giving him a squeeze of reassurance. They locked eyes, shared a nod, and entered the church.

Darcy saw nothing but Mr. Southerland's face, so focused was he on this last service for his sister. Together with Lord Llewellyn, Captain Woodhouse, and Lady Penelope, they waited as the time-honored words of the marriage ceremony rang through the space.

Finally, Mr. Southerland asked, "Algernon, wilt thou have this woman to thy wedded wife, to live together after God's ordinance in the holy estate of Matrimony? Wilt thou love her, comfort her, honor, and keep her, in sickness and in health; and, forsaking all other, keep thee only unto her, so long as ye both shall live?"

With a confident voice, Llewellyn answered, "I will."

He turned to the bride. "Georgiana, wilt thou have this man to thy wedded husband, to live together after God's ordinance in the holy estate of Matrimony? Wilt thou obey him, and serve him, love, honor, and keep him, in sickness and in health; and, forsaking all other, keep thee only unto him, so long as ye both shall live?"

"I will." Her voice was soft yet firm.

"Who giveth this woman to be married to this man?"

Darcy's mouth was dry. "I do."

It was done. He had handed over his sister to a smiling Lord Llewellyn. Georgiana would be a Darcy no more. Shaken, he took his seat beside Elizabeth. She said nothing; she only took his hand with a heartfelt smile.

For the first time that day, he relaxed.

The ceremony was quickly concluded, and Darcy found himself warmly congratulating the couple at the church door. It felt strange not to have Georgiana in the Darcy carriage, but he made no note of it to Elizabeth, knowing a tease was her sure response. Instead, he took her hand again, drawing peace and joy from her—his wife, his partner, his friend, his love.

Chapter 23

It was no surprise that the breakfast began as a rousing success. The decorations were simple yet elegant, eschewing any pomp or vulgarity. Cook had outdone herself, particularly with the enormous bride's cake. The food was plentiful, and Mrs. Reynolds organized the staff like a sergeant-major. Pemberley operated like the well-oiled machine it was.

Unlike the fashion of the day, the breakfast could never be called small or intimate, not with the unusual number of guests. That so many of the principals' families and neighbors had traveled to attend recalled ceremonies of an earlier time. And those relations included in their number those who could barely tolerate each other.

Enduring such a crush at Pemberley was never to Darcy's liking. He would have been pleased just to have the bride and groom partake of a breakfast with only Elizabeth and the Southerlands in attendance. But it was not to be.

The Matlocks and Fitzwilliams were welcome, of course, but Lady Catherine's surprising attendance was sure to cause trouble. Lord Llewellyn naturally wanted his family there, but did the Wakefords and Woodhouses have to be so loudly provocative? Both Lord Wakeford and Lady Catherine were sure to vex Lord Matlock. Mrs. Bennet was of the belief that her comments were meant to be heard by all assembled. At least the Tuckers, Bingleys, Knightleys, and Higginbottoms could converse at a reasonable level. Darcy was certain to get a headache.

But first, Darcy had an announcement to make. Upon the entrance of the bride and groom, he had everyone gather in the music room. With Elizabeth at his side, he took Georgiana's hand and began by welcoming all to Pemberley. He then moved to the subject of his speech.

"I am happy that if I must lose my dear sister's company, it is to Lord Llewellyn's care I entrust her. With her goes her dowry."

There were gasps of surprise that the ever-proper master of Pemberley would ever raise such an ill-mannered subject. Darcy carried on, a slight grin teasing at the corner of his lips.

"I do not speak of money or jewels but of something far more precious." He gazed at his sister. "Her music. To commemorate the marriage of Lord and Lady Llewellyn, Mrs. Darcy and I are pleased to present them a new pianoforte."

The guests erupted in applause while the stunned couple rushed forward, Georgiana embracing her brother while Lord Llewellyn shook his hand.

"Brother, I do not know what to say," Georgiana managed through her happy tears.

"You have gifted me with your music all of your life, sweetling," he said. "Now it is Lew's turn—and your family to come." To his new brother, Darcy stated that the instrument should arrive from London in about three weeks.

"We shall be away on our tour, but I shall inform my servants to expect it. I insist you and Elizabeth must be the first to come to Ambervale to hear Georgiana play it," Llewellyn declared.

Elizabeth assured him they would. No sooner had she kissed Georgiana's cheek than the throng descended upon them, offering congratulations. Before Darcy knew it, the ladies had departed *en mass* into the ballroom, Elizabeth and Georgiana were whisked away by Kitty and Lady Penelope, leaving the gentlemen to follow. Mr.

Bennet was nowhere to be seen. Darcy expected Elizabeth's father had surely escaped to the library.

Fortunate man!

Peace reigned for the moment in the ballroom, mainly due to the less-demonstrative members of the Fitzwilliam family. Sir Richard and Lady Fitzwilliam waited upon Lady Catherine at one end of the room, while Lady Matlock, Lord Fitzwilliam, and Lady Eugenie occupied Lord Matlock on the other. Also, since the lock on the nursery door was finally securely reinforced, Chloe remained above stairs.

Darcy and Llewellyn drifted over to the Matlocks and the Fitzwilliams, where Lord Matlock declared with stentorian good cheer, "Welcome to the family, my boy!"

"Thankee, my lord. It is an honor."

"Dash it all, lad, none of this 'honor' business! You are now *family*. I am Uncle to you."

Lady Matlock kissed Llewellyn's cheek. "And I am your aunt. But where is Georgiana?"

Darcy gestured to the other side of the room. "She is greeting the ladies."

The countess narrowed her eyes. "And Lady Catherine. Ah, well. Come, Eugenie. It seems we must bear the slings and arrows of our relations if we are to speak to the bride."

Lord Wakeford bowed as the ladies departed. He then turned to the gentleman. "Matlock, we are finally relations! Ha! Do you know my boys here?" He indicated the two young gentlemen who accompanied him.

"We met last night," the earl grumbled. In a more polite tone, he said, "Captain Woodhouse, Mr. Woodhouse."

The officer and cleric bowed as Wakeford continued. "You have a boy in the army as well, do you not?"

"I do. My son, *Sir* Richard, retired as a colonel of Hussars after Waterloo." He eyed Captain Woodhouse's full-dress uniform, taking in the few metals adorned thereon. "Artillery, is it? Tell me, did you serve in Belgium?"

"Ah, no, unfortunately." Captain Woodhouse seemed taken aback at Lord Matlock's harsh tone. "I command a training battery at the Royal Artillery Barracks in Woolwich." He chuckled. "Must teach the fellows their business, you know."

"Yes, of course," the viscount contemptibly drawled.

Sensing trouble, the captain excused himself, and the two Woodhouse brothers took themselves off with their father.

Lord Matlock turned to his new nephew. "Forgive me my beastly manner, Llewellyn. I meant no disrespect to your father or Mr. Woodhouse."

"Say no more, sir. Neil is my mother's favorite and is a bit spoiled. I advised him not to wear the uniform, but he insisted. How did you know he did not serve with Wellington?"

"He was not wearing the Waterloo Metal. I believe Richard is prouder of his than his Bath Star. Not that he wears his uniform any longer." He nodded at Sir Richard across the room. "No, that is all behind him now, thank the Lord."

Andrew slipped an arm around Llewellyn's shoulder. "Come, Cousin, I must properly induct you into the family. Let us get a drink."

"Did we not do that last night?"

Andrew laughed. "Still feel it, do you? Ha! A hair of the dog is in order."

A moment after they left, Darcy was approached by Mr. Knightley. They fell into the usual compliments of the day while Lord Matlock looked on, but Darcy could see his friend was distracted. He kept turning his eyes towards Mrs. Knightley on the other side of the room.

"I say, Knightley, is anything the matter?" Darcy inquired.

Caught out, Mr. Knightley shook his head. "Not at all. I am perfectly well." He lowered his voice. "I am just concerned over

Mrs. Knightley. She was rather ill this morning—rather ill indeed."

Darcy looked at Mrs. Knightley. "Did last night's dinner disagree with her?" She did not seem ill. In fact, she appeared the opposite—rather giddy, he considered.

"Oh no," Knightley assured him. "I admit it was my first thought, yet now she is all smiles. She has quite recovered." He squinted. "Say, that is unusual."

"I beg your pardon."

"Sorry, Darcy. It is just that Emma waved away the kippers, something she usually enjoys. I find it strange."

Darcy smiled. He recalled when Elizabeth's tastes in food changed. Then, with a start, he remembered *why*.

But before he could decide whether it was proper to enlighten him as to Mrs. Knightley's possible condition, they and Lord Matlock were joined by Mr. Tucker, and the conversation turned to politics.

"A PIANOFORTE, IS IT?" QUERIED LADY CATHERINE. "A SUITABLE gift, I suppose. You do plan to continue your practicing, do you not, Lady Llewellyn? I cannot abide the habit of young ladies abandoning their accomplishments upon marriage." She eyed Elizabeth.

"I plan to play every day, as my new responsibilities allow," Georgiana stated. "I shall follow Elizabeth's example."

Lady Catherine did not look best pleased at that. "Yes, well, it is a shame you did not spend more time at Rosings, particularly after Anne's marriage to Sir Richard. Her example in managing a house is outstanding. You can learn much from her. You must change your wedding tour plans and come to Rosings. You will stay a month complete. I insist upon it. I will not hear of anything less."

"Lady Catherine, I am sorry to say that our plans are fixed," Georgiana quietly responded. "My lord husband is very firm on that, and it is my duty to obey his wishes."

Elizabeth was quick to see her sister's jest and added, "And Lord Llewellyn *is* a viscount, milady."

As expected, Lady Catherine flushed at that. "Very well! Lord Llewellyn will hear from me over this, I declare! Firmness from one's husband is one thing—cruelty is quite another!"

Anne stepped in. "Mother, I think you mistake the matter."

"Not at all! I am celebrated for my clarity of thought and understanding! I see Lord Llewellyn is indeed a tyrant! I am most *seriously* displeased."

While Lady Catherine grumbled over her perception of the state of Georgiana's new marriage, the lady in question moved off with Elizabeth, Kitty, and Lady Penelope.

"I cannot believe my brother is harsh with you, Georgie!"

"And he is not, Penny!" Georgiana lightly laughed. "I only wish not to spend my wedding tour under the thumb of Lady Catherine."

"And one cannot help but tweak her nose a bit," added Kitty.

Elizabeth was proud that Kitty perceived their teasing. "I have found the best way to deal with her ladyship is to take amusement at her remarks rather than offense. It makes for a more pleasant conversation."

"Quite right, Lizzy! Is that how you conversed with my brother when you first met?" Georgiana's eyes twinkled.

Elizabeth's smile faded a bit. "Yes." *And it was a great mistake*, she recalled. *If I had been honest with Fitzwilliam from the start, many misunderstandings would have been set aside. He would have learned sooner that his aloof manner gave offense, while I would have earlier come to see his sterling character. We both were so blind. We might have come to an understanding in Hertfordshire! A year of happiness was lost.*

"Lizzy, are you well?" Kitty asked.

"Of course," Elizabeth returned instantly, her smile firmly back in place. *Think only of the past as its remembrance gives you pleasure.* "Come, ladies, we must mingle with our guests."

DARCY DESPERATELY WANTED TO SPEND TIME WITH GEORGIANA before she departed Pemberley with her new husband, but his sister always seemed out of reach. Other guests demanded his attention—some he wished to ignore but could not, such as Lady Catherine. Her loud, unpleasant voice was just the thing to capture his notice. To his dismay, she was berating Lord Llewellyn, and Sir Richard was doing little to stop her.

"What are you about, my lady?" he demanded of her, earning a weak smile from his new brother.

"I have just learned of *this gentleman's* tyrannical manner!" The grand dame snarled. "It is not to be borne! I will not have it!"

"I must insist you lower your voice. Now, what is this all about?"

"Lady Catherine has accused me of oppressing Georgiana, I think," replied a confused Llewellyn.

Of all the accusations Darcy could possibly level against Llewellyn—immaturity, rashness, fervency—tyranny was a consideration so outlandish as to be inconceivable. He turned to Sir Richard. "What prompted this?"

The former colonel grinned. "It seems Lady Catherine is not happy Lew refuses to oblige her and change the wedding tour to her satisfaction. She requires they come to Rosings."

"Imagine my dear niece forbidden to visit me. I am almost her nearest relation! And it is all *his* fault!" She pointed one bony finger at Llewellyn.

Llewellyn tried to placate her. "Lady Catherine, our schedule is quite set and—"

"You WILL come to Rosings! You WILL!"

Darcy glared at Richard. "Why are you not saying anything?" Darcy was disappointed with his cousin, who seemed more eager to take amusement from Lady Catherine's outlandish pronouncement rather than correct her misguided thinking.

Richard shrugged. "What can I do? She never listens to me."

"What is my sister going on about now?" Lord Matlock entered the fray.

"Is this about Lew and Georgie's trip?" injected Lord Fitzwilliam. "Are they not going to Scotland?"

Darcy glared at him. *What the devil is he about? He knows that is no longer the case.*

"Scotland!" cried Lady Catherine. "You are taking my niece to *Scotland*?"

Llewellyn threw up his hands. "No, no! That is all changed."

"Who is going to Scotland?" asked Lady Wakeford.

"So, that is why you wanted my hunting lodge," said Lord Matlock mischievously.

"A HUNTING LODGE?" Lady Catherine was beside herself.

"Please, everyone," cried Darcy. "No one is going to Scotland. Lew and Georgie are traveling to the shore after visiting my uncle, who is in poor health. Then, they will enjoy a fortnight alone." Darcy almost gagged on those words. "Pray, let us end this discussion." He glared at his Fitzwilliam relations. This was not the time or place to make sport of Lady Catherine! "Andrew…" He jerked his head to the other side of the room.

"Right, old man. Come, Father. Remember your promise."

The earl grumbled but left with the viscount to return to his chair. Darcy got Richard's attention and motioned with his eyes toward Lady Catherine. The knight sighed.

"You know this time is for Georgiana and Llewellyn. I am sure they will visit Rosings in the near future." Richard turned a pleading look at the viscount.

"Of course we shall."

Darcy saw that Lady Catherine was not placated, but at that moment, Anne returned. After demanding and receiving a brief report of the disagreement, Lady Fitzwilliam confronted the grand dame.

"We spoke of this, Mother! You cannot have your way in all things. No, do not interrupt me! You will apologize to Lord Llewellyn and wish Georgiana and him a happy trip. And pray recall *I* issue invitations to Rosings. Do we need to speak of *that* again?" The new mistress of Rosings gave her mother a *de Bourgh* glare.

Lady Catherine deflated. "No, we do not." She took a breath

and wished the young couple joy on the trip politely if reluctantly. Darcy and Llewellyn bowed and retreated.

"I am sorry about that, Lew," said Darcy.

"Georgie warned me, so I am not offended." He glanced back. "Quite the handful, is she not?"

"You have NO idea. Now, where are our wives?"

Llewellyn looked about. "I do not see them."

The pair were then waylaid by the Wakefords.

THE NEW LADY LLEWELLYN WISHED TO MAKE HER FAREWELLS TO the children, so Elizabeth accompanied her to the nursery. Chloe's response was heartrending.

"No!" she cried. "Angel aunt stay! Stay!"

"Oh, my sweet one," Georgiana declared, taking the young girl in her arms, "I must go with my husband to his house, but it is not far. Less than half a day's travel. We shall see each other quite often, I am sure."

Chloe was not consoled. "No, no! Mommy went away. Aunt Georgie stay!"

Elizabeth, with Bennet on her hip, drew close. "When a lady marries, she goes to live with her husband. But Georgiana will not be on a big ship and sail across the ocean. Her new home is nearby, and I promise we shall visit."

"We have many horses," Georgiana added.

A tearful Chloe, finger in mouth, eyed her warily. "Horseys?"

"Yes, dearest. Many horses!"

"I ride horseys?" Chloe brightened.

"If your uncle approves, yes you will," said Elizabeth.

A more comforted Chloe permitted her cousin to kiss her, an action she repeated with Bennet.

The ladies then retired to Georgiana's former room to repair their appearance for Lady Llewellyn's departure.

"Sir," said the butler in Darcy's ear, "we have a small issue that requires your attention."

Darcy took a few steps away from a boring conversation dominated by Baron Higginbottom. "What is it?" he returned softy when out of earshot.

"The grooms outside, sir. Would you please come with me? It seems there is a disagreement involving the loading of the guests' trunks." The two left the ballroom and headed towards the servants' stairs and the rear of the house.

Darcy halted. "What sort of disagreement could there possibly be?"

"Please, sir. The dispute is getting rather heated. I shall try to explain as we go."

As they descended the stairs, the butler continued. "The carriages for the visitors are being loaded, but only Lord Llewellyn's is ready for departure. The dispute is between the Wakeford footmen and Lord Matlock's people. They are arguing over whose carriages and luggage carts take precedence."

"Precedence? That is ridiculous!"

"Undoubtedly, sir. Unfortunately, all involved are somewhat into their cups from the celebratory punch."

They had reached the door. "The punch? Cook should have placed hardly any spirits in it at this time of day."

"You are correct, sir. However, a guest—Captain Woodhouse, I am told—insisted on adding whisky to the concoction."

"Good Lord! Why on earth would he do that?"

"I cannot say, sir."

A moment later, Darcy beheld bedlam. Several groups of liveried footmen, in Wakeford, Matlock, and even Darcy colors, shouted at each other, hands waving and fingers pointing. The underbutler attempted to restore order without success. Mayfield servants sat on their vehicles, laughing at the antics, while Pemberley stable hands stood by, seemingly disgusted by the whole exhibition.

"Hold fast!" cried Darcy. "There will be no more of this!"

"An' who th' devil are ya?" demanded a man in Wakeford livery.

"That's me master, you rascal!" shouted a Pemberley footman. "Watch ya tongue or you'll be eatin' me fist!" Several of his companions cried out in agreement.

In his best lord of the manor comportment, Darcy strode towards the tumult. "What seems to be the issue here?"

Immediately, the argument renewed. Darcy crossed his arms and listened. It was as reported. The carriages were to be loaded and there were not enough men to load all of them at once. They would have to take turns, and therein lay the problem. Wakeford and Matlock people disagreed over who took priority. Argument turned again to shouting, and alcohol-fueled violence threatened.

An appalled Darcy only vaguely noticed the stable master move to his side. "How'd ya want me to handle this, sir?" asked Mr. Campbell.

"There will be no fighting, Mr. Campbell. Get me their attention."

At that, the stable master loudly demanded that everyone cease their squabbles, the stable hands joining their chief. It took a few minutes before order was restored. The footmen and grooms stood quietly, some swaying dangerously. Only then did Darcy speak again.

"Men, this is conduct unworthy of your station. You wear the colors of three fine houses. Is this how to uphold the honor of your masters? We *will* have order.

"It is clearly apparent that many carriages and luggage carts must be loaded. If we work together, the job is soonest done. Agreed?"

"Wakeford first!" drunkenly yelled the Wakeford footman who had first challenged Darcy.

"Not on your life! *Matlock first!*" cried one of his uncle's men, and the commotion restarted.

Darcy rubbed his forehead. "Mr. Campbell, pray quiet them again."

GEORGIANA AND ELIZABETH RETURNED TO THE BALLROOM. "AH,

there you are, sweetheart!" greeted Llewellyn. "All set to go?"

A radiant Georgiana smiled. "Oh yes. Let us say our goodbyes."

The couple quickly made the rounds of the room, exchanging kisses or handshakes, before the party moved to the front entrance hall.

"Where is my brother?" asked Georgiana.

Llewellyn looked about. "I do not know. I have not seen him lately."

Richard sidled up to the couple. "I think he was called away to deal with a small problem."

Elizabeth called to a footman. "Find Mr. Darcy and have him come to the front hallway. Lord and Lady Llewellyn are leaving."

"MR. DARCY, A-A WORD, SIR."

Darcy was irritated at being disturbed. They had finally quieted the men, convincing them to load the carriages in order of departure. The Matlock wagons were almost finished. He turned from speaking to Mr. Campbell to see a young, nervous Pemberley footman—a new man, he recalled. "Yes, what is it?"

"I was sent to fetch you, sir. The young lady, Miss Darcy—oh, I should say Lady Llewellyn, now, shouldn't I?"

"Yes, she is Lady Llewellyn."

"Right, sir. Well, I was told to fetch you because Lady Llewellyn will be leaving Pemberley."

Darcy knew yelling at the man would not help. "That is so."

"I-I mean, sir, that Miss Darcy—oh, drat it—Lady Llewellyn is leaving, sir. With Lord Llewellyn."

The moment Darcy dreaded had come. "Ah. Very well. I shall come directly."

"Er, uh, they are boarding the carriage now, sir."

"*What?* Oh, Good God! Why did you not say so?" Darcy rudely pushed the footman out of his way and dashed to the back door, only to stop for a moment. "Mr. Campbell, see to the men!"

He then threw open the door, scaring a maid half out of her wits. Mumbling his apologies, he squeezed by and ran full-out towards the front of the house, almost slipping on the highly-polished wood. The entrance hall was filled with well-wishers. Darcy was forced to slow down and carefully make his way through the throng.

"Darcy! There you are!" cried Knightley. "You had best not tarry."

"Yes, I know—pardon me, Bingley—pray let me by, Baron—excuse me, Uncle."

Finally, Darcy found himself at the top of the steps, only to watch Llewellyn's carriage pull away. He was too late. He waved furiously, thinking of calling out, when he spied Georgiana's lace handkerchief fluttering from the coach's window.

She was gone.

Darcy slowed his steps, mindlessly making his way to his wife's side, watching his sister leave Pemberley forever.

"Fitzwilliam, you just missed Georgiana's leave-taking! What delayed you?" Elizabeth asked.

"Solving an issue with the servants," he answered woodenly, his eyes locked on the departing carriage.

"What has happened?"

"I shall tell you later. But, do not be surprised if I murder Captain Woodhouse."

Elizabeth said nothing in response, easing her hand into his. Darcy felt his frustration and disappointment diminish. *She always knows how to comfort me. God, but I love this woman!*

Darcy and Elizabeth stood on the front steps of Pemberley, flanked by their family, the flowers and flags festooning the grounds swaying in the cloudy, chilly afternoon air. They all waved as the coach carrying the newly married Llewellyns disappeared around a bend of trees. Darcy sighed as he turned to re-enter the house.

Elizabeth squeezed his hand. "All will be well, dearest."

Darcy's expression was bleak. "I know. I only wish I could have said goodbye to her."

Chapter 24

With the bride and groom's departure, Pemberley began to empty over the next few hours. The first to leave were the Matlocks, for the countess was eager to put distance between the earl and Lady Catherine. Traveling with them were Lord Fitzwilliam and Lady Eugenie.

The Woodhouses and Knightleys soon made their farewells. They were to overnight at the Ambervale Lodge dower house before setting off for Surrey in the morning. The new Lord and Lady Llewellyn would not be disturbed, as they were to spend their wedding night in the main house.

Later in the afternoon, the Bingleys and Bennets set off for Mayfield, and the Southerlands returned to Kympton. Remaining for the night were Anne and Sir Richard, Mrs. Jenkinson, Tucker and Mary, and an almost-gracious Lady Catherine.

Dinner passed unremarkably, and the entertainment afterwards could not overcome Darcy's melancholy. True, his sister Mary now played with great skill, and Elizabeth's voice was enchanting, but neither approached the ability of one who would never live there again. The party then retired for the night.

Darcy shook his head at his stupidity as he climbed the stairs to the family wing. Surely it was foolish and selfish to wish Georgiana were still at Pemberley rather than on her honeymoon tour! Llewellyn was a responsible young man and the choice of Georgiana's tender heart. Still, it was distressing to know that, except for the occasional family party, the halls of Pemberley would be devoid of his sweet sister's beautiful music.

Approaching the nursery, he could hear the dulcet tone of his wife speaking to their son. "Go to sleep, my sweet boy. The angels will watch over you."

At once, Darcy realized his mistake. There would be new and different music in Pemberley now, in its own way just as delightful. Through the opened door, he watched Elizabeth kiss Bennet's forehead.

"Uncle! Kiss goodnight!" Chloe had her arms outstretched impatiently, her blonde hair bouncing about her face.

Darcy dutifully performed as requested, hiding a smile. "We have spoken of this. It is time for sleep, not speaking. Be a good girl."

Chloe simply giggled. "Love you."

"I love you too." Darcy meant every word.

She laughed anew after Elizabeth bestowed her kiss. The Darcys then retreated to their apartments. In affectionate silence, they moved to their separate dressing rooms and prepared for the night.

Robe donned and valet dismissed, Darcy poured the wine as Elizabeth—her rich, curly, chocolate tresses plaited—padded into the sitting room.

"How do you fare, dearest?" she asked, her brown eyes concerned as he handed her a glass.

"I assure you I am well. I own to being a bit preoccupied is all. Melancholy is to be expected. It is not every day one's baby sister marries."

Elizabeth made herself comfortable on the small sofa, her robe opening as a result. Two children had added curves to her light and pleasing figure. Darcy had no complaints whatsoever over the changes.

"I shall come to accept Georgie's absence in about five years or so," he said as he sat next to her.

She laid a comforting hand upon his. "She is happy, and Llewellyn is perfectly besotted. We have nothing to fear."

"I am not concerned." Darcy tried and failed to hide his disquiet with a sip.

"Of course, you are, my dear. It is only natural that you should be. She was your responsibility for over ten years. Now she is Llewellyn's. It is the way of the world."

"I suppose you are right." He sat back. "I shall say I am not looking forward to this with Franny. Can she not take the veil?"

Elizabeth laughed. "No, she will not. And neither will Chloe." She smiled at his questioning look. "Our niece adores you."

"Truly?"

"Fitzwilliam, for such an excellent man, you still cannot understand women. You are fast becoming Chloe's father in her heart, if you are not already."

Darcy shrugged. "I promised she would be under my protection when we took her in."

"You care for her more than you say."

"I…I cannot deny it."

Elizabeth smiled sweetly. "You are a good man, Fitzwilliam Darcy. It is time you received your reward for your sufferings today."

Darcy was about to declare that today was far from being painful when he noticed *that look* in his Elizabeth's eyes. "Oh yes, today was an agony. You will tend my hurt?"

"I shall do my best." She wound her arms about his neck and whispered in his ear, "Take me to our bed, Fitzwilliam."

Who was he to deny his love's command? Darcy set down his wine, swept Elizabeth up in his arms, and carried her into the master's bedchamber.

LATER THAT EVENING, THE LIEGE-LORD OF THE KINGDOM OF PEMberley lay back in his bed, his hands behind his head. Darcy always knew this day would come—the day Georgiana left Pemberley and him forever. Now that it was done, he felt something strange, something unexpected. He expected he would be unhappy or worried or concerned. He was a bit of all those things, but there was another feeling too. He was *content*.

And why should he not be? Georgiana, now Lady Llewellyn, was married to one of the few he could wholeheartedly trust with his dear sister's happiness. He regretted he had not the opportunity to see her off, but it was of no moment, he told himself. Surely, they would be in company frequently in future. Yes, Pemberley had lost a princess, but he had gained one—nay, *two* princesses to replace her, Franny and Chloe.

He turned his head to gaze at his beloved queen sleeping sweetly beside him. How could he not feel contentment? Elizabeth was the source of all that was central to his life and all he could possibly want in the future. Through her, he gained a son, a daughter, and a ward. Elizabeth was the heart and soul of his kingdom. She was his and he was hers.

Darcy smiled in blessed happiness. It lasted but a moment before there was a knock on the chamber door.

"Mr. Darcy," came Witherspoon's light call, "I have a message for you."

Glancing at his wife, still asleep, Darcy quietly but swiftly removed himself from their bed, pulled on a robe, and made for the door. Opening it but slightly, he received a letter from his valet. A glance at the envelope caused a knot to grow in his stomach. His name was in Georgiana's hand.

"I am told it was urgent; otherwise, I would never disturb you," said Witherspoon.

Preoccupied with fears and concern, Darcy mumbled his thanks, closed the door, and after lighting a candle, he opened the note at once.

Dearest Brother,

Forgive me this note. I fear you might take alarm, so allow me to tell you at once that we are perfectly well and are safely ensconced at Ambervale. We depart in the morning for Westminster on our way to our lodgings in Worthing.

I am very sorry we left without properly farewelling you. Lizzy is an excellent sister, but there is much I should want you to know directly from me. These brief lines must make do, inadequate as they are, until we meet again.

Fitzwilliam, you are the best brother in all the world. For most of my life, you have tried to be both my friend and parent. I have wanted for nothing while in your care. I do not speak of mundane things, such as dresses and pianofortes. Your attention, care, love, and example are beyond price. In my darkest hours, you comforted me. When I was tempted to betray my heritage, you rescued me. When I needed an ear, you attended me. By the example of you and Lizzy, I have seen the very picture of a marriage filled with devotion, respect, and affection, and I have every intention of making such a one with Lew. You will reject all thanks and gratitude, I am sure, but you have mine in any case and always will, as well as my undying love.

I left your house for Lew's—willingly, happily, and without regret—but know that you, Lizzy, and Pemberley will forever have a place in my heart. Remember, we are but a half-day away.

I close, signing my new name for the first time.

> *I remain your loving sister,*
> *Georgiana Llewellyn*

Through his tears, Darcy read Georgiana's missive several times. "Dearest, what is it?"

He looked up, not realizing that Elizabeth was awake and sitting up in their bed. He lowered the paper to his waist and walked to her.

"I received a note from Georgiana."

Alarmed, Elizabeth cried, "What has happened?"

"Nothing, nothing at all. She writes to say—" Unable to finish, Darcy handed Elizabeth the note. He watched as she read, fighting his own jumbled emotions.

Elizabeth, by turns seemed concerned, relieved, and finally pleased. "She writes to say thank you."

Darcy nodded.

Elizabeth drew back the sheets, "Come and let me comfort you."

Slipping into the bed and her embrace, he sighed as she ran her fingers through his hair.

"All will be well, Fitzwilliam," she softly murmured in his ear.

Darcy kissed his queen's forehead.

"Yes, it will."

THE END

Afterword

This book marks the end of an eighteen-year journey, one that could not be made without the help of several delightful people.

When I originally wrote *The Three Colonels: Jane Austen's Fighting Men* in 2004–05, it was posted as fan fiction. I wanted to explore the monumental events that occurred during the Regency, particularly the Hundred Days Crisis of 1815 and the Battle of Waterloo, using Jane Austen's immortal characters. To do so, I did something audacious: *I insisted that Miss Austen's characters in all her novels knew each other.* That opened up an immense universe of possibilities. The novel was a joint sequel to Jane Austin's *Pride and Prejudice* and *Sense and Sensibility*.

I followed *The Three Colonels* a year later with a sequel to *Persuasion*, *Persuaded to Sail* (under its original title *The Unexpected Passenger*). Thus, I created a companion novel—my **Jane Austen's Fighting Men Series**. In 2010, I wrote a third companion novel, *The Last Adventure of the Scarlet Pimpernel*, a joint sequel to *Northanger Abbey* and *The Scarlet Pimpernel*. I believed that was the end of the story.

I was wrong. In 2010 I was encouraged to have my works published. The rest is history.

But the characters in the Jane Austen's Fighting Men universe would not be silent. They demanded closure. That required two more books: *Brother of the Bride* and *Rosings Park: A Story of Jane Austen's Fighting Men*.

Now, after five novels and nearly half a million words, it is time to turn the page. The Jane Austen's Fighting Men universe is done. The stories have been told. But before I walk away, I must thank those who were with me every step of the way, the primary editors of my work: **Debbie Styne, Ellen Pickels,** and my lovely wife and muse, **Barbara**.

Just because *Brother of the Bride* marks the end of *this* journey doesn't mean there are not more journeys to come. There are many books to write, some in Regency England, some in my home state of Louisiana, and some in other places and times that excite my muse.

I hope you will join me.

Jack Caldwell
Prairieville, Louisiana
November 2022

Suggested Readings

Austen, Jane. *Pride and Prejudice.*

—. *Sense and Sensibility.*

—. *Northanger Abbey.*

—. *Persuasion.*

Caldwell, Jack. *The Three Colonels: Jane Austen's Fighting Men.* Naperville: Sourcebooks Landmark, 2012.

—. *Mr. Darcy Came to Dinner* – a Jane Austen farce. Prairieville: White Soup Press, 2013.

—. *The Companion of His Future Life.* Prairieville: White Soup Press, 2014.

—. *The Last Adventure of the Scarlet Pimpernel*, Prairieville: White Soup Press, 2016.

—. *Persuaded to Sail*, Prairieville: White Soup Press, 2020.

—. *Rosings Park*, Prairieville: White Soup Press, 2020.

About the Author

Jack Caldwell is an author, amateur historian, professional economic developer, playwright, and like many Cajuns, a darn good cook.

Jack is the author of twelve Jane Austen-themed historical novels. **Pemberley Ranch** is a retelling of *Pride & Prejudice* set in Reconstruction-era Texas. **Mr. Darcy Came to Dinner** and **The Companion of His Future Life** are *Pride & Prejudice*-flavored farces.

The **JANE AUSTEN'S FIGHTING MEN SERIES** is made up of five novels. **The Three Colonels: Jane Austen's Fighting Men** is a sequel to *Pride and Prejudice* and *Sense and Sensibility*. **The Last Adventure of the Scarlet Pimpernel** is a mash-up of *Northanger Abbey* and *The Scarlet Pimpernel*. **Persuaded to Sail** is a sequel to *Persuasion*. **Brother of the Bride** is a sequel to *Pride and Prejudice*. **Rosings Park: A Story of Jane Austen's Fighting Men** is the concluding chapter to the series.

In 2015, he released the first four books of a series of historical novels about New Orleans, titled **THE CRESCENT CITY SERIES**. **The Plains of Chalmette** begins the series, commemorating the Bicentennial of the Battle of New Orleans. Jack marked the tenth anniversary of Hurricane Katrina with three modern novels: **Bourbon Street Nights**, **Elysian Dreams**, and **Ruin and Renewal**.

When not writing or traveling with his wife, Barbara, Jack attempts to play golf. A devout convert to Roman Catholicism, Jack is married with three grown sons. Jack's blog postings—**The Cajun Cheesehead Chronicles**—appear regularly at **Austen Variations**.

Web site: **Ramblings of a Cajun in Exile** –
https://cajuncheesehead.com

Blog: **Austen Variations** – http://austenvariations.com/

Facebook: https://www.facebook.com/pages/
Jack-Caldwell-author/132047236805555

Twitter: @JCaldwell25

By the Author

Jane Austen's Fighting Men Series

THE THREE COLONELS

THE LAST ADVENTURE OF THE SCARLET PIMPERNEL

PERSUADED TO SAIL

BROTHER OF THE BRIDE

ROSINGS PARK: A STORY OF JANE AUSTEN'S FIGHTING MEN

The Crescent City Series

THE PLAINS OF CHALMETTE:
A Story of Crescent City

BOURBON STREET NIGHTS:
Volume One of Crescent City

ELYSIAN DREAMS:
Volume Two of Crescent City

RUIN AND RENEWAL:
Volume Three of Crescent City

Pride and Prejudice Variatioons

PEMBERLEY RANCH

MR. DARCY CAME TO DINNER
A Jane Austen Farce

THE COMPANION OF HIS FUTURE LIFE